CREATION'S CAPTIVE

Melody Joanne

Creation's Captive

Book cover design by Krafigs Design

Paperback ISBN: 9798876753823

TRIGGER WARNINGS

Your mental health matters. This book is not meant to glorify these topics.

- Violence
- Bullying
- Trauma
- Parental neglect
- Narcissistic parent
- Death of a friend
- Murder
- Car accident
- Depression
- Blood
- Choking
- Dubious consent
- Domination
- Hair pulling
- Praise kink
- Depiction of a dead body
- Domestic violence/abuse
- Gaslighting
- Breeding (mentioned)
- Slavery
- Cliff-hanger ending
- Stoning
- Restraining
- Drowning

- Kidnapping
- Possessive MMC
- Animal cruelty (a character squeezes a small animal for a moment)

AUTHOR NOTE

Warning - Contains some plot spoilers.

Creation's Captive delves into dark themes, especially those involving trauma, narcissism, and abusive relationships. The male main character in this book is *not* a good man. This is just the first book in a trilogy, meaning we have a long road ahead for character development. But one thing I do guarantee - our heroine will fall in love and get her happily ever after.

Still with me?

Perfect. Buckle up and enjoy the ride.

DEDICATION

To the dark romance readers,
I don't know what kind of fucked up shit you've
survived but welcome home.
Now, turn the page.

Good girl.

CHAPTER 1

Four Years Prior

THE FIRST TIME I SAW A GHOST, I ALMOST PEED myself.

It's not that I'm particularly jumpy. I just had no inkling that today would be the day I finally lost it. But maybe these things sneak up on you.

Still, a girl would appreciate some kind of ominous warning before the laws of the universe decide to take a turn for the supernatural. I wasn't even graced with a dark and stormy night.

It's late afternoon, and besides the fact that my resume is about to become tailored to becoming a ghostbuster, I've been having a decent day. Jazz band practice has just let out, and I'm walking home, still happy in my cocoon of perfect sanity.

It's one of those first warmer days of spring. It's the kind you bundle up for in the fall but will outright reject anything with sleeves after the winter snow is gone. Because yeah, Vitamin D deficiency will drive you to do some crazy stuff.

I've gotten into the habit of cutting through the soccer fields behind the school when walking home. It adds another ten minutes to my commute but saves me from walking through an extra two blocks of suburbia.

The fields are empty since they're still soaked from the spring melt. I like empty. Empty is far better than dealing with people, especially when everyone in this town has or is currently in the process of peaking in high school.

This aversion to my community is what motivates me to gladly brave the flooded fields, rather than risk getting pulled into an awkward social situation. The icy water seeps into my shoes, but I trudge on. My toes may never forgive me.

I almost walk into her.

Or through her. Honestly, I don't know which is more likely.

The sun is just starting to set, and the growing shadows make it harder to judge puddle depth. I've just stepped over a particularly deep-looking puddle and am focused on not falling into it. It isn't a graceful effort.

At this point, my walk has become a heroic effort at keeping my calves dry. I have one leg comically extended behind me and bringing it over to the other side of the puddle. That's when I look up and see a person inches from my face.

Having a solid person this close to me would have been freaky enough. But I'm already aware that I'm not a lucky person. The girl in front of me has an eery light blue glow to her, and I can see trees beyond her – through her.

Ghost.

I scream and try to step back. Only I'm not fully balanced from getting over the last puddle, so I fall back, my butt landing hard in the icy water. I scramble back, looking more like a crab than I think I ever have.

I'm about to get up and start running when I get hit with a rare wave of logic. The ghost isn't moving. She's just standing there.

I eye her suspiciously.

Use your head, Vivian.

I try to look around for the familiar glow of a projector without taking my eyes off the girl. I have bullies. Even though they've backed off in the last year, terrifying me with a stupid prank is right up their alley.

There's nothing around me that could be casting a projection. My stomach drops. If this was a prank by my bullies, there is no way they would pass up the chance to laugh at me when I fell into the water.

The hair on my arms raises despite the chilled water that clings to them. I try to look behind me for a solid exit route. It's easier said than done, considering I still don't want to let the ghost out of my sight.

Not that this situation isn't already freaky enough, but if I stop looking at the ghost, I'm terrified she'll come at me, crawling like something out of a horror movie.

No, thank you.

"Who – WHAT are you?" I demand. Demand is a strong word. Croak might be a better approximation for my tone.

If I pee myself, no one will ever know. My ass is already soaked through.

The ghost waves her hands up and down slowly like she's trying to tell me to calm down.

Quite frankly, I'm not in the mood to take a chill pill from the undead today. Even without a solid exit route mapped out, I'm ready to take off. Only, I have a second problem. My legs are frozen, both figuratively and metaphorically.

Fear paralysis. What a shitty response to danger.

Logic, Vivian. Use your damn head.

Okay, so the ghost can move, and she isn't a prank. I mean, there are lots of other perfectly sensible explanations for what I'm seeing.

Most obviously, I've gone crazy – my mind has finally cracked. That explanation makes a bit of sense. This situation? This makes no sense.

The ghost doesn't answer me, and all things considered, I'm not too upset about it. What was it they say about your imaginary friends? 'It's okay to see them, but if they talk back to you, then you've lost it completely.'

Okay, maybe no one says that. But I'm going to run with it, regardless.

I might have one foot in crazy town, but my other foot is firmly rooted in sanity. Both could use some dry socks, though.

The ghost has the gall to smile at me. At least it isn't one of those maniacal crazy-person smiles, just a soft half-smile. Maybe she thinks she's successfully calmed me down.

Hah! Jokes on you. I just have no skills in self-preservation.

"What do you want?" I ask.

Maybe she doesn't want to talk about the whole see-through thing or trade phone numbers.

Perhaps non-corporeality is a *touchy* subject for her. See what I did there? I may not be able to move my ass in scary situations, but by God, I can crack puns.

Again, no answer from the ghost. She points behind me, then urgently waves her hands at me.

Oh God, is there something even freakier behind me?

I snap my head around, momentarily forgetting that I'm not supposed to take my eyes off the ghost. There's nothing there, and I quickly look back to see whether she is now on top of me and ready to kill me. Okay, maybe I am a bit lucky. She still hasn't moved.

Relief floods me, and it's enough to chase away the fear paralysis.

I think this is one of those rare occasions where running from your problems is encouraged.

So, scrambling now, I jump off my dripping wet ass and hightail it out of the field back in the direction I came from.

A more intelligent person would probably look behind them to see if they are being chased. I am one hundred percent the first person who will be murdered in a horror flick because I don't bother to check. I just run.

I don't slow until I've reached my house.

Finally reaching my front step, I double over, gasping for air.

My house is a small duplex nestled in a suburb's corner lot.

This is the kind of neighbourhood where the housing association takes pride in the fact that everyone keeps their grass at the mandatory length of three inches. Usually, it gives me the creeps. But right now, I'm reassured by how there's no way a ghost would dare show up on this side of manic suburbia.

Once I finally have my breathing back to a normal level, I quietly open the door. Hopefully, my mother and stepfather are deep into some television show and won't hear me arrive.

I really need to stop giving myself false hope.

A familiar, pinched face is waiting for me in the kitchen doorway. She isn't looking up at me from her tablet, but I can tell she's annoyed.

"You didn't tell me you were planning on staying out late," my mother snaps, not taking her eyes off the screen.

I'm soaked from the waist down, and all the woman cares about is that I'm late. No parenting awards are to be won here.

"Sorry, mom," I say.

It's all I ever say.

My mother finally looks up from her tablet and takes in what state I'm in. She wrinkles her nose in distaste before walking back into the kitchen. She's already back on the tablet, typing away a message. I slip off my shoes and consider whether I can reach my room before I'm grounded.

"Didn't you hear about the accident?" my mother's voice calls.

This statement has me pausing from my plan to sneak away. I try not to look completely shocked. My mother just said something that sounded like concern for my well-being.

"What accident?" I ask as I tentatively walk towards her. I didn't see anything on my way home. I think I was wheezing too hard to hear anything, either.

My mother rolls her eyes before looking away from her screen. "It's all over the news. For the love of God, Vivian, you have a phone. Use it." She's waving her tablet in my face, open to her social media feed.

My mom is one of the few successful 'business owners,' which is totally not code for a pyramid scheme subscriber.

She sells shampoos and other body care products and religiously stays on top of all social networking, recruiting other young women who want to make the big bucks working from home.

My mother is a parasite.

And from what I gather, she's a very pissed-off parasite.

"I've already had a ton of people messaging me to ask if you're okay, and they want to know if you saw the accident happen. And what could I say to them? Oh, I don't know, how about, 'Sorry, I don't know where my ungrateful daughter is right now.' That will go over so well for the reposts."

There it is – the actual reason she's upset.

My mother and I have a strained but peaceful coexistence on the best of days. She's mostly come to terms with the fact that a mini-me bleached-blonde clone didn't climb out of her vagina.

We're about as opposites as you can get. She has platinum hair, chocolate brown eyes, and a cheerleader physique honed from a death grip on her glory days. The stereotypical cheerleader attitude has stuck hard, too.

According to her, I inherited my father's looks. Dark auburn hair, a splash of freckles and dark blue eyes. She isn't being complimentary when she says it, either. She's been pushing her company's foundation on me since I was *seven*. To her horror, I also have a predisposition for curves and none of the coordination necessary to 'work them off.'

I can't remember how old I was when the calorie counting started.

Maybe that's where this mental break stemmed from. When in doubt – blame your childhood. Am I right?

She's still waving the tablet in my face and looking at me like I'm an imbecile, but it's moving too quickly for me to read anything.

"Sorry, what happened?" I frown, trying to figure out whether I've just sucked myself into a longer conversation than needed. I think I'm getting motion sickness from trying to read the moving screen.

My mother slams the tablet back down. Thank goodness for strong technology cases.

"Drunk driver." She rolls her eyes as she says it. "Honestly, the state they're letting this town go to. I knew those less expensive houses up the road were inviting trouble. Just wait. It's not going to be the end of this stuff. They'll be letting all kinds of trash into our town now."

I grit my teeth together, reminding myself that talking back is futile. I'm not looking for pain today.

My mother continues, oblivious to the damage I'm undoubtedly causing my teeth, "Your aunt shared the post. The guy lost control of his car and crashed into a tree. Right on the path you take home. How did you not see it? It happened like ten minutes ago. Emergency services are probably still there."

I peek at the post she scrolled to, and my breath catches in my throat. The car is completely wrapped around a huge oak tree. There's a mailbox next to it, and I can see the edge of the soccer field in the distance. That's the exact path I usually take.

The one I didn't take today.

My mother sees my complexion pale and is temporarily appeased. "Exactly. Can you see how this makes *me* look? My friends know you've been walking down Regin Street to get home. And then to have a major accident there and not be able to account for the whereabouts of my daughter? People will start to talk," she finishes with a hiss.

"Sorry, Mom," I repeat. "I didn't see the accident. Uhm, the soccer fields were flooded, and I fell in a puddle. So, I decided to take the main sidewalks home."

The lie comes quickly enough. Before my mother can work herself into a frenzy about what people must be saying if they saw me soaking wet, I slip out of the kitchen and quickly head upstairs.

The aftershocks of this afternoon hit once I'm in dry clothes and am wrapped in a cozy blanket.

The timing of the ghost appearing is sketchy. Isn't this a plot for some fated death movie? The main character avoids their natural death through supernatural means, only to be hunted by death itself. I shudder at the thought and make a mental note not to watch any more scary movies. They are clearly getting to my head.

Hopefully, this was my first and last brush with supernatural activity.

CHAPTER 2

I WOKE THE FOLLOWING DAY CONVINCED THAT the ghost was only a hallucination.

Am I lying to myself? Absolutely.

Anxiety – meet denial.

Of course, my plan to bury my head in the sand and pretend yesterday never happened would work much better if the ghost in the soccer field was the only ghost I would be seeing.

Silly of me to assume my life would return to its non-supernatural state. Because when I leave my house to take on what should be a super-ordinary day, I'm faced with what I guess is my new normal.

Ghosts. Everywhere.

It's as if someone has lifted a curtain, and suddenly, a new freaky world has been superimposed onto my reality.

I think the occasional ghost sighting could be tolerable, but this – this is a bit extreme.

There are ghostly figures peppered across my neighbourhood. It's easy enough to tell them apart from the living. Beyond the fact that if you look closely, they're see-through, the ghosts all have that same light blue glow. Some are following living people, but others just wander about aimlessly.

If that wasn't bad enough, they're inside people's houses, too. Judging by the number of glowing figures I see in my neighbour's windows, his house is super haunted. I wonder if he hears rattling chains when he tries to sleep at night. Maybe that's why he's so cranky.

When I was five, the old man yelled at me for accidentally walking on one of his tulips. I've thought poorly of him ever since, but maybe I need to re-evaluate. I guess being severely haunted might leave you feeling a bit grumpy. My good mood has certainly disappeared.

I'm torn between wanting to crawl back into bed and wanting to pretend nothing is happening.

Normal. Act normal.

Everything is fine. Totally fine.

It's not fine. But I go to school anyway.

I suppose there is one silver lining to this whole dead people predicament. At least the ghosts are quiet. The only noise I've heard out of them is a hushed whisper, but it's not anything I can make out. It's almost as if they speak in static or a low whispering white noise.

I make it to lunch hour before breaking my 'fake it till you make it' strategy. Rather than braving the cafeteria crowds, I head to the library. It's deserted in here, save for the glowing figure of an older woman sitting on one of the reading chairs.

I guess it's time to make stupid decisions.

I approach her.

"Hello," I say in a quiet, friendly tone.

To my surprise, the ghost looks at me with a mixture of shock and horror. I think she's more surprised to see me than I am by her. She looks distraught.

Am I some kind of harbinger of living person-cooties?

She gives me a good frown before turning her head back to her book.

I could take the social cue and leave her alone. But instead, I try again, "Uhm, hi, do you have a second?"

Nothing.

She's ignoring me. I guess ghosts are passive-aggressive.

I feel my wayward hope of a career as a ghost-whispering detective float away.

Thanks a lot for the unrealistic expectations, Hollywood.

The rest of my afternoon goes by normally. Or as normal as can be expected if you don't count me running into no less than seven ghosts that haunt my school. Every last one of them refused to acknowledge me. So, I've settled on ignoring the jerk ghosts right back.

If that's how things are going to be, we can all pretend the other doesn't exist or seriously disturb their mental peace.

Am I burying my head in the sand?

Yes.

Do I feel bad about my decisions?

No.

I'm totally fine. The twitch over my left eye has always been there.

By evening, my nerves are completely frayed. But I'm still dead set on pretending my life is not in shambles. Right now, that means prom.

I don't have much choice – not if I don't want to become a ghost. Because if I skip prom, my bestie is going to straight up kill me.

While I don't have many friends, I'm lucky to have one solid best friend. Emily, or Em as she prefers to be called, is a spitfire and a half.

When Em moved here a year ago, she told off every one of my bullies. Her smart mouth should have gotten her bullied, too, but Em has a 'get out of bullying free card.' Aka, her twin brother, Jackson.

Jackson is the popularity king. He plays just about every school sport and is set to earn a varsity scholarship.

Since the school loves Jackson, and Jackson loves his sister, people don't mess with Em. Luckily, since Em and I are usually together, that same bullying immunity translated to me. Herd immunity at its finest.

I'm not really a 'school dance' kind of person, but when you finally make a friend, you'd be surprised what you're willing to do to make sure you aren't alone in the world again.

So, I'm putting on the final touches of my makeup and trying not to pull at my dress's strapless top.

The dress is Em's doing. It's a deep purple and knee-length, flaring at my hips.

"The flare is to give the illusion that you have an ass," Em teased when she pulled it off the rack.

Em is full of shit. We both know carbs have a magnetic pull towards my butt.

I check my phone to make sure I'm not running late. Emily and Jackson are set to come pick me up in another 5 minutes or so.

Nailed it.

I move to grab my clutch when a familiar ghost appears in front of my door. It's the ghost girl from the soccer field yesterday.

This time, I don't scream. Instead, I gasp, jump about a foot, and drop my phone.

I think not screaming shows some level of personal growth.

How stereotypical would it be if I asked the ghost whether she's ever heard of knocking?

At least this time, I'm not completely freaking out. Now, I can look *past* the fact that she's see-through and get a good look at her.

Ghost girl looks young, maybe close to fifteen years old. Her hair is up in a bunch of braids crisscrossing her head – fancy braids. She's wearing some kind of gown – nope, it's a toga.

Maybe this ghost died at a Halloween party. Being forced to spend the afterlife in a costume, that must suck.

Alternatively, this ghost died a long time ago. Like not in this millennia type of long. Do ghosts get more powerful with time?

Mental note: do not piss off the boss-level ghost.

Luckily, the ghost doesn't look upset. She's looking at me with the same 'please don't scream or freak out' expression.

I peek around her to make sure my door is closed since I'm worried looking through her might be rude.

The door is shut. It's best if the people in my house don't hear me talking to myself. I take a deep inhale before breaking the ice for what will undoubtedly be another one-sided conversation.

"You again," I start, keeping my voice low. "What do you want? Also, did you do this?" I wave at the window, trying to encompass the whole dead people predicament. "Because, respectfully, I'd like the gift receipt."

Surprise, surprise, the ghost doesn't answer. She just stares at me, wide-eyed, giving no indication she understands my questions.

I try to contain my sigh of frustration. "Did you warn me the last time because I was going to be hit by the driver?"

At this, ghost girl gives a small smile.

Yes! Houston, we have made contact!

"But why? Who am I to you?" Not to say I'm not grateful, but I'm *dying* for answers.

Ghost girl averts her eyes and gives a slight shake of her head.

I purse my lips.

Ghost girl won't talk, but she answers yes or no questions. I can work with that. "Okay, but you're here now. Are you here to warn me again?"

Her eyes snap back to me. She nods before pointing to my phone and vehemently shaking her head.

"My phone? Is it going to blow up?" I warily push it away with my toe.

Ghost girl looks back at me with a look that says, 'Don't be an idiot,' before shaking her head and pointing at my phone again, this time with more insistence.

Following her lead, I gingerly pick it up, unlocking the screen to see my texts with Em.

> Em: Okay so we're picking you up at 7 tonight.

> Em: Vivvvv, Jackson wants to know if you'll be ready for 7.

> Em: VIV! You'd better be ignoring me because you're getting hot for prom.

I look back at the ghost. She keeps pointing to the screen and shaking her head. "The dance? I shouldn't go to prom?"

Ghost girl shakes her head, looking irritated that I'm not understanding. She points at my phone again.

I've always sucked at charades.

"Okay. Not the dance, then. My ride? Is something going to happen on the drive?"

Bingo.

Ghost girl looks like she might start jumping up and down as she nods. She points at the screen again before crossing her hands in repeated 'X' symbols as if to say, 'No driving – absolutely not.'

"Okay, no driving then," I answer, trying to appease her. She looks agitated, and I'm not keen on being on the receiving end of a ghost's frustration. That just sounds like a recipe for a poltergeist.

I'll pass.

Ghost girl looks satisfied with my statement. She nods her head at me once more before disappearing.

My shoulders sag, relieved that she's finally gone.

Alone again, I consider her message.

The school is only a short drive from my house. And Em lives just a few blocks away. What harm could come from such a short drive?

But then I get flashbacks of the drunk driver accident scene.

I shudder. It's better to be safe than sorry.

It takes a second for the panic to set in. If the ride is dangerous for me, is it dangerous for Em, too? I text her back, trying to sound nonchalant.

Em might be my best friend, but in the spirit of keeping my only friend, I'm keeping my freaky ghost experiences to myself.

> Viv: Hey sorry – was busy getting ready.

> Em: No problem. We're leaving in a few to pick you up.

> Viv: About driving… I was thinking we should walk.

> Em: Uhm what? Girl, you have not seen these heels.

> Em: We're driving otherwise I'll be too sore to dance.

Viv: Right, sorry. But maybe my mom could drive us?

Em: Suddenly have something against my brother?

Em: I know he has a big head and all, but it doesn't get in the way of his driving.

Em: You'll live.

Viv: No! Not at all!

Viv: Sorry.

Viv: I just don't think we should drive.

Viv: Bring extra shoes, we'll walk together!

Em: What the hell is going on with you?

Viv: Nothing!

Em: I'm your best friend. TELL ME!

I take a deep breath. Em is stubborn, and now that she thinks I've insulted her brother, there's no way she will back down.

I chew on my bottom lip, likely getting lipstick all over my teeth, thinking of a way to convince Em to walk to prom without sounding like a crazy person.

The clock isn't on my side. No genius plans come to mind.

Crazy it is.

> Viv: Okay! I have a really bad feeling about going to prom in Jackson's car.

> Viv: I know it sounds crazy, but please trust me.

Em: LOL

Em: Nice try.

Em: Is this you trying to get out of going to prom?

Em: You promised you'd come out!

> Viv: No! Not at all! Please trust me! Just please walk.

No immediate response.

> Viv: Em?

> Viv: EMILY DO NOT GET IN THE CAR!

My heart is hammering a wild beat. How can I stop this? I try texting Em again.

> Viv: EM. Please! Please don't get in the car!

> Viv: Something bad is going to happen!

Em's icon finally flashes, showing she's seen my message.

> Em: I don't know what you're playing at, but fine.

> Em: Walk weirdo.

> Em: We're on our way to prom and we'll see you there.

I feel my heart sink to my toes.
No. I'm supposed to be able to stop this.
I pull on some running shoes and run for the door.
Tearing down the sidewalk, I race towards the school. It's starting to rain. That isn't ominous at all. I pull out my phone and dial Em. No answer.
Thunder booms and the sky opens into a torrential downpour. As if I needed more motivation to run faster.
Almost there.

Soon, the school comes into view. Cars line up along the front drive, and teenagers spill out, trying to avoid the rain.

Already soaked to the bone, I stop to scan the cars, looking for Jackson's.

Nothing.

I dash inside the school, ignoring the looks from other students. My dress is splattered in mud, and I can feel my makeup dripping down my cheeks. They back away from me and start whispering and pointing my way.

Em isn't here. Maybe she hasn't arrived yet?

Ignoring the giggles, I run back outside. I stop under the awning to scan the lineup of cars for new arrivals — still no Jackson or Em.

"Come on, come on," I mutter as I pull out my phone to call Em again.

Still no answer. They should be here by now.

And then I hear it, a sound that even the torrential rain can't mask.

Sirens.

The ambulance tears down the main drive toward Em's house. My panic starts to claw its way up to the surface, and the edges of my vision eyes darken.

"Oh god, no," I breathe, shaking off the panic as I run after the first responders.

I'm soon passed by a police car, another ambulance, and a fire engine, all sporting loud sirens and flashing lights.

My tears are coming freely because I know, I just know, this isn't a coincidence.

Finally, I turn a corner and see the lights have stopped, just in front of the lake. Emergency vehicles block my view.

I'm still running when I nearly collide with an officer. He stops me from accidental assault by grabbing my shoulders.

"Woah – slow down." The officer looks at my dress and nods back up the road. "You need to get back to the school. It's not safe to be out here in this weather."

I pull back from his hold and try to look behind him. "Who is it? What happened? My friend – she hasn't shown up." I manage to sputter.

"Ahh, I'm sorry, but I can't tell you anything until the family has been notified," the officer replies.

It takes me a second to process the implication behind his words. Notifying families is something you do when someone is dead.

The officer frowns as he takes in my look of shock, likely realizing his misstep. I don't give him a chance to stop me as I dart past him, ducking under the police tape.

It can't be Em. Please don't let it be Em.

The officer yells at me to stop, but his orders are unnecessary. As soon as I round the firetruck, I freeze in my tracks.

Jackson's car is submerged in the lake. The front has completely disappeared, with only the trunk remaining above water. The firefighters are working to pull the vehicle out.

The officer grabs my arm. "Hey! You need to leave. This is an active investigation site."

"My friend!" I look back at him in terror. "That's my friend's car! Is she okay? Please! Where is she?"

The officer must take pity on me because as he steers me away from the accident, he tells me, "I'm sorry, miss. I think maybe you should call your parents. I – look, we were able to revive the girl."

Any relief I might feel at his words is lost on what he isn't saying. They revived Em – just Em, and not Jackson.

My body starts to shake as the officer leads me back to the other side of a barricade tape.

"You should call someone," the officer says again before turning back to control the crowd starting to form around the crash site.

Word must have gotten out because many students are here now, trying to get a good look at what happened.

"That's Jackson's car!" someone yells. The other students start talking, a few asking the officer if everyone is okay. The officer gives away nothing and keeps asking everyone to go home. It isn't working.

I ignore them all. My feet feel like lead, and there's a pounding in my head. The black circles are coming back, tunnelling my vision.

I can see the accident from this spot. The firefighters finally pull the car out of the water. The rear window is shattered. The front end is covered in mud and crumpled inwards. The driver's side looks like it took the worst of the impact, and I can see a shadow still in the driver's seat.

The firefighters start working to get the door open.

It takes just a few minutes, and then they pull him out. All the students stop talking in an instant. I think I hear someone scream, and the sobs start. The paramedics quickly circle the body, hiding it from sight. But it's too late.

Everyone saw him. Everyone knows.

Dead.

Jackson is dead, and I could have stopped it. My best friend's twin brother. The guy with so much life in him. He's gone, and I didn't save him.

I killed him.

The words start spinning in my head.

I killed him. I killed him. I killed him.

The officer is back to standing in front of me. I hear his voice like it's coming from a great distance as he talks to me, but I don't register it. He looks at me with concern, and I vaguely catch the word 'shock.'

It's the last thing I hear before the tunnel vision morphs into complete darkness.

CHAPTER 3

THE DAYS FOLLOWING JACKSON'S DEATH GO BY in a haze of despair. Rather than brave the sea of faces at school, I chicken out and lock myself in my room.

I don't want to talk, don't want to think. The only person I've tried to communicate with is Em, but she hasn't answered my texts.

Honestly, I can't blame her.

There are so many things I could have done differently. I failed my only friend. My eyes are burning from the constant breakdowns.

I don't know what to say if Em ever decides to speak to me again. Nothing I say won't sound superficial. There's no way to convey how truly sorry I am.

The guilt presses down on me.

It hurts to breathe.

Melody Joanne

I get a whole week of hiding before my mother decides it's time for me to rejoin society. Declaring that 'it isn't even my friend who died,' she sends me on my way.

I'm too numb to argue.

So, against my better judgment, it's an overcast Monday morning, and I'm back at school.

The classes, the teachers, and the students all blur together. Every movement feels robotic. It's like someone else is driving my body, and I'm watching from inside my brain.

Em is still absent. I feel even worse when I realize I'm relieved she isn't here. I'm still unsure what to say when we inevitably see each other.

My guilt only intensifies when I see how the other students look at me. At first, I think that without Em as a buffer, the other students are gearing up to resume bullying me – business as usual. But this is different.

This seems more personal.

At lunch, I walk by some of Jackson's friends. The group stops talking mid-conversation and purposefully turns to glare at me. Not just the normal snooty looks they usually give me. This feels like hate.

I can feel their eyes boring holes into the back of my head as I hurry to move out of their line of sight.

Already at my limit for human interaction, I find an unlocked classroom to hide in. Slipping inside, I sink to the floor, letting my back rest against the door. It's dark, and I don't bother with the lights. I don't want anyone to find me.

The glares have me on edge.

Could Em have told people about my texts before the accident? Are they all blaming me for not stopping Em and Jackson from driving?

I can feel the tears welling up to the surface again. I need to think about something else.

But what else is there? I have no idea where to go from here. Is this my life now? To be warned away from a terrible fate just to see the ones I love get hurt.

This is utter bullshit.

If I'd been in the car, maybe I could have helped; maybe Em and I could have gotten Jackson out. Anything is better than this constant questioning and survivor's guilt.

I keep my head down for the rest of the afternoon. We're studying the Salem witch trials in history class. While I think the subject matter is interesting, I'm not in a good place to be hearing about people dying.

Also, despite my best efforts not to make eye contact with anyone, it looks like whatever caused Jackson's friends to glare at me is spreading. By the last period, I'm sure at least a dozen people are looking at me like I'm a monster.

They aren't wrong.

The end of the day can't come fast enough.

When the bell finally rings to signal it's time to go home, I beeline for the doors. I'm going straight home and hiding in my room. I can't come back here.

It's a great plan, but it's turned upside down when I see who is standing outside the school. Em.

I stop dead in my tracks. Em doesn't notice me; she's talking to a handful of students — Jackson's old friends.

One of Jackson's friends sees me, pointing me out to Em. I gulp as we lock eyes. Her face is bruised, and there's a bandage on her cheeks. She looks exhausted and angry.

Cautiously, I make my way over to her.

"Em, I am so sorry," I start as I reach her.

Em narrows her eyes at me. Now that she's closer, I can see her eyes are red and swollen from tears. Even with the clear anger on her face, the venom in her voice takes me by surprise.

"I want you to know that you won't get away with this – you fucking psychopath."

Her words hit me like a slap across the face. "Wha-" I start under my breath.

Em is looking at me like I took a knife to her brother's throat. My eyes widen in disbelief at the implication.

"Em, no! You have every right to be mad that I didn't try harder to stop you guys from getting in the car. But I had nothing to do with the accident! Nothing!"

Could Em really think I tampered with their car to cause the accident? I can understand being blamed for not stopping the accident, but causing it? There's no way.

Em flushes with rage, her hands balling into fists at her sides. I think she might actually hit me. "LIAR!" she screams.

I step back in horror.

"The police didn't find any evidence of tampering, but I know you did something! I don't know what the hell is wrong with you, but you won't get away with this. I've shown everyone in our grade your messages from that night. You will pay for this!" Em finishes, her voice cracking with unshed tears as she turns and stalks away.

I can't find it in me to follow her. Clearly, Em has made up her mind and thinks the absolute worst of me.

I guess thinking I'm a murderer is easier than believing ghost stories.

All the students that had gathered to watch the show trickle away, dismissing me. I feel the telltale pain in my throat, warning me the tears are coming. I sink onto the sidewalk, hugging my knees to my chest. The tears come freely.

I couldn't stop them even if I wanted to.

When I finally have control over my sobs, the school parking lot is empty. It's starting to get chilly. I didn't bother with grabbing a coat this morning.

What's the point of bundling up when you can't feel anything?

My vision blurs again. Only this time, it isn't from tears; it's from the see-through human in front of me – ghost girl.

I don't even flinch. I have bigger problems.

She's in her usual state of worry, waving at me and trying to get my attention. But instead of humouring her, I lower my head back down, resting my forehead on my knees.

"Go away," I mutter.

All I want is to be left alone.

The eery glow doesn't disappear. I look back up to see her waving her hands wildly, indicating that I should go back into the school. Ignoring her antics, I turn away from her.

Ghost girl doesn't take the hint. She reappears, now kneeling in front of me. She shakes her head and points to the school again. Her message is loud and clear, and I should probably be worried.

I'm not.

Any sense of self-preservation I had died at the accident. All I feel is mounting frustration that I wasn't in the car to help.

"Look," I start, letting annoyance bleed into my voice. "I never asked for your help. I don't know what you want from me, and at this point, I don't care. So just leave me alone."

There. It's said. No more running from my fate. If I'm going to die today, I'm facing it head-on.

The ghost looks stricken. She wrings her hands together as if stuck in indecision.

My frustration mounts further. "Just go," I snap.

Ghost girl hesitates a second longer, anxiously looking over her shoulder before disappearing.

At that moment, a car comes tearing around a bend, headed towards the school. I expect it to slow down now that it's on the school drive. It doesn't. And it's headed directly towards me.

I scramble backwards, and the car screeches to a stop directly in front of me. My legs are shaking from the scare, but I manage to stand up and take a better look at who's driving like a maniac.

I'm in trouble.

The passengers spill out. They're all wearing dark hoodies with the hoods pulled up. The hoodies wouldn't be so concerning if it weren't for the Halloween masks. I can't see anyone's face.

One of the figures starts towards me.

Oh fuck no.

I turn to run in the opposite direction.

I'm not fast enough. I make it about two steps before I'm grabbed around my middle. The person picks me up off the ground, and I start screaming and kicking to no avail. The grip on me only tightens.

Still, I'm not giving up.

I keep screaming, desperately hoping to see someone walking down the road. No one is around to hear me.

I keep kicking out, trying to hit a second masked person, who is now approaching with duct tape. They disregard my struggles as they grab my legs, taping them together at my ankles. Together now, they carry me towards the trunk of the car – the open trunk, where another masked person waits to lock me in.

Oh god, no.

My claustrophobia flares to life, and true panic settles over me. I start screaming like a mad woman, utterly blind to everything except not going in that trunk. I flail, trying to escape, but still, I can't get free.

Someone around the front of the car yells, "Shut her up already."

There are more footsteps. Someone with a gorilla mask is standing over me now. The Gorilla person lifts a hand before something hard strikes me above the temple. Blissfully, everything goes black.

When I wake up, I can't see a thing. Everything is dark, and my head is throbbing.

I try to reach up to touch the spot where I was hit. No luck. My wrists are behind my back, tied together around something rough, maybe a tree?

I flex my legs only to find they aren't tied to the tree but are still duct-taped together. I point my toes but can't feel the ground.

Well, shit, this is really bad.

I want to scream, but there's a big cloth ball inside of my mouth – a gag.

I move my head around, trying to find some kind of light. There's some fabric brushing up against my nose and scraping over my hair. There's a bag over my head.

Did the masked people just tie me up in the middle of nowhere and leave me to be eaten by vultures? I feel like I at least deserve an evil mastermind speech.

A girl wants some closure.

When I read adventure novels, the hero always pretends to be knocked out a bit longer so they can get the jump on the bad guys.

Recall I am more inclined to be the first to die in these situations.

So, of course, I immediately start struggling against my ties, trying to slip free of them. The rope holding my wrists together is rough, and the fibres bite into my skin. I test the strength of the knots. They're tight.

My movement doesn't go unnoticed. A voice in front of me calls out, "She's awake."

I freeze, trying to recognize the voice. It sounds vaguely familiar.

"About time," another voice responds.

At the sound of that voice, my blood runs cold. I *know* that voice.

Em.

Is she seriously so convinced that I had something to do with the accident that she's ready to kill me over it?

My body starts to tremble. The irony of the situation isn't lost on me. Seeing ghosts is going to be the literal death of me. And no one will know to put that on my tombstone.

Pity.

Em's voice comes again, this time from behind me. "Vivian Ryans, you stand before us today accused of two crimes."

I can hear other footsteps as Em speaks. There must be a good amount of people here.

A party in my honour, they REALLY shouldn't have.

"Your first crime is the murder of Jackson McDaniel." Em's voice is hard, and I can hear the bitterness behind each word.

"Your second crime is a contingency. On the off chance you didn't tamper with the car, we still charge you with witchcraft."

At this, I hear snickering from the others.

Oh boy.

It looks like the Salem witch trial classes have sparked my classmates' interest. The sound of footsteps comes closer, the crunching leaves alerting me before Em's voice whispers directly behind me.

"Do you know how witches are punished, Vivian?" she asks with a sinister tone.

My heart stops.

Oh god.

Are they going to burn me at the stake? Is that what this tree is? A pyre?

I start struggling against the ties again with renewed vigour. No way, no burning at the stake; I'm not going out like this. Let them pick something less drawn out.

Em must feel satisfied by the torment she's putting me through. Because when she speaks again, she sounds like she is thoroughly enjoying herself. "Luckily for you, we aren't murderers – not like you are. So, we'll dole out your punishment. Then, we'll leave you here to rot. Maybe you'll get lucky, and someone will come along. If someone does find you, though, you will never say a fucking word about what happened here today."

Yeah, you keep lying to yourself, bestie.

I would laugh if I weren't gagged.

"Or," Em continues, "I will show every adult and authority your text messages. You'll be fully investigated, and even if the officers can't find a way to prove you tampered with the car, you'll be committed for life. Whether in a prison cell or an asylum, you'll never see daylight again – locked up in a tiny, padded room."

Em is well aware of my hatred for small spaces. She knows the effect her threat has on me.

Crushing defeat sweeps away any hope I might have for justice.

I will never, ever risk that punishment. I think I might even prefer being burned at the stake.

But Em isn't finished driving home her threat.

"I wonder if they still use those vests that don't let you move your arms."

I stop struggling, fear paralysis taking over once again.

"So, you won't tattle if you manage to break out of here, will you, Vivian?" Em all but purrs.

Apparently, revenge is her thing. Who knew?

I manage to shake my head.

If I play along, they probably won't outright kill me. Probably.

"Good," Em responds. I can hear her backing away.

"Now be a good sport and take your punishment. It's not even close to what you deserve, but it will have to do."

A male voice in front of me asks, "You want to start?"

Em answers, "Yeah, let's get this done. I don't want to be around her a minute longer than I have to."

There is more faint rustling, and then I feel a sharp pain in my leg. I try to scream, but the gag is holding.

Holy crap, that hurt.

What the hell was that? Did they just cut me?

There's another sharp pain now, only this one hitting my shoulder, and then again at a spot where the tree doesn't cover my back. Again and again, I'm hit with something hard.

Rocks, I realize with dismay.

They are throwing rocks at me, and not small gravel from the feel of it. These are decent-sized rocks, and they hurt like hell.

I can feel my blood starting to ooze down my arms – sharp rocks.

Over and over, the rocks hit me.

I thrash against the tree, trying to get away from the pain. Still, the ropes hold, and the rocks keep coming.

I try to protect my eyes by tucking my chin into my neck.

Bad idea.

My attempts at self-preservation only draw attention to my head. I get hit in the head a few more times before, and for the second time that day, I black out.

CHAPTER 4

HOLY CRAP, I HURT. EVERYWHERE.

I try not to move as I regain consciousness. I'm not sure how long I've been out.

A few minutes? A few hours?

Em and the others might still be close by. Maybe if they think I'm still out cold, they'll leave me alone.

I don't hear any shuffling or snickering.

My head is spinning, and there's a ringing in my ears. Likely the result of two back-to-back head injuries. The ringing makes it hard to hear anything.

I think it might be nighttime. I hear crickets over the ear-ringing. It's colder, too. The wind blows through my now-tattered T-shirt. If it is night, then I've been knocked out for a few hours.

I doubt Em and her friends have hung around that long, but I give it a few more minutes before I decide I'm alone.

When no other sounds come, I start struggling against the ropes. I'm shivering, whether it's from shock or the cold, I don't know. Probably both. I'm at risk of hypothermia if I don't find a way off this tree.

God, my head hurts.

I need to find a place to warm up, and soon.

I do the stupid thing and let myself feel grateful that at least I'm mostly dry. Cold raindrops splatter across my body, as if on cue with my misplaced optimism.

If there is a god, I'm clearly not their favourite.

I keep trying to wiggle out of the ropes. They're still tight, but not as tight as they were earlier. I must have loosened them when I struggled to escape the stones.

Stones.

Those lunatics actually stoned me and left me for dead.

I shove that thought back into a dark place in my head. It's reserved for all the trauma I am not ready to process. This is not the time.

Just focus on getting free.

How do people in movies get out of these situations? Right – break your thumb.

I'd really rather not. But if push comes to shove, I have that option. Let's call that one Plan Z.

My wrists are burning as I keep trying to loosen the ropes. I might be getting somewhere; I have a decent amount of wriggle room now. My hand keeps getting stuck at the thumb junction. Just a bit further to go.

It takes me a second to realize that something has changed. It just got quiet. The crickets are silent. The only noise left is the splattering of rain.

The hairs on the back of my neck stand on end. I think it's a bad sign when a forest goes silent. Doesn't that usually mean there's a large predator nearby?

I'm looking a lot like a wounded animal right about now.

I need to get off this damn tree.

I keep trying to tear my hand through the looser opening, but the ropes aren't giving. I'm so close. I can pull my hand out if I can just get my thumb through.

Reluctantly, I settle on Plan Z. I keep tugging on my hand, though, working up the nerve.

It can't hurt that badly, can it?

My internal motivation is interrupted by the sound of a branch snapping somewhere behind me. I freeze at the sound.

It's followed by a menacing growl.

Well, that's all the motivation I need.

Instantly, I crack my left thumb back as far as it will go. I scream into my gag but manage to wrench my hand through the binding. I'm still screaming as I fall to the ground in a heap.

I don't give myself time to feel the pain. I sit up, yank the sack off my head and pull out the gag. I don't bother to look behind me or get my bearings. After ripping the tape off my legs, I'm up and running for my life.

Despite being weak and exhausted from the cold, my adrenaline is kicking in full force, pushing me forward. I can feel a twinge in one of my ankles. I must have tweaked or sprained it when I fell off the tree. I try to ignore the pain that is beginning to radiate out from it and keep running.

Sprains aren't life-threatening. Growly things in dark forests probably are.

The pain in my ankle worsens. I've gone from sprinting to hobbling over branches, using trees as support. I'm not sure how far I've made it when my ankle finally gives out, and I tumble, landing hard on the wet forest floor.

Kneeling on the ground, I gasp for air.

I'd really like to know if whatever growled is following me. But I can barely hear anything over my thundering heart and the rain. Hopefully, I outran whatever is in the forest with me.

I'm doubtful, though. Even with my recent paranormal-inspired fitness routine, I'm not much of a runner.

It's dark, and I can't see anything that looks like a path. I need to get out of here. How the hell does one get their bearings at night, in the middle of the woods?

There's probably a road close to where I was tied to the tree. But going that way means I might come face to face with whatever was there with me.

I'd rather take my chances with dying of exposure. Isn't dying of hypothermia like going to sleep? I much prefer that over being mauled to death by the thing that growled.

I pull myself up, gingerly testing my ankle. Putting weight on it is excruciating, to the point where I can't feel my broken thumb or other injuries.

Instead, I get back on the ground and start fishing around in the dark, looking for a walking stick. The moon is bright, but there are enough clouds that I'm still fumbling around.

I'm still pawing at the ground when I notice a faint light in the distance – my heart soars.

Someone is looking for me!

I wave my arms and yell, trying to flag them over. The light continues to make its way towards me, but there's something weird about how it moves. It isn't sweeping or consistent like a flashlight. This light seems to blink. It's in one spot at one moment, and then less than a breath later, it reappears ten feet ahead.

My brow furrows as I try to rationalize what I'm seeing. Maybe the flashlight batteries are on the fritz?

I'm lying to myself because no human can move that fast.

I start to crawl backwards, trying not to draw more attention to myself. Considering I was screaming and waving a second ago, I recognize how stupid that is.

The creature gets closer, and it's definitely headed in my direction.

Oh fuck.

It's another ghost. But unlike the other PG-13 ghosts I've been seeing, this creature is something that has crawled straight out of my nightmares.

It has a humanoid shape, but parts of its body look like they have melted. It's as if the earth is sucking down on the creature's life force for the sake of overstaying its welcome. Its arms are elongated, and its fingers just about touch the ground.

Something is hanging limply down at its chest – a jaw. It takes me a second to realize it's a jaw because the creature doesn't have much of a face. There are two hollow, sunken-in indents where the eyes should be. The mouth opens to a gaping dark hole.

Its skin is a pallid grey, with thin black veins networking over its skin. The creature is facing my direction, and even though it has no visible eyes, I know it's looking at me. And it's coming for me.

I keep backing up, staying low to the ground as the creature advances. I try not to take my eyes off it because every time I blink, it appears a little bit closer.

As the creature approaches, I smell the stench of rotting meat.

I blindly back up until my feet hit something solid. When the rest of my body presses against said solid thing, I realize I'm an idiot.

In my panic not to look away from the creature, I backed myself into the hollow of a fallen tree. The only way out is forward and around.

Snapping my head to look back at the monster, I scream. It's directly in front of me now. Its mouth opens even wider, like a giant snake. The gaping maw hangs around the creature's waist as it descends onto me. The black void that fills the cavernous mouth looms just above my head.

This is it. It's going to eat me.

With that realization, exhausted and still stricken with grief, I give up.

I can't outrun this. I've probably escaped death far too many times at this point. Instead of letting my terror consume me right along with the creature, I stop screaming and shut my eyes.

Maybe Jackson and I can be friends in the afterlife. The thought brings me peace. At least I won't be alone anymore.

I wait for death to come.

Another breath.

Death is taking its damn time!

After a few more breaths, I open my eyes to see what the holdup is. The creature is still there, its eerie blue glow illuminating the otherwise dark forest. It's standing very still, as if confused. Its jaw slowly closes.

Seeing the massive mouth, I feel another stab of fear. Bad idea.

The creature hisses, and its jaw opens again.

I slam my eyes shut and take a calming breath. Okay, so maybe the creature responds to fear.

I force my fear down into the same place I'm keeping all my other trauma. I'm compartmentalizing.

I need another emotion to hang onto – something to distract me from the terror. I settle on detached curiosity.

I'm just going to pretend I'm reading about this creature and not facing it alone in a dark forest.

I can do this.

I peek my eyes open again. The creature looks relaxed. My fear theory has merit.

Cautiously, I study the creature, forcing myself to feel only mild interest. It helps not to look at its face. The body isn't as creepy once you get past the disproportional limbs.

It looks vaguely human. It's wearing a dress, but it's all ripped up and shredded down the front. The creature's legs are exposed, and its knees are scratched up. The scratches continue up its thighs.

Her thighs. This creature was human once.

With that realization, I'm hit with a wave of overwhelming anguish. I gasp, looking back at the creature's face. That emotion didn't come from me.

My mind is flooded with distant voices as I lock eyes with the creature's unseeing eye sockets. I can hear her in my head, a woman screaming to please stop and to let her go.

Bile rises in my throat as I put the pieces together. This creature was human. And, from the sounds of it, she was assaulted the night she was murdered.

My heart goes out to her, erasing any lingering fear I was trying to repress. No one deserves what this woman went through, to die so horrifically, only to find no peace in the afterlife.

The voices start again, replaying the same sounds and feelings.

It's as if she's trapped, forever reliving her trauma.

I'm not sure she can understand me, but I try anyway, "I am so deeply sorry for what happened to you."

I'm not sure why I do it, but a part of me feels compelled to let her know her pain is not invisible. That her suffering is seen, and she isn't alone.

As the words leave me, there's a prickling sensation along my skin. A wave of warmth rises from somewhere deep inside me and radiates through my body. Looking away from the creature, I lift my arms before me, trying to make sense of what I'm seeing.

A silver light pulses off me, coating my exposed skin and projecting outwards.

Well, this is a new level of weirdness.

I look back at the creature, thinking perhaps the light is coming from her.

My mouth drops. The creature is gone, replaced by the ghost of a woman. She's wearing the same dress, only it's no longer in tatters. The silver glow radiating from my skin is mirrored on hers.

How is this even possible? I look back at my skin, but the silver glow is gone.

The woman seems content.

"I…" I stammer, trying to let my brain catch up. "What just happened?"

Maybe this ghost can answer me. She certainly isn't avoiding me. The ghost only smiles and beckons me to follow her.

I think there's a hard and fast rule about not following ghosts in a spooky forest. But at this point, I'm pretty low on options.

How many times have I avoided death today? What's one more?

I try to stand, but as soon as I put weight on my foot again, I grimace. "My ankle, I'm not sure I can keep walking on it."

Have you ever tried hopping through a forest with only one good hand to grab onto things? It's not ideal.

I look around, thinking maybe the ghost will wait for me while I crawl around and find a decent walking stick. As if having the same thought, the ghost woman looks around and whisks away a few paces before picking up a long stick from the shadows.

That gives me pause. The ghost picked up a physical object.

Well, that's new.

The woman glides back to me and holds out the stick. I graciously accept, testing its strength. "Thank you," I say.

I use my good hand to hold onto it and take a step forward. I can make this work.

At that, the ghost smiles at me again before turning and slowly starting to float in the direction she came from. She stops to look back at me, beckoning me again to follow.

It's time for a leap of faith.

I shrug and slowly set off, following her ethereal glow.

We don't walk for long before the ghost stops. Reaching her side, I look ahead to where she's staring. Not a dozen feet away, the forest opens to a road.

I could cry, but it would take more energy than I have left. "Thank you," I breathe. My words come out choppy since I'm still shivering. The ghost smiles at me once more before continuing and fading out of existence.

I don't bat an eye at her sudden disappearance. I've seen enough crazy things over the last week to last me a lifetime.

With renewed drive, I hobble over to the road and make out the faint glow of a town not too far away.

Still frozen and tired, I decide I want to live, and start walking.

Chapter 5

Four years later, present day.

MY FEET SKID DOWN THE STEEP EMBANKMENT to the beach, the rounded stones providing little traction. Fog is already rolling in off the water, making it difficult to see the other side of the cove. With the fog comes a damp chill, and I tighten my favourite thrifted sweater around my neck.

I need to come to terms with the fact that fall is not too early to start wearing a scarf, at least not in this part of the country.

The northern shores of the East Coast have become my haven for over two years now.

When I finally made it home the night of my attack, I kept my lips sealed, refusing to share any details of what happened to me.

Luckily, my mother was so appalled by the threat of a scandal that she'd insisted on the spot not to involve the police. I was in complete agreement – no authorities needed.

I think some pain meds would have been nice, given my broken thumb, multiple lacerations, and sprained ankle. But, under the same umbrella of 'don't let the neighbours know your kid is fucked up,' my mother insisted I was fine.

So instead of receiving medical care, I sucked it up and went to my room.

I didn't leave the house again for another year and a half.

In the days that followed, I fell into a deep depression. I outright refused to return to school, which made it impossible for me to complete my last high school term.

Instead, I was forced to wait until the following fall so I could register for my school's online courses. Once I completed my final courses, I applied to every college that was located far from my hometown.

In all that time, I never once stepped foot outdoors.

I had absolutely no desire to risk seeing Em or recognize one of the voices of my attackers. Instead, I became a complete shut-in, seeing only my mother and stepfather, even months after the last of the bruises had faded.

While the bruises faded, the stones left scars up and down my arms and across most of my body. The rocks had cut deep.

My mother couldn't bear to be brought into the rumour mill over my latest 'cry for attention' and had agreed I shouldn't be seen in public.

The only thing that kept me going all that time was my unlimited collection of smutty romance novels – courtesy of my town's online digital library.

Escapism at its finest.

The day I got my acceptance letter to a coastal college almost 30 hours from home was the happiest day of my life.

I worked hard enough while online learning that my acceptance letter came with a substantial scholarship. I mean, there was no excuse not to nail your classes when you had literally nothing else to do.

The same day my acceptance letter arrived, I secured a student loan and line of credit. Hours after that, I rented a fully furnished apartment near the college, sight unseen.

Luckily for me, people out East 'did things a little differently' – their words, not mine, and no co-signer was needed – just a damage deposit, paid for by courtesy of the aforementioned student line of credit.

I was on a bus and moved into my new place two days later.

No heartfelt goodbyes, no going-away party. Just more pain when my mother took that opportunity to disown me.

The college is small, not particularly well-known, and remote. So very remote. And that suits me just fine.

In this town, I'm just another tourist or student; who knows for sure? The girl I left behind is a ghost. Here, I had a chance to be reinvented.

Here, I'm normal.

Of course, normal may be a bit of a stretch to describe my current state. While I'm determined to be utterly ordinary in this new place, no shade of beige will make the ghosts and creepy faceless creatures disappear.

There must be something wrong with my internal wiring because once I noticed more of the creepy creatures here, I couldn't ignore them.

I nicknamed them 'the faceless,' namely because they lack many facial features. I get zero points for creativity. But apparently, I have an overactive conscience when it comes to monsters.

And so, I didn't do the sane thing and ignore the clinically terrifying beings. Instead, I honed my ability to release their spirits.

I liken the experience of freeing spirits to helping them 'go to the light,' as some popular television shows call it.

Not that I binge-watched every paranormal show I could get my hands on during my shut-in period. But if I did binge-watch them, it was solely for educational purposes.

The fog that rolls into the cove now surrounds me.

You would think as a very claustrophobic individual, the fog would make me uncomfortable. But strangely enough, the fog feels more like a security blanket.

Sure, I can't see further than an arm's length ahead of me, but that means no one can see me either, and that suits me just fine.

However, the cave that looms ahead of me will be a trial. The caves are a local legend. This cove is less than an hour's drive from my apartment, so I was all in when I heard a few tourists talking about the destination.

Melody Joanne

I love to walk the coastline by my apartment every night before bed. Over the last two years, I've freed at least a dozen faceless along that path. But I know that if I want to help more trapped spirits, I need to start looking into new places.

That's where the cave comes into play. The cove is surrounded by steep cliffs, except for one slightly less death-inducing hill on the far-left side. Usually, access to the cove is completely blocked off by churning waters.

The tides here are some of the highest in the world. The cave is only accessible at the lowest tide, and even then, not for very long. As the tide ultimately rises, the cave becomes fully flooded again and invisible to the world.

Local legends say the cave was once used as a smuggling ground for pirates.

Even now, with the full knowledge of where the cave is, you need perfect timing and a decent understanding of tide charts to get inside it.

Reaching the cave entrance, I nervously glance at the timer I've set on my phone. The timer tells me exactly how much time I have left before my path to the cove's other side is again flooded.

Less than a quarter of an hour now. This is going to be a short exploration.

I'm guessing that if pirates used this cave to smuggle things, without the advent of the smartphone and timers, there would probably have been some trial and error in determining safe windows to enter the cave. And through that trial and error, some pirates may have passed on in a traumatizing way – potentially a good hotspot to find more faceless.

Am I recklessly endangering myself by wandering into a death cave alone in the middle of nowhere?

Maybe.

But quite frankly, there isn't much in my life that has any real meaning other than freeing the faceless. So, death caves it is.

I might still be a bit depressed.

Not letting my anxiety paralyze me, I enter inside. It's dark, and I switch on the flashlight app on my smartphone.

While some fog penetrates the cave, it's less dense here. I can make out the shells of thousands of snails and other sea life plastered to the still-damp walls.

The cave's opening is massive but rapidly splits into multiple smaller tunnels. I keep moving at a steady pace, choosing one of the paths, taking care to always take the right-hand path when I find a split between two networks of caves.

I expected it to be quiet here, but the echoes of dripping water are amplified. The tunnels are tall enough for a person to walk through and not too narrow. I can barely touch both sides if I extend my arms.

It's wide enough that my claustrophobia isn't bothered.

So far, there's no evidence that people have ever been here. Not that I deluded myself into thinking I could find any kind of treasure. I know die-hard treasure hunters have combed every last crack in these caves.

But still, there's a thrill in thinking of the long-ago people that may have frequented this place.

As I make my way even deeper into the cave network, I finally see a faint glow ahead.

Bingo.

The glow isn't still but instead blinks from one location to the next, steadily making its way toward me, continuously reappearing slightly closer.

Quickly, I squish down the fear that wants to come out. I don't care how often I've helped faceless creatures. Their habit of blinking in and out of view, coming closer and closer, always freaks me out.

It only took me a few instances of trial and error to confirm that the faceless feed on fear. Luckily, I'm a quick learner and have yet to take a dive into one of their black hole mouths.

As most trauma survivors can attest to, I'm excellent at compartmentalizing.

Rather than letting my fear stick around, I focus my mental headspace on who I might be dealing with today.

The faceless looks like a man, and he's wearing some kind of armour, leather by the looks of it. He's shirtless under the armour, and I can see intricate tattoos clawing over his body.

Are those Celtic knots?

Something like that, at least. Did the Celts ever make their way to these shores? Maybe, but no, that isn't right. I spot the telltale knotwork hammer on one of the tattoos.

This faceless must be Norse.

Looking back up at the smoothed-out face of the faceless spirit, I'm thoroughly curious. It stands still before me, staring at me with vacant hollow eyes. If it did have eyes, I'm guessing it would look disappointed that I'm not a walking happy meal of fear.

Sorry, bud, no fast food today.

Stepping closer, I start to hear them – the moments the man experienced before his death. He'd been exploring the cave when he noticed the water gathering around him. Panicked, he'd started running, trying to find his way back out again, only to get lost and swallowed by the unforgiving waters.

My own emotions go out to the faceless and the terrible death he suffered. As the feeling of empathy leaves me, I feel that same warm light from within me, slowly reaching from my chest toward the creature.

The silvery light envelops the faceless, and the creature is replaced by a man. His hair is long and braided down his back. His face sports the same runes that are inked across his body.

Viking. I found an honest-to-goodness Viking.

A hot one, too.

My excitement would have been longer lived except for the feeling of ice-cold water in my shoes. Turning my phone's flashlight to the ground, I realize the ground is now covered in over an inch of water.

Crap.

Switching back to my timer app, I see that, sure enough, I don't have more than a few minutes left to get out of the caves.

Otherwise, I'll be filling in the now vacant position of 'idiot who stayed in the caves too long and had their soul trapped for most of eternity.'

No thanks.

Spinning on my heel, I start running back the way I came in. In hindsight, I did not leave myself much time to get back to shore.

Stupid, stupid, stupid.

I keep cursing as I run faster, always remembering to turn left when I meet a split in the cave.

Rounding a corner, I step on a particularly smooth stone – funny thing about wet, smooth stones. They're slippery. And with that wise realization, I go down, falling into the water that has now very quickly risen to at least six inches.

The fall doesn't damage me, but the same can't be said for my smartphone. As I fell, I tried to grab the wall and accidentally launched my phone into the water.

Evidently, smartphones and water don't work so well together. My phone is now hidden in the steadily rising water, and I can't see any hint of its light.

While I would love to paw around the dark water to try and find it, I really don't want to die today. So, instead, I pull myself up and start running with one hand against the left-hand side of the cave wall. I try to keep a mental map open of how far I am from the cave entrance.

I know I must be getting closer. The water that swirls around my feet feels stronger, but I can't trust the currents. Who knows how many eddies and other swirly water patterns are created when tides enter underground caves?

I sure as hell have no idea.

Faster now, I keep moving. Without my phone, I have no idea how long I've been in here. But even with my flashlight, I knew I would need to run to get out of here on time. I'm much slower without the light.

I fucked up.

Pushing ahead, I see a faint silver glow.

Moonlight!

I feel almost giddy at the sight and flat-out run towards it, splashing through now foot-deep water.

Disappointment hits with a ferocity when I realize what I'm seeing isn't the moon. It's the hot Viking ghost.

Well, shit.

My mind races. Did I skip a few tunnel turns when I ran towards him?

I don't have time to turn back. I don't have time for much of anything.

Even though I haven't communicated with any freed faceless ghosts since the woman in the woods, I shoot my shot.

"Please help." My tone is pleading. Hopefully, that breaks through any language barriers.

The Viking ghost says nothing. He disappears until I see his faint glow up ahead. I take off running again towards him.

It isn't lost on me that I'm trusting my life to a Viking who evidently couldn't find his way out of the cave when he was alive. I can only hope he mapped it out better in his creepy ghost phase.

After a few more moments of chasing Viking lights, I'm finally at the mouth of the cave.

I want to sink to my knees with glee that I won't drown in the cave.

But I can't because I'm still very much at risk of drowning in the open air. The currents are dangerously strong as they pull against my knees. I push forward, heading for the only side of the cove that isn't a cliff.

The fog hasn't cleared, and I can only hope I'm taking the quickest route possible.

My mental mantra starts up again.

Stupid, stupid, stupid.

Maybe I'm turning into an adrenaline junkie. I can see the draw. I certainly don't feel numb now – the desire to live courses through my veins with renewed vigour.

Finally, the water grows more and more shallow. I don't stop, even when I reach dry ground. I know the tide will catch up to me momentarily. Instead, I wheeze as I make my way back up the embankment, questioning my life choices.

I collapse onto the ground once I'm well above the tide lines. When I look down into the cove, I see the light of the Viking spirit fade away into nothingness.

I try to smile – it's difficult to do when you're gasping for breath and shivering.

While I can't undo my past, this is something I can do that makes a difference, even if it's only in the afterlife. I can help spirits find their way out of their tortured prisons, even if my own guilt keeps me in mine.

CHAPTER 6

WHILE I LOVE MOST ASPECTS OF LIVING ON THE northern coast, the wind here is going to give me white hair.

Sure, you could laugh at the fact that a self-declared ghost-whisperer is afraid of wind. But when every building literally shakes from the force of the North Atlantic 'breeze,' a bit of wariness seems valid.

My apartment isn't too far from campus, so I walk to save on parking and gas. Unfortunately, my quickest route cuts through a forest. And while this is usually a beautiful and relaxing walk, today's wind is clearly out to destroy my peace of mind.

I hustle down the path, glaring at the thin, spindly trees that rattle and sway like wacky inflatable tube men.

Don't you do it. Stay rooted where you belong.

Yeah, I mentally threaten trees. I'm not perfectly sane, I know.

The campus and the forest next to it both face the ocean. Logically, I know these trees have been buffeted by these gusts for longer than I've been alive. The evidence is in the dark green moss that hangs from every branch.

Today, the moss combines with the dappled sunlight from the overhead canopy to give the illusion that the forest is shivering. Or maybe that's just my body – it's cold enough.

I finally caved this morning and busted out my scarf and rubber boots – or my 'all-seasons' as they're called out here.

I pick up my pace, eager to be well away from the dancing trees. All around me, I can see branches – some at least as thick as my arm, littering the forest floor.

Well, that's slightly foreboding.

The path is empty, save for me. Maybe locals know better than to walk through forests during windstorms.

Or maybe a tree has already taken them out.

I should get these intrusive thoughts under control.

More than likely, most people are doing the sane thing and are still in bed, not out at the crack of dawn because a demented professor is a "morning person."

I guess getting crushed by a tree would save me from my morning tutorial.

I'm in my third year of college, and the classes in my schedule this term are mostly fun to learn about. I'm double majoring in history and English, so I have the advantage of being able to pick and choose most of my classes. A perk of double majors, the prerequisites are a bit more loosely defined than single majors.

Still – there are some unavoidable classes. This morning's modern history class is a prime example.

The class would be a bit more enjoyable if a psychopath didn't teach it. Said psychopath is Dr. Richard Parnard, the man who specifically instructed the department to schedule his class and tutorial at the worst possible times.

This man wakes up before dawn to get a run in before Monday tutorials and even invites his students to join him.

Sweet, but absolutely insane.

The insanity of Dr. Parnard is why I'm just arriving to campus now, at 7:30 on a Monday morning, and am surrounded by the faces of my exhausted peers.

Slowly, very slowly, we shuffle into class, most of us still half-asleep. I'm pretty sure some of them still smell like alcohol.

I guess the kitchen parties ran into Sunday.

While this small college town is low on bars or clubs that usually draw in students, there is enough wacky Atlantic culture to keep any rowdy student full of alcohol and drunken fiddle music.

Not that I'm judging. I might not be big on parties, but I did my civic duty and was screeched in with the best of them.

The room is built as an auditorium, with two-person desks set up across the eight levels. The room's right side has window seats facing a boardwalk and the ocean.

Before another student gets the same idea, I hurry up to my favourite spot in the back right-hand corner of the class. At least people-watching will help keep me awake.

A bang on the desk jolts me.

I'm greeted by the somewhat maniacal smile of my friend Sarah. Sarah is lean and athletic, with short-cropped brown hair framing her round, not-tired-looking face. While Sarah and I met in our first year, we only became friends well into the tail end of our second year.

That's one fallback of having a double major – when you don't share almost every class with the same group of people, it's more challenging to make friends — especially if you happen to be introverted.

"Goooood morning, sunshine!" Sarah exclaims.

She's holding a tray with four cups of coffee and hands me a cup. Her voice is bright and chipper, and I see a few students grabbing their heads closer to the front of the class to make the loud noise stop. Hangovers can be a bitch.

"You're a lifesaver," I answer, taking the cup and taking a long inhale of the sweet caffeine. "How did you know I needed this today?"

Sarah smirks. "I saw your chat icon last night, it said you were still online at 1 AM. Please tell me you were with a man."

Sarah has a habit of checking in on my sex life. She likes to note that even a nun would be bored by my complete lack of dating.

I decide to shake things up. "As a matter of fact, I was! And he was sweet, sexy, thoughtful, and great in bed..."

Sarah cuts me off, rolling her eyes, "And completely fictional. Right? You were reading."

She sees right through me. I laugh, "Guilty."

Sarah turns to face me, making sure she has my undivided attention for the gospel she's about to grace me with. "Vivian, you're literally a knockout. If I had your ass, I'd be getting laid every night."

Conner, another friend of ours, arrives just in time to hear Sarah's comment. Without asking, he grabs a coffee from the tray and takes a seat in front of us, commenting as he does so, "Sarah, I'd gladly do you, even with your flat ass. The sass that comes out of those lips would make it more than worth my time."

Sarah rolls her eyes. "Dream on, playboy."

Sarah's isn't wrong. With his blond, sun-kissed hair, broad chest and winning smile, Conner is an incorrigible flirt and class A playboy. Luckily, he also happens to be funny and a somewhat decent human if you can get past the incessant sexual innuendos.

"Ahh, it's okay, Sarah. We all know Vivian is my true love anyway. So, tell me, Viv – when are you going to let me show you what your sex books are all about?"

My cheeks heat, and I consider sinking into my chair out of sight.

ONE TIME!

It only took one time when I let my friends crash at my apartment after a night of drunken debauchery. After Sarah and I passed out on my bed, the guys, who were banished to the floor, decided to raid my bookshelves. They got a very explicit image of what I like to read.

They have never let me live it down since. "Not any time soon, Conner – sorry, you're just not my type."

Conner smiles at me salaciously. "Shame," he says as he eyes me up and down, "red-headed nymphs with ocean-blue eyes are *exactly* my type."

Sarah rolls her eyes for what must be the third time this morning. I think she's going for a record. "Conner, anyone with boobs is your type," she sasses, saving me from any further embarrassment.

Conner seems to want to argue but is cut off when Dr. Parnard addresses the class to quiet down. Making sure to give me an exaggerated wink, Conner turns back to look at the board.

We all have to pinch our lips to stop smiling when our friend Isaac, who looks half-dead, walks in just as the class settles down.

Isaac keeps his head down, making no eye contact as he's forced to make the walk of shame across the front of the class and up the stairs to our spot.

Dr. Parnard doesn't appreciate tardiness. He makes sure to give Isaac the class's undivided attention while he unpacks his laptop and gets settled. By the time Dr. Parnard starts to speak again, Isaac looks like he may have a sunburn from the shade of blush on the back of his neck.

Today's tutorial isn't exactly exhilarating – we're covering the dawn of the digital age. I try to stay focused as Dr. Parnard begins writing a timeline on the board.

The professor doesn't believe in lecture slides. If he only writes his material on the board, students are pushed to attend his class rather than try to understand the material from home.

A lot of this tutorial is review. I spent most of my Saturday afternoon preparing my notes. The yawns are already starting and are spreading through the class faster than the common cold. To avoid the yawn plague, I turn my attention from the professor to the scene outside.

Students taking classes with less insane professors are starting to arrive on campus. While most hustle from one building to another, others are content to sit by the central fountain, enjoying their morning coffee.

The school isn't very old, maybe 50 years from what I remember seeing on a plaque outside. I haven't found many ghosts in the school buildings, probably due to its recent founding. I can only imagine how haunted some of the older colleges might be.

After learning how to help free the faceless, I took another shot at communicating with the local ghosts. I had an abundance of local history assignments in my first year. I was hoping some of the older ghosts I'd seen around town would be able to offer some insight.

My efforts were in vain. No amount of coaxing, smiling, or bribing would get the ghosts to give me the time of day.

How does one bribe a ghost, you ask?

Apparently, not with wine.

The ghosts' attitudes just mirror those of the ghosts in my hometown. If I dare to look at them, it's like I've grossly invaded their privacy. So, I've left them to their own musings and adopted the 'I'll pretend I can't see you if you pretend you can't see me' strategy.

I still think my life would be cooler if I could at least talk to them.

Stupid jerk-faced ghosts.

When the tutorial finally ends, most students are slow to get up, their muscles cramped from sitting still for so long. Sarah stretches lazily beside me, and I'm content to hang around in my seat, as the guys get up and turn towards us.

Our little group consists of four people. All history majors, Sarah, Conner, and Isaac became friends while

72

partying in our first year. They only 'adopted' me months later.

My adoption was less than subtle.

I'm sitting at one of the larger library tables, pouring over some study notes, when the three hooligans plop down next to me.

I feel like a deer caught in headlights when the overexuberant energies of Conner and Sarah sit on either side of me. Isaac sits in front of me, offering a shy smile. That's the only thing I notice about him because a second later, Conner and Sarah demand my undivided attention.

Sarah introduces herself, noting that she's seen me in many of their classes and that it's high time we become friends. She then pushes her phone in front of my face and asks for my contact info because we will be hanging out.

She's as subtle as a freight train.

I'm shocked and speechless, but I enter my contact info as asked, only to be added to a group chat with the three of them a moment later.

Conner doesn't miss his opportunity to hit on me, but Sarah swats his hand, demanding he not scare me off and make me think they're weird. This instigates a heated yet playful argument between the two, which only finishes when Sarah declares that I'm off limits as a hookup for at least a few hangouts. Just so that they can show me what a great group they are.

Conner relents, and as they leave, Sarah tells me she'll be saving a seat for me at our next shared class.

Who in their right mind could resist that kind of friendship offer?

A few months later, during one of Sarah and I's favourite wine and homework nights, I got up the nerve to ask why they'd decided to invite me into their group. I hadn't been actively looking to make friends. The traumatic memories had ensured that, and their interest in me had seemed entirely random.

Sarah grinned as she responded, "I love introvert friends; you all seem so innocent and shy, but once you're in with them, they are the craziest, most fun people out there."

I laughed at that, unsure I bought into the crackpot theory, but I was grateful, nonetheless.

Sarah interrupts my train of thought, bringing me back to the present, "Breakfast?"

"PLEASE," Conner answers, like a man starved. He looks like he's about to keep talking but is distracted, turning to smile at a girl walking past us.

She turns to me, "Vivi – breakfast, you coming?"

I shoot my friends an apologetic look. "Sorry guys – I either live frugally or need to get a part-time job, and I would much rather avoid working at a drive-through."

For the moment, I'm getting by with only working during the summer term and living off those savings, in addition to scholarships and student loans during the school semesters.

"Awe, Viv, but think of the perks – all the fries you can eat – and all the fries you can feed your friends!" Conner answers.

I laugh, "Then YOU get a fast-food job."

Conner gives me his most winning smile. "And miss all the extra time hanging out with you, gorgeous? Never!"

I shake my head, smiling. He's a flirt, but he's harmless. If anything, he's desensitized me to male attention.

Reluctantly, we head out of the empty class, heading for the main building doors before the next hoard of students ambles in.

"Okay, so Conner, Isaac, and I are getting breakfast. We don't have any other classes together today, Vivi," Sarah states. I know from her tone that she's up to something. "What time are you done today?" she continues.

"Just after 11," I answer. There's suspicion in my voice. Sarah is notorious for talking us into crazy adventures.

"Perfect!" Sarah exclaims. "I have a fun activity planned for us, and before you say no, it's free, and you owe us because you bailed on partying this weekend."

I did bail on partying, and I do feel a bit guilty. But my favourite author had just released a new novel, and I couldn't put it down.

"Alright," I relinquish. "But I need to go and get a new phone first. I uhm, dropped mine in the ocean over the weekend – so by the way. I have no phone; I'm not ignoring you all." I pause before adding, "Can I at least know what we're doing?"

"Of course!" Sarah says, giving the group a devilish smile. "You know how I love to surf, and you all never come surfing with me because rental equipment costs cash? Well, I went on a few dates with Tommy. He works at the surf shack on the beach. Nice guy, TERRIBLE taste in movies, and anyhow, he said that Monday afternoons are really slow, so I can bring you guys over, and you can all try to learn how to surf, free of charge!"

She's practically bouncing with excitement. No, scratch that; she is, in fact, bouncing. The girl loves to surf and usually goes out at least twice a week.

I'm not sure how great I'll be at surfing, but I can swim, and it sounds like a fun challenge. "Alright, I'm in!"

What's a bit more adrenaline-inducing activities? That's my new code for near-death experiences. I'm swearing off those.

Isaac is beaming. "Yessss!" he exclaims. "I'm so stoked; I've wanted to get in the water and try the waves since we got back from summer break!"

I notice Conner looks a bit concerned. "You okay, Conner? Don't feel like surfing?" I ask him.

"Ahh, well..." he starts, looking embarrassed. "It's just that I'm not a great swimmer. All muscle, you know? I don't float too well."

Sarah is quick to jump in, "They have life jackets! Don't worry, bud; we would never make fun of you for not being a strong swimmer. Not when we have soooo much other material to go off when it comes to you."

Conner looks relieved but ruffles Sarah's hair anyway for the sass she threw him. They love poking fun at each other.

Once again, I'm reminded that beyond the jokes, my friends genuinely care for each other, and I suppose that includes me, too.

The thought gives me a pang of unease. It isn't easy to let people in. But the more time that goes by, the better I get at letting my guard down.

"Okay, so it's settled. Vivi, meet us at the surf shack at noon. No wait. Make that one. The phone store guy will probably want to hit on you, and it will take extra time.

Bring a bathing suit and a towel. Byeeeee!" Sarah finishes by turning and walking towards the main street that holds multiple cafés.

Isaac follows her, but Conner can't help flirting one more time. "Viv in a bikini – if the water doesn't drown me, the heart attack surely will," he finishes before winking and then turning to catch up with the others.

I laugh again. It's nice having a group of friends. I think that with them, maybe, just maybe, I can be okay again one day.

CHAPTER 7

CONTRARY TO SARAH'S PREDICTION, THE STORE clerk does not hit on me. That might be because the person working the counter today is a very pregnant woman, but I don't feel the need to give that information.

I blanch as I mentally recalculate my budget while walking home. Smartphones are not cheap, but if you can't have internet access to look up the random questions that come to mind every day, what is even the point of having a phone?

It looks like I'm going to need to cut back on more than just breakfast out with friends over the next few months. That leaves the grocery budget or the book budget, you know – the essentials.

Oh, the difficult choices of a broke college student.

I make it to the beach with a few minutes to spare. Scanning the shores, I'm relieved to see no ghosts or faceless here. I take that as an encouraging sign that no one has died here in a long time.

I head down to the sand in front of the surf shack.

Conner is already waiting in his pink flamingo swim trunks. He's shirtless, and I can tell he's cold.

"You're going to turn into a popsicle if you don't put more clothes on," I exclaim as a greeting.

On the other hand, I am wearing my favourite baggy sweatpants and a black hoodie over my bikini. Even with the layer of protection from the weather, I'm still wrapped up in my towel to try and stop the wind from digging into my bones.

Conner laughs. "Well, at least I'll be a popsicle with some damn sexy abs on display. They'll be able to put me up in a museum as the perfect male specimen."

He starts posing in different positions, flexing every muscle he can think of.

"A museum job! So prestigious. I can see the writing in front of your plaque now: Most failed attempts at asking friends out," I tease as I try to push my hair behind my face into a French braid.

Okay, maybe Sarah's assessment that I would come out of my shell more when I accepted the group as 'my' people wasn't too far off. Or maybe Conner is just the easiest person to joke around with in the world, so not even I can resist.

Not that I will *ever* admit that to him, of course. The guy does NOT need someone to put his name and 'irresistible' together in a sentence, no matter the context.

The wind that worried me during my morning walk has shown no sign of slowing down. It's making it impossible to get my hair under control, with more strands getting caught in my mouth than the elastic. A French braid isn't happening today. Giving up, I let the waves whip around me wildly.

The wind is welcome here, though. There is a great swell in the water. The waves crash onto the shore, and fog is starting to descend over the water.

The town is positioned on a small strip of land, with one side bordering a sheltered bay while the other opens to the vast Atlantic. We're on the non-sheltered side now, and you can't see the horizon from the fog that quickly rolls in.

Conner isn't ignoring an opening to hit on me again, "That may be my plaque, Viv, but I'm certain I'll grow on you. If I hit on you enough, you'll eventually come to appreciate my charm."

"Hey guys! Sorry, we're late! Isaac wanted to give me a speedo fashion show before we came here," Sarah calls as she and Isaac hurry towards us.

I'm relieved at their interruption.

Conner gives me a heated look before turning to our friends. I'm starting to wonder if maybe the man is being a bit more flirtatious with me than usual.

Isaac laughs and blushes a bit as he shakes his head. "Nah, sorry guys, I just had trouble finding my swim trunks. I hadn't unpacked them yet," he finishes, running his hand through his hair again with a sheepish grin.

"He refused to wear one of my bathing suits." Sarah pretends outrage. "I told him I have like seven, and tough guy wouldn't hear of it."

Isaac gives Sarah a wolfish grin. "Sarah, if your bathing suit is on my body, then you'd better be wearing it."

I bite my lips together to stop from laughing. I wonder if Isaac and Sarah are starting to have a thing between them. Isaac isn't usually a flirt. Then again, maybe hanging out with Conner is finally rubbing off on him.

Conner and I both side-eye each other, eyebrows raised, acknowledging the change.

Sarah laughs and turns away from Isaac. I swear her cheeks are a little pink.

Interesting.

"Okay, well! I'm going to talk to Tommy and get some wetsuits for you guys before you all chicken out," she calls before running away from the group.

And yes, she is literally running. Sarah doesn't move slowly; she has the energy to rival the energizer bunny.

As Sarah makes her way to the surf shack, a tall, thin guy comes out to meet her. He's holding wetsuits, but his eyes are glued on Sarah, who is already geared up in her own.

Isaac notices Tommy noticing Sarah, and his posture becomes less relaxed. He crosses his arms and slightly lifts his chin as he stares at Tommy, irritation evident on his face.

Right, Sarah is dating Tommy.

Not ideal if Isaac is starting to be interested in our friend.

Sarah is oblivious to Isaac's posturing. She's bubbling with excitement about finally getting her friends into the water. "So, everyone, this is my friend Tommy. Tommy, these are my friends Conner, Isaac and Vivi!"

At the introduction, Tommy reluctantly pulls his eyes from Sarah as he approaches us to hand out the wetsuits. "Hey guys, uhm, I tried to guess your sizes from the surf shack."

As he hands Isaac a wetsuit, Tommy looks momentarily taken aback by Isaac's hostile look.

Thankfully, Conner, ever the people person, holds out his hand to shake hands with Tommy. "Hey man, thanks so much for doing this."

Tommy quickly glances at Sarah before looking back to Conner. "Yeah, no problem. Sarah is out here all the time, and if you guys love surfing just as much, I'm sure we'll be seeing more of you, too."

He and Conner then start having what is undoubtedly a riveting conversation as they both walk toward the surf shop entrance to find a life jacket for Conner.

I'm relieved about the complementary wetsuit and not needing to show off more of myself than I'd like. I'm pretty careful about keeping my scars covered up.

One night, out of morbid curiosity, I tried to count them. There were at least fifty that I was able to see. Some have faded over time to become barely noticeable, but others are larger and leave clear marks over much of my skin.

I might like my new friends, but I'm not ready to talk about my past. I'm not sure I'll ever be.

I turn to Isaac and Sarah. "I'll be right back; I'm going to change in the bathroom at the beach entrance."

Sarah laughs, "Too shy to show off your bikini body? Come on, girl! I would kill for your curves!"

I laugh with her, "Oh, come on, Sarah, you've got the fabulous lean, athletic look. Like a sexy gazelle."

Poor Isaac is taking a drink of water just as the words leave my mouth, and he spits it out as he bursts out laughing.

"A gazelle, Viv?" he asks, tears in his eyes as he wipes his face on Sarah's towel. They aren't used to me being vocal with my humour.

Hey, good things take time.

"A *very* sexy gazelle," I deadpan before turning towards the bathrooms.

I'm relieved I was able to distract them from asking more questions about why I'm not changing with them on the beach.

The wetsuit is a deep grey and quite literally skin-tight. It's the full-body kind and thick enough that it will likely at least offer some protection against the cold. I stuff my sweater and sweatpants into my schoolbag and head back to my friends, who now stand beside the surfboards Tommy has brought out.

The surf shack keeps a small, fenced-in courtyard at the back where all the surfboards are stored. Placing my bag with my friend's things, I head to a free board lying in the sand.

Conner is wearing a yellow life jacket over his black wetsuit and eagerly questioning Tommy about his different tips for us.

Tommy is notably not in a wetsuit.

Isaac is impatient and interrupts them, "So about the lesson..." he begins, the annoyance bleeding into his tone.

Oh boy, there is zero diplomacy in that tone. It sounds as though our typically mild-mannered Isaac is ready to fight someone.

Tommy looks back to Isaac and crosses his arms, doing some posturing of his own. "Well, I believe there's no way to learn like experience. So, get out there and learn. Besides, Sarah will be with you. Just copy her," he finishes. His expression isn't exactly hostile, but it certainly isn't friendly.

Great.

Male rivalry has cost us our lesson.

But apparently, Sarah thinks this is a genius plan. She picks up her board and starts running to the water, calling behind her, "You heard him, guys, trial by fire! Woo!" With that, she's running over the shallow waves and paddling out.

Conner, Isaac, and I exchange looks. "Well, you heard the woman." Conner shrugs. "Last one in the water has to ask Parnard what kind of cologne he uses," he yells as he takes off after Sarah.

"Oh, hell no!" Isaac yells as we chase him.

We quickly catch up to Conner and beat him to the water.

I've taken up jogging every now and again since moving here. I'm still not a runner, but I'm not as painfully out of shape as I used to be.

"Dang it," Conner exclaims as he hits the water seconds after us.

We're standing in less than knee-high water now. "Come on, Isaac, you can fish me out of the water if the undertow takes me down," Conner instructs as he and Isaac pair up, walking further into the water before getting on their boards and paddling out.

The guys make their way out, and Conner slips off his board and splashes into the water before he even tries to stand on his board.

Giggling, I decide to take my time as I make my way into deeper water. The waves are deafening as they crash around me, and with the fog, I quickly lose track of my friends.

Soon, I can feel the undertow pulling at my feet and decide I'd better get onto my board. It's a bit of an awkward effort. At five feet and five inches, I'm not very tall and apparently even less coordinated in water than I am on land.

Finally, after more attempts than I care to admit, I sit up on my board and find my balance.

Am I supposed to stand on this thing?

Fat chance.

But I'm no quitter and willing to make an absolute fool of myself trying. Come to think of it, though, with this fog, the only person who will know how monumentally I failed at surfing is me.

Silver linings are like the hot sauce of life. You need to put that shit on everything.

Scanning around me, I try to find Sarah, but to no avail. The fog is thick, and it's hard to see more than ten feet ahead. Squinting, I figure I'll paddle out and try to find the others.

You'd think I would at least be able to hear Conner. The guy is loud and never stops talking. But I guess even the ocean wants to drown him out.

Picking a random direction to paddle out to, I gingerly lay down on my board, trying to avoid letting more of my body touch the water. The water is freezing, and I'm not keen to jump in just yet. When I finally place my hands in the water, a shock courses through my left hand.

Holy shit!

I wrench my hands back.

The water around me ripples away through the waves, heading out to deeper water.

What the hell was that?

Gingerly, I inspect my hand. There's nothing wrong with it, and there's no damage that I can see.

I thought maybe I was stung by a jellyfish, but the pain was gone in an instant. There are also no telltale red strips indicating I'm in for a world of hurt.

Glancing back into the water, I try to see below the dark surface. Do electric eels live in the Atlantic Ocean? Are there other fish that can shock you?

Unlike our unenthusiastic surf teacher, I'm not keen to find out through experience.

Unfortunately, I've caught a bit of a current, and my board has floated out further than I anticipated. As I look behind me for signs of shore, my stomach drops. It's going to be challenging to get back without paddling.

By challenging, I mean near impossible.

Unless there are other currents nearby that push you in, but even then, I need to get out of this current.

Once again, I look around for my friends. I can't see far enough through the fog.

Hopefully, whatever shocked me is long gone and not headed for them. I chew on my lips for another minute before making up my mind.

There's no helping it; I need to touch the water again.

Very gingerly now, I place my hand back under the water. My wariness is quickly transformed into surprise.

Small tendrils of blue light extend from my left hand. Like little strings, I can see them glowing, leading off into deeper water.

I frown, trying to make sense of what I'm seeing. At this point, I have a pretty high weirdness threshold, so I'm not scared, just a little taken aback.

Personal growth for the win.

Slowly now, I pull my hands from the water. As my left-hand leaves the water, the lights disappear.

Examining my hand again, I confirm there's still nothing there.

Am I graduating from ghosts and faceless to some new freaky business?

I'd really rather not.

My supernatural social card is full.

As usual, the universe doesn't care.

Placing my hands back into the water, I see that, sure enough, the blue lights are back, shimmering underwater until they disappear up ahead. I rack my brain for any possible explanation.

Maybe I'm the love child of Aquaman and Spiderman, and no one ever bothered to tell me.

That could be fun.

I flex my left hand to see if I can shoot the tendrils out like water-webs but without luck.

Shame.

I glance at my right hand and am relieved that whatever spooky business is going on seems to be affecting only my left hand. I watch the shimmering blue lights a moment longer before I feel it.

A faint tug.

The sensation reminds me of when I went fishing as a child, and a fish was giving 'bites' to the lure but not taking the hook.

Again, another faint tug on my hand – like someone is toying with the other side of the blue tendrils, beckoning me forward.

I could go back to shore and pretend this didn't happen, but – something in my gut is telling me to follow. Like an itch I can't scratch, I feel compelled to find out what is on the other side of the strings.

Maybe whatever is on the other side can help explain why I suddenly started seeing ghosts and why I was warned from my death. I want – no, I *need* answers. Also, I've learned the hard way that ignoring cues from the supernatural doesn't pan out well for me.

So, who am I to argue if the spooky lights want me to paddle out into the deep, dark, and likely very dangerous waters?

Again, I'm totally not setting myself up for another near-death experience.

Those are off-limits.

Instead, I mentally convince myself this is a fact-finding mission.

Besides, supernatural things usually lead *away* from my death.

It's fine. Totally fine.

I wave my hand back and forth, the blue lights dancing with my movements but still leading in the same general direction before fading from view under the fog.

Answers.

I repeat the word in my head as I start paddling out, following the strings of light. The further out I get, the stronger and more frequent the tug becomes.

That's either encouraging or worrisome. I can't decide.

The fish and lure comparison suddenly feels a bit more foreboding.

What if I'm not the one holding the fishing pole, and this thing is reeling me in?

The waves are getting bigger now, crashing over my head as I try to duck beneath them to avoid getting pushed back. It takes more than a few tries to get it somewhat right.

How did Sarah make this look so easy?

The surf is deafening and disorienting. So far, I'm managing to stay on my board. I'm completely soaked and freezing. Still, I paddle further out.

The tugging on my left hand is getting much stronger now. I'm just ducking below another wave when, suddenly, the pull becomes a yank.

I'm wrenched from my board and pulled into the inky depths.

All I can see are bubbles as I'm tossed around in the dark, turbulent waters.

I flail around but am entirely disoriented. My fingers claw out blindly, trying to feel for the cold breath of surface air. Despite my increasing panic at my new 'no breathing' lifestyle, I spot bubbles forming as another wave crashes down.

Up.

I try to swim in that direction but can't lift one of my arms. My left hand still has blue lights extending from it and is being pulled in the opposite direction. I try wrenching it up, but my hand keeps getting pulled down, trying to carry the rest of my body with it.

That isn't right. I need to go up, not down.

My thoughts feel fuzzy as a deep cold settles over my body. My vision starts to blacken. Something is in my face now, darkening the world around me.

It's blocking my ability to find the surface.

My hair.

I try to use my free hand to push it from my face as I keep trying to swim to the surface, using only my legs and one non-spooky hand.

It isn't working.

The tugging on my left hand intensifies and starts pulling me deeper. Whatever has me doesn't want to let me go. Frantically, I kick harder, trying to get to air.

My panic peaks as I feel two hands wrap around me.

Shit, shit, shit. It's got me.

But no, whatever is around my waist is pulling me up. The tugging on my left hand stops, and I start clawing back to the surface, desperate for air. I'm moving fast, helped by whoever is holding me. As my head breaks the surface, I take a gasp of life-saving air.

Wiping the water from my eyes, I see Sarah's terrified face. She doesn't let me go but grabs my arm as we quickly beeline over to her surfboard.

"Are you crazy?" she yells at me over the pounding waves. "We need to get out of here; these waves are too much for a beginner!"

"My board..." I stammer. My teeth are chattering.

"Forget the board," Sarah yells back as we both hold onto her surfboard and swim for shore.

Once we're crawling onto the beach, Conner, Isaac, and Tommy run towards us, but Sarah and I ignore them. Together, we collapse onto the sand.

Sarah must still have some energy because she quickly sits back up as if fuelled by her frustration. She whirls on me. "Why the hell would you go out that far?"

She apparently isn't ready to hear an answer because she continues, "And in this fog! What if I hadn't seen you? You could have drowned! The boys and I met up on the beach after ten minutes because the weather was getting worse, and we couldn't see you anywhere! It was sheer luck that I managed to catch a glimpse of your red hair, and then I saw you go under a wave, and you didn't come out! I've never been so scared in my life!"

I don't know what to say. I've never experienced this before.

Sarah isn't upset because I might have embarrassed her in some way. She's genuinely concerned for me.

Guilt washes over me at this new experience. "I – I'm so sorry Sarah."

This is it, I realize. My friends are going to abandon me for the stupid mistake I made, and I'll be on my own again.

I sit up and hug my knees to my chest, cradling my face into my knees as I try not to cry. But then someone wraps a towel around me, and an arm comes around my shoulders.

Sarah cuddles up next to me, "Just don't do insane stuff like that again before saying something, okay? I'm all for chasing thrills, but let's make sure we stay alive to chase the next one."

I'm still trying to process what just happened. Sarah isn't staying angry with me. She forgave me just like that.

Conner drops in front of us and is quickly followed by Isaac, huddled under their towels. "What happened, Viv? Did you decide you were the little mermaid and figured you'd try aquatic life?" Conner asks, his perpetual goofy grin still on display.

So, he isn't angry either?

"No, Conner, I told you," Isaac answers. "She decided drowning was better than writing Dr. Parnard's term paper."

I can't believe this. Not one of my friends is turning on me. Instead, they look concerned and are trying to lighten the mood after such a stressful event. It warms my heart – which is good because I'm pretty sure I'm turning into solid ice out in this freezing wind.

"I..." I stammer, "I was looking for you guys. I had no idea how far out I was with all this fog."

I feel guilty for not telling them the full truth, but there is no way in hell I'm going to tell anyone about the lights. No matter how supportive my new friends are, nothing is worth taking that chance again.

"That fog really did settle in on us quickly, didn't it?" Sarah notes, and the guys nod their heads in agreement. "Alright, well, I think we should get dry before we get hypothermia."

She stands and helps me up, but when we turn towards our things, Tommy stands behind us, looking grim. He's now sporting a dark blue raincoat with the hood pulled up against the wind. It contrasts against his bright board shorts. "Look, uhm, Vivian, is it? I'm sorry to do this, but the board you were using hasn't washed back onto shore, and I am going to need to charge you for it, or my boss will wring my neck."

He looks terribly uncomfortable, and I feel bad for him. The guy already bent the rules, letting us try the equipment for free.

Sarah looks shocked, and by the scowl that comes over her face, she's about to tell Tommy exactly where he can shove his surfboards.

I step in front of her and quickly answer, "Of course, I completely understand. Do you mind if I put on some dry clothes first? I'll have trouble paying if my entire body has frostbite, and my wallet is with my clothes."

Tommy is quick to agree, seemingly relieved that I'm not putting up a fight against paying for the missing board. Ten minutes later, I'm back in my dry clothes, wishing I had brought a winter hat.

Once again, I'm trying not to let my jaw hit the floor from monetary shock.

"Five hundred dollars? The board is five hundred dollars," I ask again, just to make sure.

"Sorry, Viv," Tommy answers. "It was one of our newer training boards and has hardly been used."

My head spins. This, combined with my replacement phone, will take a considerable chunk of my remaining student loans for the fall semester. I suppose I can get a job at the library, which should help me get through the winter term.

Still, I'm grateful I at least have the cash to pay for this. I would feel bad if Tommy's act of kindness got him fired. Even if I'm pretty sure Tommy's lust for Sarah spurred on said act of kindness.

Apparently, lust for Sarah isn't on Tommy's mind now. Once I finish paying, I catch Tommy eyeing me up and down appreciatively. "Look – uhm, I'd love to take you to dinner sometime to make up for this whole fiasco. Or I could give you a personal, one-on-one surfing lesson." The look on his face is lecherous.

My cheeks heat. Isn't this creep supposed to be dating my friend?

I pick up my bag and look up at Tommy. He is trying to school his lecherous look into one that oozes confidence. He's failing.

I give him my sweetest smile before answering, "Thanks, but to be perfectly honest, I would rather try surfing alone, on my period, in a school of sharks before going on a date with some asshole who is playing my friend."

I barely catch Tommy's look of utter disbelief as I exit the surf shack.

Tommy doesn't come out to say goodbye to us.

"Took you long enough," Sarah says as we start towards her car.

"Sorry," I answer. "Please tell me you won't be seeing that creep again."

"After he screwed over my friend?" Sarah answers in disgust, "Oh god no. He didn't even have the balls to come out and say goodbye. What a worm."

I catch Isaac's grin as we reach the car. There is definitely something brewing between those two.

Sarah offers to drive everyone home, and exhausted from the cold, we happily agree. She drops off Conner and Isaac first and is just pulling up in front of my apartment when she turns to me, looking worried.

"You're sure you're okay? I know we haven't been friends all that long, but if you ever want to talk, I'm here, okay?" Sarah says.

I feel the blood drain from my face. I thought I'd been able to fool my friends into thinking I was just looking for them in the water, but it seems like Sarah saw through it.

"I'll be okay. Thank you, really. For everything today. It means a lot," I answer, and I mean it. She literally saved my life out there.

"Okay then," Sarah answers, not one to prod. "Get some sleep. I'd suggest a hot bubble bath, but I doubt you've got a sexy man waiting for you in there to pull you out of the water if you decide to try drowning again."

I laugh as I exit the car. "Thanks again! See you tomorrow!" I wave and then turn to head to my apartment.

My home is on the fourth floor in the middle of a long hallway. While the rooms aren't big, the apartment complex has everything I need.

There's a communal, coin-operated laundry facility down one side of the hallway, with a snack machine to boot. Along the other side of the hall, there's a staircase that leads down four flights of stairs to the front door, but best of all, further down the staircase, there's a second door that leads to the building's underground parking garage.

While I typically walk to school, the winters here are treacherous, and the city's only bus service runs twice a day – first thing in the morning and late at night. So, after one horrible winter of trudging through freezing rain and nearly breaking my neck half a dozen times, I spent the following summer working as many hours as possible.

I found work at the library and helped at a café during the tourist season. The pay wasn't phenomenal, but it was enough to put aside some living money for the school semesters and enough to buy myself a used car.

However, since parking passes are expensive, I have resolved to drive only during the winter term and walk during the spring and fall months.

I'm nailing this adulting thing. I should get a sticker for my efforts.

I flip on the lights in my apartment and feel ready to collapse onto my bed for the night. My bachelor apartment isn't much to boast about. It has a tiny kitchen that opens to a small bedroom and a micro-bathroom off the front door.

Even though it's small, I was able to fit two bookshelves that I found in the trash during my first semester here. Their shelves are bowing from the multitudes of books that weigh them down.

It was a toss-up between the shelves or an old couch I'd found since there wasn't room for both. Ever the bookworm, I feel like I made the right choice.

Forgoing the couch, I elected to buy a few extra pillows for my bed so that I could prop myself up when I wanted to sit.

My bed is slightly larger than a twin – I bought the double bed from my neighbour after sleeping on an air mattress for a month. It's a bit lumpy but is now covered with a few rainbow-coloured quilts and an assortment of colourful pillows.

I further brightened the space by adding twinkle lights up and down my walls, a reading lamp next to my bed, and some bright purple black-out curtains.

It's small, but to me, it's perfect.

I drop my bag onto my only barstool. The apartment is too small for any kind of dining table, so I use my kitchen counter as both a table and a desk.

Switching out the main lights for my twinkle lights, I finally let myself fall into bed. My body feels bone weary, but no amount of exhaustion can stop my mind from racing.

What on earth were those blue lights today?

I lift my left hand to the lights, half expecting the glowing tendrils to come forth again now that I'm alone.

Nothing.

I frown, letting my hand drop over my head.

None of this makes sense. The ghost girl warning me about my impending doom all those years ago, the other corporeally-challenged creatures that appeared shortly after that, and certainly not this afternoon's paranormal insanity.

Why me?

I know I didn't imagine being pulled down into the ocean today. No amount of stress-induced mental breaks can explain the tugging sensations that were pulling at me.

But it wasn't just physical. There was a mental draw, too. Like some part of my unconscious mind, buried deep below, knows something and wants to find whatever is in the water.

I close my eyes, trying to peer deeper into my mind. It feels like I'm forgetting something. Like when you leave the house and get the nagging feeling the oven is still on.

I rub my face in frustration and concede that whatever forgotten thread of memory I'm trying to bring up can't be forced.

Glancing at my new phone, freshly charged during my little field trip, I'm shocked to see it isn't even dinner time yet.

Today has been a complete drain, but I know I'll be awake all night if I fall asleep now. Sighing, I pull myself out of bed and rummage through the kitchen.

I settle on old faithful – ramen noodles. Five minutes later, I'm sitting at the kitchen counter on my barstool, wolfing down the delicious empty carbs as I scroll through my email.

I groan when I note the reminders I've set for myself, loudly displayed on my home screen.

Read two chapters of Roman History by Tuesday morning.

Ps – if you don't feel like doing it, then please feel free to practice your stripping.

Pps – once you've realized you are so uncoordinated you'd starve as a stripper, just do the homework.

Reluctantly, I place my empty soup bowl in the sink before fetching my textbook.

Reading the two chapters and taking detailed, colour-coordinated notes takes me well into the evening. I love organizing my note topics by colours and own at least two dozen different coloured pens. It's a guilty pleasure and an excellent study aid.

Stretching, I pull my mind out of hyperfocus mode and check my phone messages. I have three. They're all from Conner.

Conner: Can I trade a muffin for your Roman History notes tomorrow?

Conner: I can't even with the Rome chapters. Promoting horses to senate, guzzling gladiator fluids. HOW DID THE EMPIRE LAST THIS LONG?

Conner: Okay – Muffin AND a coffee. Final offer.

I laugh as I text him back.

Vivian: Make sure it's a chocolate chip muffin.

Conner is quick to respond.

Conner: Done. You're the best! Xo

I snap some photos of my notes and send them to Conner before putting my phone back on the counter and walking over to my bookshelves. I still have a bit of time before bed. I was thinking I might read, but I'm still nursing a major book hangover after finishing the toe-curling novel from my favourite author the night before.

Sighing, I decide instead to put on some laundry. I don't want to leave my wet, salt-soaked bikini to dry in my apartment.

I bring my laptop with me and stream two hours of trash TV while leaning against the dryers before returning to my apartment.

My brain feels utterly spent. At least I was able to turn off my thoughts for a while. Mind-numbing television was the perfect remedy for my racing mind.

Finally ready to end the day, I take a steaming hot shower to rinse off whatever ocean water is left on me before cozying up to my mountain of pillows and quilts.

I'm asleep in just a few breaths.

CHAPTER 8

THEY CAME IN THE NIGHT.

My sisters scramble within the moon goddess temple, frantically hurrying to hide our most precious artifacts before the battle makes its way up to us.

The temple is embedded into the mountainside, and from my vantage point, I have a clear view of the city expanse below.

Though daylight is just now breaking, I know with near certainty that no guards are coming to protect us.

Last night, my sisters and I watched in horror as the water beyond our city's walls lit up like fireflies as hundreds of ships waited to attack us.

Many other attackers have tried to take the city by sea before, but these invaders are better prepared.

From the open gates and lack of gaping holes in the city walls, I know they must have come in through the secret passages to open the gates unseen. By the time the city guards mounted a response, our enemies had full, unfettered access to the city.

When our citizens were evacuated through secret passageways, they were slaughtered by the invaders waiting within. The invaders are not interested in survivors.

Surrendering is not an option.

The screams of our people reverberate across city walls and echo up the mountain. The blood of Atlantis seeps into the cobbled stone paths, and our great buildings are crumbling.

The invaders are not here to take over the city. They want it to crumble to nothingness.

This isn't conquering. It's annihilation.

Much of my great city has grown quiet now, except for the occasional scream as another survivor is found and massacred.

I steel myself and touch my short swords, once again assuring myself I'm armed. Though the invaders have yet to set their sights on the temple, the muted sounds of the city tell me it won't be long before they turn their attention to the final Atlanteans, who still draw breath.

A savage grin spreads across my face at the glorious thought that these men can bleed too and that soon, their blood will be mine to spill.

I turn my attention from the battle below and lock eyes with one of the senior priestesses.

"You're ready, Cassandra?" she asks me.

I nod, grimly determined.

A single tear falls down the priestess's cheek. She wraps her arms tightly around me, her voice quivering, "We always prayed this day would never come. When we sent you off to train as a Guardian – never did I think. No other before you have ever needed to complete this duty."

I hug her back, an ache settling in my chest. "I'm prepared to do what I was destined for."

At this, the priestesses' eyebrows furrow, and she releases me, giving me a troubled look. "I want you to remember something, Cassandra, and to always keep this wisdom with you. Your destiny is your own. It is not something to be chosen by outsiders but from the force of your own will." She looks incensed. I'm confused but nod to appease the elder.

The priestess nods her head approvingly before stepping back into the temple.

Just as she's shutting the door, I call out, "Barricade the doors, and then get them out. All of them. The children know the way."

The elder priestess looks surprised, but she nods before shutting the door. She isn't fast enough, and I catch a glimpse of something new in her eyes.

Hope.

I'll remain outside the doors and buy them as much time as possible. There is a passage off this mountain that only I and a few of the children that remain here know of. It's a dangerous passage, but we're out of other options.

The city will fall.

But I will make sure the mountain bleeds with the blood of those who dared to take my home.

Alone now, I'm left with my thoughts as I wait for the invaders to set their sights on the mountain. I knew there was danger coming.

I was warned.

My lover had come running to the temple to tell me that I was in terrible danger and that my city would fall. I may serve the Goddess, but his power is said to rival that of the divine.

He embraced me when he broke my heart.

I asked him how we would fight the danger, and he insisted that he could not fight this battle for the city. He showed me a satchel he'd packed with food and clothes. I noticed a dress in the satchel, and my heart shattered even further. He wanted me to abandon my very people and stressed that my staying was certain death.

I moved away from him then, shaking my head softly. While this divine creature may profess his love for me, if he thought I would leave my sisters and temple children to face death alone, he knew nothing of my heart.

But then again, he never knew me at all.

While he had shared his powers with me and shown me how he could grow life into being, I was not so forthcoming, ashamed of how my own nature so sharply contrasted with his.

From an age earlier than I remembered, I was chosen by the elder priestesses to act as the guardian of the temple. Guardians are not simply a title but a promise held in absolute secrecy until the moment is dire. Whereas my fellow sisters swore to do no harm and are pacifists, I was sworn to the dark side of the moon.

I was sent from one temple to the next, across our kingdom, to be trained by the greatest warriors known to humanity. Scrolls of ancient fighting thought lost to the world were kept in the vaults of temples, only accessible to the guild I was selected for – the Guardians.

The Guardians are called on to protect their faith and those who live in service of it. We are exceptionally skilled with all forms of combat, and our true identities are kept hidden to stop outsiders from picking us off.

We are monsters in people's clothing.

I've never breathed a word to my sisters about what I am, and only a few remaining elder priestesses know the truth. I'm their weapon, the living embodiment of our warrior goddess.

My lover has undoubtedly never even heard of the Guardians. The guild has never even become a whisper of a legend; such is their dedication to secrecy. He could only know me as a pacifist, no doubt accepting my impending slaughter.

Instead, I urged him to stay and fight. To protect our home and not abandon us. But he'd shaken his head, pleading that I leave with him.

I turned from him and went to wake my sleeping sisters without another word to him. I left him in the temple hall, and when I returned sometime later, armed with my short swords and dagger, he was gone.

That was hours ago, and I know my last moments are drawing near. I'm not so vain to think I can take out the entire army. But I will make sure that I spend my final breaths trying.

I may be alone, but I have the advantage.

The path that winds up around our mountain is barely two feet across. The path twists so that your right arm is pressed against the wall as you come up. Any right-

handed soldier climbing the path will have a minimal range of motion and difficulty swinging their weapon.

My robes wave in the light wind, and my red hair is secured around my head in intricate braids. I can hear them now, in the lower part of the mountain, yelling and making their way up the path.

I hope the long trek up the mountainside will exhaust them.

The soldiers are fresh from battle, their armour soaked in blood. They aren't moving quickly, and I can hear their laboured breathing. I disappear beyond the turning of the path, lest they draw arrows on me.

As the first soldier rounds the bend, I stab him in the neck at the junction of his leather armour. He's dead before he even sees me.

The invader behind him hasn't noticed his companion stop. His head is down, and his cheeks are flushed, panting from the steep climb.

I kick my foot out at the man I killed, knocking him back off my sword and into the still-staggering second invader. The force is enough to push them both off the cliff, and the other soldiers yell and panic as their two comrades fall to their deaths.

The following soldiers now approach more carefully, unsure of what just happened. Once again, I strike from beyond the bend in the path. My blade slices through his lower stomach, and he doubles over. He bleeds out quickly and blocks the way for the others.

The other soldiers yell, pushing the wounded soldier off the path and out of their way as they rush towards me in single file. Their swings are awkward as they try to maneuver the narrow space.

And so, my dance begins.

I favour quick slashes with my weapons as the soldiers come around the corner, conserving my energy. When they do manage to swing their weapon, I'm ready to block with one sword and slash with my other.

I kill ten in a matter of minutes.

Wiping my weapon on my robes, I peek around the corner. I can't see any more soldiers making their way up the path, but when I look over the ledge, I can see a crowd of the invaders gathering around the crumpled bodies that fell off the ledge.

I duck back before they have a chance to look up and spot me.

My heart beats at a wild pace. The blood spilled thrills me.

Normally, I don't feel the urge to bathe in the blood of my enemies, but I know what fate lays ahead for my sisters if the temple is breached before they've vacated the area – rape, brutalization, and death.

I'm ready to kill as many as it takes to help them and avenge the souls of my people that were stolen this night.

More soldiers make their way up the mountainside path now, their steps echoing towards me. The bodies below must have alerted others that something went wrong at the temple.

I wait with bated breath, remaining invisible for as long as possible.

When the soldiers finally start to round the bend before me, I'm again ready for them. And the cycle continues.

The invaders come, and I lay waste to them. Some don't even reach me, instead tripping over the bodies that now litter the narrow strip of earth before me.

After I've killed over four dozen soldiers, I must capture the attention of some of their commanders. I hear yelling below as arrows slice through the air, trying to reach me without luck. The temple is high and dotted with crags and jutting rocks, blocking access to me. I grin at their failed efforts.

The soldiers are coming in at a slower pace now as they try to devise strategies to take me out. A massive soldier barrels around the corner, holding his huge sword like a spearpoint over his head.

I swear I feel the ground shiver beneath his thunderous steps, and I take a knee just before he rounds the corner. By the time he notices me through the slats in his helmet, I've lodged my blade into his groin. He falls back with a croak of pain.

More come, but I slaughter them all.

One hundred dead now, but still they come. I know the enemy must have forces in the thousands, but now they are only sending up unseasoned, young fighters, likely in an effort to exhaust me.

If only their lives could be so simple.

The Guardians kept me awake for days, forcing me to dodge arrows and parry unexpected attacks with nothing to sustain me. Again and again, they broke me until I could be reshaped into something fierce.

I will not tire of spilling blood.

I've killed well over two hundred of their soldiers when I hear movement behind me.

I whip my head around to see that soldiers have scaled the mountainside behind me using ropes and hooks. A dozen of them are standing in front of the large, circular entrance to the temple.

I scream as two of them try to push open the doors. I run towards the group, my swords drawn.

I will not let them take the temple. Not yet.

This group of soldiers is not unseasoned. I can see scars littering their bodies where they've removed their armour for the climb up.

I'm happy to add my artwork to their collections before rendering them to corpses.

I spin from soldier to soldier, parrying blows, striking, and spinning to parry another soldier as the previous soldier falls to the ground. One soldier knocks me down, slicing my left arm.

Shrieking in pain, I tumble backwards, dropping one of my swords. Quickly, I right myself and unsheathe my dagger. They don't slow their attack. Again, I block their strikes, my back to the temple doors. I can feel myself weakening from the blood loss in my arm.

I will not fail my sisters. I will not fail the children.

Faster.

I need to kill them faster before I become too weak.

I lunge out from the door, dodging a soldier's sword and coming chest to chest with him. I ram my dagger into his neck.

A final soldier stands before me now. His face is wild with rage from seeing his friends die before him. He runs for me. I meet him halfway but throw myself onto my back at the last possible moment, one hand discarding my dagger to hold myself up. My other hand grips my short sword, and I slice through the junction of the soldier's inner thigh and groin as he overshoots and runs over me.

I right myself and run to cut the rope that is secured on the ledge of the mountainside. As I reach it, I feel something puncture my chest.

Looking down, I see an arrow tip protruding from my breast.

I look over my shoulder to find my attacker but can't see them.

Again, another arrow pierces me, now in the shoulder. I feel my body go limp as the force of the arrow knocks me from the cliff's edge, and then I know no more.

CHAPTER 9

I WAKE WITH A START, MY ENTIRE BODY covered in a cold sweat. That might be the most vivid dream I've ever had. My heart beats wildly, and I try to take deep, calming breaths.

I'm safe, still nestled in my protective fort of throw pillows.

That dream felt perfectly real. It didn't feel like the nonsense my subconscious memory likes to conjure up.

There was none of the typical horror where I get chased by a giant tube of toothpaste. This dream was something new.

Sitting up, I inspect my left hand yet again. I still can't see any remnants of the eerie lights.

To be honest, I'm not mad about that.

I think back on my dream, unable to shake the familiarity. Maybe I read it in a book a long time ago and just can't remember. Still, I've never dreamt so vividly about the books I read. Otherwise, I'd be getting to bed much earlier most nights.

There's something familiar about the robes my dream self was wearing and how my hair was braided. I know I've seen it before. Rubbing the sleep from my eyes, I yawn before reaching out to check the time. The glowing light reads 5:45 AM.

Gross.

Still, I know I'll be even more exhausted if I go back to sleep and wait for my 6:30 alarm. So, instead, I crawl out of bed to splash some water on my face. It almost makes me feel human.

My eyes have dark circles under them. I guess that's what you get when you spend your night fighting your dream enemies. Still though. It was so familiar. I feel like I'm missing something obvious – as if the answer is staring me straight in the face.

Realization hits like a ton of bricks.

Ghost girl.

The outfit I was wearing in my dream, the robes, the hair, all of it matched the outfit ghost girl wore.

But how is that possible?

Did the ghost girl somehow imprint one of her memories onto me? Then again, I haven't seen her in years. Whatever is going on must be tied to the glowing blue threads that led me into the water. But what?

Sometimes, I feel like my entire life is a movie, and I keep falling asleep for parts of it. So, when the crazy stuff happens, I'm left asking, 'What did I miss?' but there's no one there to explain the plot holes. And I am desperate for some answers.

I sigh, trying not to fall into the slippery slope of self-pity. I don't think you ever become cured of depression. It's a bit like addiction. You always need to stay vigilant of your triggers to make sure you don't fall off the wagon.

So, instead of getting pulled into some pre-6 AM despair, I focus on what I can control. That may be a trick I picked up from a self-help book. It's not therapy, but hey, it's effective.

Taking in my sleep-deprived condition, I consider putting on some makeup, but a quick weather check tells me not to bother. It will be another cool, foggy day, and any makeup I put on will melt off my face by noon.

Instead, I dress for a cozy day, choosing my favourite black high-necked sweater, a tan A-line skirt, and thick black tights.

I look back at my bed longingly before deciding I need to get out of the house. With my newest spooky life developments, I'm feeling on edge. Hopefully, being out in public will help that.

I grab my textbooks and laptop, shoving them into my schoolbag before heading out. The morning air is crisp, but the wind has died considerably since yesterday. As a result, the fog hangs around like a stagnant blanket. Droplets settle on my face, and I am grateful I didn't bother with makeup.

I head towards the small coffee shop where I worked last summer. Even after spending far more money than I should have yesterday, I figure I deserve a coffee as a treat for not dying.

After all, you need to celebrate the little things.

The coffee shop is only three blocks from my apartment. It's close enough to the ocean that I can take the boardwalk to the college afterward rather than doubling back.

Even though it's still mostly dark outside, the sidewalks are well-lit, and the streetlights are still on. The closer to town I get, the more pungent the smell of saltwater is.

It's not even half past six, but the town is already waking up. Fishermen in their trucks line up at the shop's drive-through, eager to caffeinate before hitting the docks. I keep my head down as I pass them, pretending to be engrossed in something on my phone.

East coasters are friendly, and I'm not awake enough to chat about the weather with a stranger. It's also a 50-50 split between getting pulled into conversation with a friendly, harmless older man or a creep.

Those aren't odds I'm willing to play with.

The coffee shop holds a dozen or so small tables and comfortable faux-leather chairs of every colour. The walls are a light yellow and dotted with framed prints of local artwork. It feels cozy and warm. Sohanna, the barista on cash, lights up when she sees me come in.

"Vivian! What's up, girl? I've missed your face ever since you went back to school. Also, I finished the book you recommended, and I cannot even. I'm going to the bookstore later today to buy the next one. I think I might have to say goodbye to my social life. Spicy romance novels are way more interesting." She throws her hands into the air like she's entirely at her wit's end.

Sohanna likes dramatics, even at the crack of dawn.

I sympathize, "I wish I could say it gets better, but the second book is even better than the first. Sorry for feeding the new addiction." I walk up to the counter, tucking away my phone now that I'm in a safe place.

Other than Sohanna and me, it's empty in here.

"HAH!" Sohanna laughs. "You aren't sorry, and you know it. Now we get to talk about books all the time when you come back to work next summer, and you know you'll love it."

I beam. "Actually, yes, that sounds wonderful. We can have a spicy barista book club."

Sohanna laughs again. "Alright, deal. So, just your usual this morning?"

I nod and gratefully accept my cup of steaming coffee. Thanking Sohanna, I head to my favourite table by the shop's front window.

I have some time to kill before my 8:30 AM class. Luckily, it isn't busy, and I don't think Sohanna will mind me loitering.

Fishing my laptop out of my bag, I'm careful not to wobble the table and spill my coffee. With my luck, I'll fry my computer and have to buy a new one of those as well. I make a mental note to back up my work later – just in case.

I stare at my empty screen as I sip on my coffee. My back is to the wall, and anyone walking by would assume I'm engrossed in whatever I have open. But instead, I let my mind wander, trying to connect the dots between the paranormal activity I've experienced.

Ghost girl saved me twice and then tried to save me a third time. That at least makes a bit of sense. Someone is looking out for me.

It's a bit unexpected, but I can rationalize it.

Whatever happened yesterday is throwing me a bit for a loop. Something pulled me underwater.

I think I was well on my way to drowning but didn't get any danger warnings from ghost girl. So, maybe she hasn't been keen on helping me since I blew her off four years ago. Or perhaps I wasn't in danger. The burning in my lungs and panic at being dragged into the deep water certainly felt like danger.

Chills steadily make their way up my arms to the back of my neck. I take another sip of coffee and try to distract myself from the memory by looking outside.

The ghostly figure of a woman stands in front of the flower shop on the other side of the road. The ghost doesn't look at me and disappears through the shop's front door.

Right, I see dead people.

Dead people that want nothing to do with me.

My life makes no sense.

I grit my teeth together at the thought, agitated. Why did I randomly start seeing ghosts after my first escape from death? I didn't come close to dying, and it isn't like I can communicate with them.

All of this feels so pointless.

What is the point of seeing ghosts if you can't even talk to them?

Drumming my fingers on the tabletop, I mull over the thought. Then, I get hit with a crackpot idea that might be too out there even for me. Powering up my laptop, I look up how to talk to ghosts.

Over the years, I've tried physically speaking to them, pointing, shouting, writing notes – nothing has worked.

But there's no way I'm the first person interested in contacting the dead.

Maybe I'm one of the first to see the ghost's facial expressions when trying, but thousands of people must be obsessed with speaking to the other side. I've never put much stock in paranormal activity besides the occasional scary movie or book plot.

I wasn't even sure there was an afterlife until I walked among its citizens, albeit unwillingly.

My search returns a multitude of websites, all touting the best way to communicate with the dead. There's even a phone app that states it can unscramble ghost speak. I read a few blogs, each claiming to hold the best techniques. I skim through them.

The method I keep seeing is Ouija boards. I've heard of them, though I've never used one. Refining my search, I find that while you can buy the board, they're also easy and free to make.

Bingo!

Free is looking very good these days.

I jot some notes on how to put it together as well as some best practice tips. The website recommends using a group of people.

Fat chance.

The website also notes that the spirit world is most active at night. Well, that's sensible enough. If anything, I think it would feel weird to communicate with ghosts during the day.

Daytime is exposing, unlike the protective cover of darkness.

When I finally feel like I have a plan moving forward, I buckle down and get some classwork done. I get into my writing groove, and after what feels like a couple of minutes later, my phone alarm starts buzzing, letting me know it's time to walk to campus. I would one hundred percent have kept working and forgotten about attending class if I didn't set alarms.

Hyperfocus is fun like that.

Sohanna is now masterfully fielding a long line of people, so I give her a quick wave before heading towards the boardwalk. The sun lights up the sky, though most shops are closed except for restaurants.

As I draw nearer to the boardwalk that trails above the beach, I feel a tingling in my left wrist again. It's not quite a shock like yesterday, but more like a prickling static charge.

Yet again, I lift my hand to examine my wrist but can't see anything on it—no lights, not even a mosquito bite. But the closer I get to the water, the more I can feel it, a faint but incessant tugging. It's just enough that I can't ignore it.

Stuffing my hands into my pockets, I increase my pace to the school. I keep getting intrusive thoughts about getting dragged into the water, schoolbag in tow.

Not ideal.

Despite my hurried pace and dedication to ignoring the latest developments in my paranormal problems, the pulling doesn't stop.

If this Ouija board thing could work, that would be great.

I'll try to get some answers tonight and hopefully not invite a hoard of demons into my apartment.

Honestly, my quota for paranormal life-crashers is full.

No vacancies.

Arriving on campus, I find Conner, true to his word, waiting by our Roman history class door with a coffee and a massive chocolate chip muffin. He holds them out to me as I approach him.

"As promised," he grins as he hands them to me. His hair is tousled like he just climbed out of bed. Lucky bastard. "One cup of coffee, one muffin – the one with the most chocolate, and, of course, one hot stud muffin for you to do with as you please."

As I take my proffered goods, he places an arm around my shoulders and kisses my head.

I laugh and try not to let him see how taken aback I am by his show of affection. "Alright, lover boy. I want this stud of a man to let me go so we can get some good seats." I shrug off his arm and head into the classroom.

What the hell is wrong with me?

Conner is someone I should be attracted to. The man has no issue getting dates. Yet still, I want to shrink away from his touch, even if that simple head kiss was the most action I've ever gotten.

Broken, I must be broken.

Conner doesn't show remorse over his flirting but doesn't try to touch me again as he follows me. I'm relieved.

"Hey, you always gotta shoot your shot," he says as we make our way to our seats.

Roman history is in an auditorium-style room, similar to most of our classes. However, this class holds rows of seats with foldable personal desks instead of tables. I spot Sarah and Isaac in one of the upper rows. Unfortunately, the seats next to them are taken. It's a popular class and usually a full house. Instead, we claim the two seats in front of them.

Sarah taps my shoulder. She's sporting her hair in a high ponytail and looks radiant without any makeup. "Good morning, sunshine!" she says with a smile. "I hope you got some decent sleep after yesterday's surfing fiasco. I still can't believe that jerk charged for the board when HE didn't give lessons. Complete negligence."

I smile back, grateful my friend isn't still interested in that asshole. "He's a piece of work. And I'm doing okay, thanks. I was up early, though."

Sarah snorts, "Obviously. Your eyes aren't half-closed like they normally are in morning classes. Did you finally take up sunrise running? Can we go together? Please be my running buddy!"

I snort at the sheer absurdity of Sarah's statements.

A morning person? Not happening.

I'm too drawn to the cozy atmosphere of twinkle lights, candles, and a full moon to dream about going to bed early.

"Not gonna happen," I answer as I flip my notebook to my latest page.

Conner is talking to Isaac but pauses and turns to me, looking surprised. I was confused about what might have stunned him when I realized my notebook was open to the Ouija board outline. I move to turn the page, but Conner is faster. "Thinking about calling some ghosts? I have to say, you never fail to surprise me."

Sarah and Isaac lean over to see my sketch as well. Isaac can't help but give his two cents, "Obviously, none of the guys here meet her fantasy romance standards, so she's conjuring up a dead one."

He and Conner both burst out laughing. Sarah almost smiles but stops herself in time.

My cheeks are on fire. It would be nice if the ground could open up and swallow me whole. Sarah notices.

"I think it's cool," Sarah remarks. "I made one once in high school after my Nan died." She has an undertone of defensiveness, like she's daring the guys to keep making fun of me.

Isaac stops chuckling at his joke and kicks the back of Conner's chair to get him to stop. "Oh yeah, did it work?"

"I'm not sure. Nan was blind in the end, and the letters spelled out a bunch of jumbled words, so... maybe?"

Conner turns back to me. "So, who are you trying to call, Viv?"

"I – I'm not sure," I answer truthfully. "I just read about it this morning and thought it looked interesting."

"Can this be our first spooky season activity?" Sarah asks excitedly.

"I'm in!" Isaac chimes in.

"GHOSTBUSTERS!" Conner exclaims as he pumps his fist into the air.

"I'm not sure that..." I begin to respond, but honestly, I have no idea how to object to this. The website said it's better if there are at least two people. My friends are all staring at me with eager excitement. "You know what? Awesome, yes. Let's do this. My house tonight?"

The others agree just as the lecture begins. Roman history is a great class. Our teacher asked us to pair up as she explained the assignment. We are to pretend we have a time machine and will be travelling back to Rome. We can bring any items we want, so long as they fit into a 1-meter square box.

The goal is to take over the government and establish yourselves as new rulers. Item lists and our 'Evil Plan to Take Over the World' are due at the end of class.

Conner and I team up since we're already next to each other. We settle on a box of vaccines (at my insistence that if Malaria can take out Alexander the Great, then we sure as hell aren't going to take chances), along with instructions for making gunpowder, canons, and war techniques from empires a few hundred years following the Romans.

We plan to become indispensable to the military and then stage a coup. We fill the rest of the box with pizza, chocolate, and other necessities because we aren't leaving the best parts of the twenty-first century behind without some mementos to tide us over.

All in all, it isn't a bad effort. I'm unsure about the whole pizza and chocolate addition, but Conner made a fair point that sound mental health is imperative to our focus on the mission. And while comfort food might not fix the problems we will face in Rome, it will surely make us feel better.

I stay in the auditorium with the others after class to solidify our evening plans. "My place, eight tonight?"

"It won't be dark enough by eight," Sarah muses. "Ou! Let's make it a pizza/movie/ghost trio!"

I raise an eyebrow at her. "You do remember I don't have a TV. Or a couch?"

"That's fine with me," Sarah responds. "Your bed is big enough to fit all of us, and we can watch a movie off your laptop, or hey! Isaac! Your laptop is obnoxiously massive. Bring yours!"

Isaac is offended. "There's nothing wrong with the size of my laptop; it's a gaming laptop. Now, if you want to see massive..."

Sarah puts her hand on his mouth to stop him. "Woah, now, okay, so bring your laptop. I'll bring pizza, Vivian, you make the board and Conner, you get the wine."

Sarah has a big heart; she knows that she and Conner are college-fund kids, while Isaac and I are a bit less well-off and rely on student loans and summer jobs.

Well-off or not, I object, "I'm happy to pitch in for pizza or booze."

Sarah shakes her head and won't hear of it. "I know you're purposefully not telling us how much that surfboard cost yesterday, and those things are NOT cheap. So, you get a pass on pitching in tonight."

"Fine," I begrudgingly acquiesce. "But I'll get some chocolate."

"Done!" Sarah responds, and with that, we set off on our separate ways.

Walking to my next class, I feel a surge of excitement at the thought that maybe this will work.

If anything, I'm pumped to have my friends with me. I don't relish the idea of something scary happening in the middle of the night while I'm alone.

I know that's a bit hypocritical coming from someone who goes out most nights, trying to find scary, trapped spirits. But my apartment feels different.

It's my haven, my safe place.

But I want answers, and hopefully, I will get them tonight.

CHAPTER 10

THE DAY FLIES BY, AND AFTER A FULL afternoon of back-to-back classes, I have just enough time to run to the store before hurrying home to clean up.

I also remember to hide some of my darker romance novels in my drawers. Seriously, the guys do not need ideas about stalker romance.

Making a Ouija board is simple enough. I spell out the alphabet in two rows, trying to leave enough space between the letters to help distinguish whatever might be spelt out.

I include a 'Yes' and 'No' on each corner of the top of the board and then include a row of numbers from zero to nine underneath the alphabet. Finally, I add 'Hello' and 'Goodbye' in the bottom corners.

I'm going all out. I busted out my Sharpies and used my favourite silver colour to give it all an extra 'spooky' edge. For the sake of the ambience, I turn off the main lights, save for my fairy twinkle lights. Spooky season vibes abound.

I'm contemplating whether I have time to add stars to the board when the apartment intercom goes off. No stars it is.

"Hey, girl!" Sarah calls as she walks in, placing two large pizzas on the counter.

Isaac follows her, laptop in his hands. "S'up, nerd?"

I roll my eyes and grin. "Takes one to know one."

Conner carries four large bottles of wine. "I've got two reds, two whites, and no class in the morning. So, who's getting ghostbusters-hammered with me?"

Oh boy.

Tonight should be interesting.

Sarah walks over to the bottles and claims a bottle of red. "Thanks, Conner."

"Not running tomorrow morning?" I ask.

"Nope," Sarah answers. "But I was assigned three more papers today to get done by the end of reading week, and if that's not a reason to drink, then I don't know what is."

"Ouch," I sympathize. I forgot next week is reading week. "Are you guys all going home for fall break?"

Conner squeezes in beside me to get some pizza. "I am. My mom wants to wash my sheets. Can't imagine why."

I laugh as I reach for a fruity-looking bottle of white wine. I know this label – it tastes like juice and is just sweet enough to make you forget the hangover it will bring.

"Maybe she wants to cry over all her lost grandchildren," Isaac answers, grabbing three slices of pepperoni. "I'm going home too. My folks need help cleaning the gutters, and I'm looking forward to not worrying about cooking or doing groceries for a week." He grabs the second bottle of white wine.

Sarah has already propped herself up onto my small army of pillows. "I'm leaving Thursday. Mom got us tickets to go to some resort, and she wants all the kids there for family bonding time."

"Always so fancy," Isaac says as he places his plate next to her and sets up his laptop at the foot of my bed to play the movie.

"What about you, Viv?" Conner asks. He's still in the tiny kitchen with me, eyeing me curiously. "Are you headed home for reading week?"

The kitchen can barely fit us, and I can feel his warmth beside me. Conner is gorgeous with his messy blond hair and hazel eyes. He's built like a tank, thanks to his ruthless gym worship.

I should be at least a bit excited that his attention is focused on me. And yet, there's nothing. There is no spark, not even a tickle.

Have I mentioned I think there's something wrong with me? Maybe I'm so damaged from my past that I only feel safe enough to be aroused by fictional men.

Conner waves a hand in front of my eyes. "Earth to Viv. You still with us?"

I blush. "Sorry – what did you ask me?"

Conner puffs up with extra confidence, clearly thinking he's the reason I lost my train of thought. He's not entirely wrong – but boy, would he be disappointed at hearing the specifics.

"I asked if you were going home over fall reading week," he reminds me.

"Oh!" I stammer, trying to wrap my head around an answer that won't make me sound weird. I'm too socially awkward to be that clever. "Oh god, no. I'll never go back there if I can help it." I shudder before walking out of the kitchen.

I sit next to Sarah, so Conner has no choice but to sit on the opposite end next to Isaac. Conner looks like he's about to pry into my personal life when Isaac shushes us and puts on the movie.

The movie is about a person whose house is haunted by killer ghosts. I appreciate the irony, though I've yet to meet any malevolent ghosts. Unless you can call ignoring someone malevolent, but it's more passive-aggressive than anything. Right now, I think I would welcome an angry ghost. If it cares enough that I exist, maybe we can have a chat.

As the movie ends and the credits start to roll, I stretch from the bed and turn to the others. Sarah is snuggled into Isaac's arm, and Conner looks half asleep, head propped behind his arms. I am ninety-nine percent sure he just flexed when he saw me looking at him. I quickly turn my attention back to Sarah and Isaac.

"You guys ready?" I ask as I move my eyebrows conspiratorially. The more I hang out with these goofballs, the more I feel myself relaxing and coming out of my shell. I'm broken, but maybe it isn't permanent.

Sarah jumps from the bed, half-empty wine bottle in tow. "So ready! Especially since it's your place and not mine. After that movie, no Ouija boards at my house – ever."

Giggling, I fetch the board and lay it in the center of my bed. It's still too dark to see the letters with just my twinkle lights on, so I light some candles on my dresser and night tables.

"Setting the mood, Viv. Love it," Conner remarks as we all shuffle to sit around the board.

The room is glowing from multiple sources around us, and the flickering candlelight makes our shadows dance across the walls. I reach over to my bedside table and pick up a shot glass to place in the centre of the board.

Always classy.

"Okay," I start. "So, we need someone who will take notes, and then three of us will place our fingers on the shot glass to try and communicate with the other side. Any volunteers for note-taker?"

Isaac reaches over behind him and re-opens his laptop. "I'm in for note-taking." His laptop screen adds a blue glow to the room.

"Okay then." I smile. I try to squish down the tiny bit of hope that is blossoming in my chest over finally getting some answers.

Don't get your hopes up.

Realistically, there are very few ghosts in my apartment complex, and certainly none in my apartment right now. But hey, maybe it's like picking up the phone. I just have to call, and someone in the mood to chat might decide to turn up.

I place two fingers on the shot glass, and Sarah and Conner do the same. Sarah has a faint wobble – the wine is starting to hit her.

Conner looks amused as always but, for once, doesn't crack a joke. Maybe the movie got to him a bit. The killer ghosts did manage to kill the main character's playboy love interest.

We wait a few seconds before Conner whispers, "So, what next?"

"Well…" I whisper back, thinking back to the website I read that morning. I'm halfway through my wine bottle and am trying to keep it all straight in my mind. "Okay – next, we have to say hello and ask if there's anyone who would like to talk to us. So, uhm, yeah. Here goes nothing."

I'm not sure where to address the ghosts, so I settle on looking up. I figure it's a better omen than looking down.

"Hey, if there's anything out there, any ghosts, we'd love for you to come by and have a chat with us. I'm Vivian, and these are my friends Conner and Sarah. We uhm – we have wine and pizza if you're into that," I finish and try to bite down my laughter as I look at Sarah, who is vibrating from trying not to laugh. Conner has less control and snorts.

Isaac looks half asleep, and I elbow him gently with my free arm. "Still with us?"

Isaac nods. "Just resting my eyes until company shows up."

I'm about to respond when suddenly, I feel the shot glass start to move. My eyes lock on it instantly, and I watch as it slides over to the 'Hello' portion of the board.

"Hello," I answer. "May I ask who's here?" I look at Conner and Sarah as the shot glass starts to move again. Their eyes are locked on the glass, looking a bit afraid and confused. They don't look like they are pushing the glass, but then again, you never know.

The shot glass stops over the letter N, then continues over to the letter E. It rests there a moment before sliding into the open area of the board and coming back to rest on the letter E. Finally, it moves again to the letter D.

"Isaac, you getting this?" Sarah asks.

"Yup," Isaac answers. "I'm just the right amount of drunk for this."

"Need –" I read and pause for a moment, confused. "Need what? What do you need?"

The shot glass starts moving again, more quickly. When I see what's being spelled out, I take my fingers from the glass and cross my arms. "Conner, is this you?" I'm irritated. The glass spelled my name.

"No! Honest!" Conner responds, removing his fingers to cross his heart.

"Need Vivian," Sarah says, chuckling. "That sounds like a Conner thing to say to me. Are you just trying to scare us? It isn't working, dude."

"Guys, I'm not. Look, I won't even touch the glass this time. And to prove you aren't doing anything, you should both take turns closing your eyes while it moves. Just to see if it still makes sense."

"Seems like a good plan to me," Sarah says, looking back up to me. "You okay with that?"

"Let's do this," I say, placing my fingers back on the shot glass.

Sarah closes her eyes first, and Conner keeps his hands on his lap, true to his word that he won't touch the shot glass anymore. The glass moves. I didn't expect it to. I thought Conner was messing with us.

It settles on the letter K, then E and then stops on Y. Sarah opens her eyes, looking curious.

"It seriously moved again? What did it say?" she asks.

Isaac answers, "This time, we got 'key.' Okay, so does the ghost need Vivian or a key?"

A smile is pulling at the corners of my mouth. I'm trying hard not to show how excited I am. I have no idea what ghostly key something needs, but I'm taking this as contact.

"Only one way to find out, and I'm still not convinced Conner didn't spell my name." With that, I close my eyes. I feel the glass start to move immediately from one place to another. When it stops, I ask if I can open my eyes.

Conner clears his throat like choking before answering, "Yeah, you're good."

"Well? What did it spell?" I look at Sarah; she's gone pale as a ghost.

"Your name, again," Sarah says. "Alright, I think that's enough spooky stuff for now. Viv, will you be okay tonight after that scary movie and with a ghost that wants to steal your keys?"

I'm still trying to process the fact that the ghost spelled my name again. Someone really does want to talk to me. This is fantastic, and maybe I can finally get some answers if I try again on my own.

I grin at my friend. "A roommate who won't hog the bathroom, what's there to be upset about?"

Sarah laughs but still looks uneasy. She yawns as she stands up from the bed. "Alright then, I'm headed home. Are you guys coming? It doesn't look like it's raining or anything, so it should be a decent walk."

Isaac also stands, albeit a bit unsteady on his feet. "I'll walk you home, Sarah."

Conner and I follow them to the front door. A mostly drunk Sarah and Isaac stumble out, but Conner stays put. He calls out to their slowly staggering figures, "I'll catch up with you guys later; I want to ask Viv something."

A small curl of dread settles in my stomach. I surely don't have the necessary people skills for what is coming.

Sarah and Isaac wave at us as they continue down my apartment hallway. Conner closes the door behind them and leans his back to it. He isn't very tall, but he's stocky, and his frame takes up most of the doorway.

I stand before him, unsure what to do with my hands. I settle on crossing them over my chest. That body language means you aren't interested, right?

Conner notices, and his eyes stay on my breasts for a second too long before moving back up to meet mine. He looks at me with a mixture of longing and determination.

My cheeks flush.

I'm about to ask him what he wants when he starts, "Look – Viv. I know you've got to know I'm into you. And not in a playful, I love all women kind of way. I want *you*."

I frown, opening my mouth to let him down quickly, but Conner rushes on, "Just – just let me get this out, okay? I know you don't date, and I can't imagine why, but from what you told me tonight about not going home, you've got some troubled history, and I just want you to know that I'm here for you and would take amazing care of you. I'd treat you like a goddess, and I would never hurt you."

He leaves the doorway and stands directly in front of me. I'm about to back away to put more space between us when Conner notices I look uncomfortable and backs off.

"Sorry – uhm yeah. Just think about it, okay? You don't need to answer me tonight. Take your time," and with that, he opens the door and lets himself out.

I stand rooted to my spot for a good minute before locking the door.

I should be thrilled. Conner would probably make a great boyfriend. But I'm not.

The only thing making my pulse race right now is the anxiety of knowing that I'll have to let him down. Maybe I should give him a couple of days to think I'm taking his offer seriously. I don't want to bruise his ego.

I look back over to the Ouija board sitting on my bed. It's almost midnight now, but after Conner's words, I just want to escape this reality for a while and turn off my brain.

I put away the board and change into some comfy sweats and a tank top before settling into bed with one of my favourite romance novels. It isn't comfort food, but it has the same effect.

I fall asleep an hour or so later, the book still in my hands.

CHAPTER 11

I'M NOT SURE HOW I'VE MADE IT THIS LONG without dying.

What kind of idiot adult falls asleep with not one, not two, but SEVEN candles still burning?

I'm a walking hazard.

Luckily, I only slept for a few hours before waking up in a hazy panic. It's probably my subconscious asking me what the hell is wrong with me.

Putting my book down on my bedside table, I get up to blow out the candles when I see her. It takes every ounce of my willpower not to scream.

There is a ghost sitting on my barstool.

When the ghost sees me looking at her, she smiles warmly before standing to greet me, "Hello, Vivian."

My jaw drops. If there are any fruit flies in my apartment, I'll be getting an extra hit of protein tonight.

Closing my mouth, I sit back at the edge of my bed, trying to look relaxed. This ghost just spoke. She spoke, and she knew me.

We are on a whole new playing field.

I ignore the obvious tremble in my voice when I answer her, "Hello, uhm – who are you, and why are you in my apartment?"

There's something off about this ghost. She seems – more solid. Like the ghosts I'm used to, she's glowing, only the light coming off her is a bright white that shimmers off her skin.

The ghost-ish woman slowly comes to stand before my bed, her long white dress billowing around her. She has long, nearly white hair, and it's braided down one of her shoulders.

I'd make a crack about the ghost being an Elsa-wannabe were it not for her eyes. They are completely white, reinforcing my thought that this is no ordinary ghost.

Maybe she's another boss-level ghost?

If that's the case, then I'm betting she's at an even higher level than the original ghost girl.

"We met earlier, though I don't believe that form of communication will do. I've been meaning to contact you for quite some time now. It's always a bit difficult to pinpoint Keepers when they start out. But when you opened the portal, I was able to spot you immediately." The ghost woman serenely folds her hands before her, knowing I'll have more questions.

"I – wait, what? I didn't open any portals?" I'm confused. There's a lot to unpack here, but that comment got my attention. I immediately have a mental picture of swirling circles and people walking through them.

I can confirm there are definitely no portals here.

"Yes, the board you made was infused with your energy. And when you asked for someone to come through – I heard your call in the Otherworld, loud and clear. I'm sure many other realms heard, too."

I want to ask about the Otherworld but stop myself. First things first, I need to know who this ghost woman is and if she's dangerous. My body is on high alert, and the hair on the back of my neck is standing upright. I'm not sure if it's because the ghost can speak, but I'm getting some major fight-or-flight vibes, and at this moment, I'm leaning toward flight.

Which begs the question, how do you outrun a ghost?

What did they use in the movie to banish ghosts? Holy water? Sage? I suspect that no amount of smoke will make this ghost leave before she feels like it. There's an aura around her that radiates something. It feels like power or authority.

I choose my following questions carefully. "Who are you, and why have you been looking for me?"

"Of course, you must not have realized we've already been introduced. I am Need, and I've been looking for you because you're holding on to something very important."

Need takes in my utterly flabbergasted expression before continuing, "Apologies, it's been some time since I've had a new Keeper." She pauses as if trying to figure out where to start before diving in, "You see, the universe depends on balance. Good and bad. Dark and light.

Without balance, we would fall into chaos and ruin. Keeping this balance is my duty. I watch the realms and ascertain when the scales are tipping too far from one side to another."

I nod to let her know I'm keeping up. She continues, "When that happens, I send in one of my agents — either a Creator or a Destroyer. Creators help bring humanity into new, bright eras. The Renaissance, modern medicine and the ability to write were all sparked by my Creators. However, when enlightenment has gone too far, and the scales are tipped too far into the light, I send in a Destroyer. They bring down civilizations, spark plagues, and cause natural disasters."

"Both are beings of absolute power. A single Destroyer could erupt every volcano on your planet with just a thought. As a safety precaution, we keep their power bound. We collar them. The collars were forged so that Creators and Destroyers could only access their powers when the lock on their collar was opened. And when they are not needed, we put them to sleep, somewhere far out of humanity's reach, lest they are found."

I digest Need's words. This all sounds like too much for my world. Even after all my experiences with the paranormal, I'm not sure I can buy into all-powerful beings and magic collars.

Maybe this is the ghost version of a pyramid scheme pitch. They make you believe some crazy, outlandish claim. All this ghost is missing is the hook where she tries to get me to recruit ten boss mortals.

Need watches me closely, assessing my reaction. I try not to be too obvious about my doubts, but even with her opaque eyes, I'm guessing Need can see clearly and isn't going to pretend otherwise. "I can see you aren't fully convinced."

I look at my rug and clear my throat, now carefully choosing my words. I'm trying really hard not to offend her. "I mean no disrespect. The thing is," I pause, hoping this won't come off as insulting, "this all sounds a bit crazy."

Please don't go all freaky faceless on me and try to eat me.

The ghost woman – Need, arches an eyebrow, a smile tugging at her lips as if someone not believing what she says is absurd to her.

"Such a mortal thing to say," she starts, her head tilting slightly to the side as she considers me.

At this angle, she resembles a child looking at a bug and wondering whether or not to step on it.

I would love not to be crushed. That would be ideal.

"It's not enough to have a spiritual being of great power appear in your house. You need *proof.*" She doesn't raise her voice, but I flinch anyway. She doesn't sound too pleased with me.

I'm about to let her know she isn't the first ghost to show up in my room, but before I can react, Need's hand shoots out and clamps down on my shoulder. I don't even have a chance to scream before my body feels like it's being wrenched into a tight tunnel, stretching and pulling in ways that are entirely wrong.

In my next breath, my feet are once again touching the ground, and I stagger to stay upright as Need's hand releases me.

I gasp and want to ask Need what the hell she's just done, but I'm rendered speechless when I take in my surroundings.

I'm no longer in my apartment.

I'm standing barefoot on cobbled stones. All around me is a wall of jungle, its sounds piercing the air. Most impressive, though, is the sight that lies before me – a massive stone pyramid. It's notably absent of vendors or tourists.

Through my shock, I mentally tried to figure out which civilization the pyramid belonged to – Aztec maybe?

My guessing is interrupted by an impatient-sounding Need. "Well, Keeper, shall we accept that I am not making up stories? Is this *proof* enough that this universe has more magic than you know of?"

I reach out and touch a jungle leaf, just to be certain. It's real. I nod, still at a loss for words.

Satisfied, Need grabs my shoulder again. This time, I'm a bit more prepared for the weird stretching sensation that follows.

A breath later, I'm standing in my apartment again. Shivering slightly, I walk over to my closet to pull on a sweater. I'm not used to anyone seeing my exposed arms, and years of self-conscious hiding are hard to break.

Once covered and warm, I walk back over to Need, who is back to looking regal, even as she sits on my only barstool. Standing in front of her, I ask the obvious, "But what does this have to do with me? Why have you been looking for me?"

Need looks at me like I'm an idiot. "Surely you've noticed your power awakening by now."

Her tone is getting more clipped by the moment. Clearly, this ghost feels that her time is valuable, and I'm now infringing on it.

I want to ask how my ability to see ghosts has anything to do with whatever she's talking about, but Need continues before I have a chance, "Each of our Creators and Destroyers has a Keeper, a handler if you will. These beings hold the key to their Creator or Destroyer. Keepers ensure their charge is not released at the wrong time. The consequences of that would be disastrous."

Need pauses for added effect. She stares at me with her opaque eyes as if to ensure I understand the gravity of what she's saying before she continues, "Now, you've undoubtedly begun to feel the pull of your key towards the Destroyer you've been chosen to watch over."

At that, my eyes widen and dart over to my left wrist. Perceptive as ever, Need smiles knowingly. It's eery, not knowing where her eyes are looking.

"A Keeper and their Creator or Destroyer are bound by fate. You are drawn to each other by the energy between the key and the collar. The bond makes it so you will find each other when it is decided the Creator or Destroyer is needed."

I'm a bit irked at hearing someone is choosing my destiny. I've never been one to believe in fate, but if there's a mystical puppet master up in the universe, I have some choice words for them.

Forgetting that I'm supposed to be trying not to be crushed by this evidently very powerful ghost, I ask, "But who decides anything?"

"That is not something for you to concern yourself with," Need answers.

I frown.

I'm pretty sure Need just rolled her eyes at me, even though I can't tell for sure. She continues, her tone now reeking of condescension, "There is a Council of us." And like a skilled politician, she layers on her assurances thickly. "We are beings of great power, and our duty is to watch over the realms and maintain the balance. Your soul took our notice in a previous life, and it was decided that you would become our next Keeper when the time arose."

The mention of my past life brings me pause, but I squish that thought down and focus on my current life. Hopefully, there will be room to get more answers later.

Need said, I hold the key to a Destroyer. Frankly, I'm not keen on unleashing death and destruction on innocents. No matter what supernatural creature thinks it's a good idea. "But why now?"

At my question, Need's expression changes to one that's uncomfortable, if not a bit embarrassed. Her discomfort is quickly masked behind a cool façade of superiority.

"This is a bit of a delicate situation, and it requires some urgency. You see, one of our Council members has decided to leave the Council. She holds the key to our oldest Destroyer and has taken it with her. We are worried that she will use the key and unleash the Destroyer onto the realms. She is a dark being. There is some political discord going through the Council. We believe this may be a power play to place the realms permanently into darkness." Need's face crinkles in disgust as if the mere thought of having an unbalanced world might make her lose her lunch.

"And that, dear child, is where you come in," Need continues, "You must find your Destroyer, and together find the disgraced Council member – she is called Morgana and her Destroyer. Once you've found them, you must unleash your Destroyer. It is the only way to end the life of the Destroyer she is commanding."

The blood drains from my face. "You want me to kill someone?"

Need's façade of calm fractures. "Not someone – something. The Destroyer is a weapon. This is a necessary evil. We cannot allow someone entrenched in darkness to have unlimited access to such power." She storms up to stand in front of me before continuing.

"Think Vivian. Think of the damage they can enact on your *fragile* –" she emphasizes the word "world. This being can kill everyone you love with a thought. They can begin a new world war or cause major earthquakes at every fault line. And they will do it, Vivian. It's what they are." Her tone is urging, and she holds obvious distaste for the creatures she controls.

I think of my friends, of the life I've built for myself. A major earthquake could cause a tsunami that would wipe this entire town out of existence.

I'm not sure I have it in me to kill anyone, but then, I wouldn't be doing the killing, would I?

I shake my head at that thought. I'd just be just as guilty as someone who pressed the nuclear bomb button.

Swallowing, I ask, "Why does it have to be me? You said you have a Council full of people. Why can't one of you clean up the mess." I stop myself before calling it 'your mess.'

Need calms again at the question and takes a step back. "Like I said, Vivian, it's a time of political discourse in the Council. I don't know who can or cannot be trusted. But you, you lived honourably in the past. And you have every reason to want to see the rogue Destroyer put down. You can be trusted with this assignment, and once you have succeeded, you will be released of your keyholder bindings."

I'm relieved to hear that this is only a temporary arrangement. Quite frankly, this sounds like a paranormal dog-walking job. Only the dog is actually a terrifying attack creature who may or may not blow up my world.

Who's a good boy?

I'm about to ask how I'm supposed to do any of this when Need looks over her shoulder, frowning. "I've already stayed too long. The fewer members of the Council that know you exist, the better. Morgana will be looking for you, too. She'll want to make sure you don't stop her. She undoubtedly heard your call through the portal earlier as well. This is a matter of urgency, Keeper. Find your Destroyer, awaken it, and then find Morgana's and put it down. It's the only way to save the world as you know it." And with that, she disappears.

I stand blinking at the spot where Need just stood, gobsmacked. Well, that wasn't part of the description on the Ouija board blogs.

I look at my wrist, squinting to see anything that looks like a key. Nothing. Not even a cool faded tattoo.

Shame.

Sitting back down at the edge of my bed, I consider my next steps. Magic is real. And apparently, I have some.

I've never considered my ghost-sight ability to be a power, though I didn't get a chance to ask Need about that particular ability. Maybe the Destroyer is invisible – and I need the ghost-sight to see it.

However, opening a portal to other realms is a whole new level of supernatural.

Realms.

Need mentioned realms, as in plural. Is the Otherworld a realm?

What a terrible name for a realm.

Does that mean there's another realm called 'Thatworld,' or maybe 'Thisworld'? Truly, the possibilities abound.

After doing that thing where I try to make light of potentially terrifying life events, my thoughts circle back to the inevitable, more troubling things.

Is there really a Council of people or creatures that choose people's destinies? What's the point of living if everything is already mapped out and nothing you do makes any difference?

This sounds like prime material to bury your head in the sand from — or at least process when I'm less drunk and more awake.

I glance at my safe, inviting bed. Going back to sleep and pretending this was all a drunken dream sounds really good right about now.

That is until I remember Need's urgency.

Others will be looking for me.

Other what? Other magical creatures? How am I supposed to defend myself against supernatural beings? I don't have any fancy magic kung fu. Hell, I can't even ask my passive-aggressive ghost buddies to lend a hand.

Feeling disheartened and a little anxious, I tentatively lift my left hand, point two fingers at my wall, and whisper – "Bam."

Nothing. No magic spells. No firebolts.

Shame.

Powers awakening, my ass.

Back to the drawing board.

While I might not have magic handguns, I'm not entirely out of luck. This so-called Destroyer I'm supposed to release, they have power.

They might not have cool magic handguns, but hey, I'm not feeling picky at the moment.

Do I have any other options?

I could stay home and hope nothing finds me at night – but it took Need no time to find me after I used the Ouija board. I don't know if the other magical beings are as strong as Need, and truth be told, I'm not keen on finding out.

I need to find the Destroyer ASAP and then get on with all this saving the world business.

It isn't what I originally planned for my evening, but hey, adaptability is the best ability.

I'm pretty sure I read that on a fortune cookie once.

CHAPTER 12

ARMED WITH A 'SAVE THE WORLD OR DIE trying attitude,' I slip into my sneakers and pull my hair into a ponytail before grabbing my keys and heading out the door.

The hallway is deathly quiet, so I peek at my oven clock before shutting and locking the door. Three AM, no wonder it's quiet. Even the other college students are in bed.

I try to be as quiet as possible as I tip-toe down the hall towards the staircase door.

Whatever decent weather was around when my friends left is long gone. As per Atlantic standards, it is a torrential downpour.

I consider doubling back to get my car, but then remember the bottle of wine I drank.

Maybe driving isn't the best idea.

Besides, if I'm going to follow the pull of the Destroyer's collar, that means I need to get in the water. And unless the Destroyer is somehow closer to shore now, I will need to find something to borrow to let me get out that far.

Seeing as it's *a bit* late, said borrowing will likely be without permission. So, it's probably better not to risk having my license plates seen by any cameras that might be kept in the beach area.

Lifting my hood so that my hair is fully covered, I start jogging down to the beach, where I nearly drowned not even two days ago.

It's a bit unreal to think that almost drowning isn't the craziest thing that's happened to me in the last 48 hours. I've gone from being an almost normal person who can see ghosts to being entrusted with the fate of humanity.

How does one list such a promotion on their resumé?

Mind you, I'm not sure I'm qualified for the promotion, but given the choice of sitting back and possibly letting some supernatural creatures obliterate all my loved ones or standing up and trying to do something, I'm going to choose option B.

Every time.

I make sure to avoid the streetlights as I walk on the sopping wet grass instead of the sidewalks. I'm already soaked, but considering the next steps in my evening, getting rained on seems like a proverbial 'drop in the bucket.'

Finally making it to the edge of town, I reach the forest edge that separates the university from the busy shops and restaurants. I follow along the edge, being careful to avoid any broken branches.

I have no flashlight and chose not to bring my phone. The financial repercussions of bringing my phone to my last paranormal oceanside adventure were lesson enough – when dealing with spooky things and water, the electronics stay home.

The wind whips at my face, and I tuck my head down, effectively doing nothing for the icy chill that sweeps under my sweater. At a minimum, I figure that it will help ensure any cameras on campus won't see me.

While I doubt there are any cameras in most parts of this small town, I have enough rule-breaking anxiety to hold a high degree of paranoia.

After a few more minutes, I finally reach the boardwalk that skirts the beach. My wrist starts to tingle. Whatever bond connects me to the creature I'm supposed to find is evidently taking notice I've arrived.

Creepy.

I follow the boardwalk toward the surf shack, and my wrist starts to feel increasingly tingly, with the slight pulling beginning again. Luckily, whatever blue lights appeared in the water the other day are still nowhere to be seen.

The tide is up, but the waves are much smaller than the last time I was here. Approaching the water, I consider my next steps.

Consider is a strong word.

I already have an idea as to how I can get far out enough in the water without drowning, but I'm not sure I have the guts for it.

Stalling, I crouch down and place my left hand in the water. Instantly, the wispy blue lights erupt from my hand and reach out under the water, further than I can track.

Yeah, there's no way I'm swimming out that far. I splash my hand a bit in the water. "Here, boy," I whisper.

Nothing happens.

Well, it was worth a shot.

My stomach curdles. I know what I need to do, and it's making my anxiety peak.

Turning away from the water, I make my way to the Surf Shack, again careful not to get too close. I scan the small building for cameras but find none. I aim for the small, fenced-in area around the back. The fence is high – eight feet at least, but it has no barbed wire or anything jutting out from the top.

A smart person would have thought to bring something to clip the fence links.

Since I'm not a smart person, I kick off my shoes so that I can fit my socked toes into the chain link fence holes. I start to climb. The wires dig into the underside of my toes, and I hustle to get over the fence.

I try to use my hands to hold my weight as much as possible. I don't look like a cat burglar, but I make it over the top. I let myself drop onto the other side.

Landing, I still for a breath, waiting to see if there are any alarms. When there are no death lasers, attack sharks, or blaring sounds to alert the town that I'm a dirty, rotten thief, I start looking at the boards.

It only takes me a second to realize I'm a complete idiot.

The boards are chained together. Of course, the owners wouldn't trust a flimsy fence with thousands of dollars of equipment on a deserted beach. Unlike me, they are not idiots.

I mentally kick myself as I feel along the chains, testing whether they are locked up tight. Tommy wasn't very committed to Sarah; maybe he wasn't too committed to his job, either.

It's a long shot.

Walking down the row of chained-up boards, I start to feel discouraged until I finally find a board that isn't chained up. On closer inspection, I can see why. It's broken, missing a small part of its back end.

Gingerly, I feel along the broken side, hoping it isn't broken from a shark bite. It's only a moment later when I realize something else about the board.

This is the same board I used the other day.

I'm livid.

That two-timing, good for nothing, Tommy found the board – the board I paid for. And he didn't make any attempt to contact me and return my money.

Well, now I have much less guilt about what I'm doing. I'm just taking back what belongs to me.

Fuelled by indignation, I lift the board and push it up the fence, reaching up as far as I can on my tippy toes to let it fall to the other side.

I'd love to say that I've found my groove in thieving, but of course, I'm not tall enough, so the board just falls back down and hits me in the head.

I have no career in this industry.

Chewing my lip, I settle on Plan B. I lean the surfboard up on the fence and start to climb. Once I'm at the top of the fence, I reach over and start pulling the board, lifting it to the other side.

I let it drop down into the sand and quickly follow. Assuming I don't drown, my feet and hands will be sore tomorrow. I slip my shoes back on before dragging my not-really-stolen board back to the water.

The rain is still coming down, but I know my clothes will only weigh me down if I slip from the board and end up fully submerged in the water. And so, I strip down to my bra and underwear, leaving my clothes and shoes in a heap far from the water so that the waves won't take them, even if the tide continues to rise.

I gasp as I touch my toes to the water. I shouldn't be surprised, but it's still frigid. A nice warm rain would help with the cold.

The rain is not warm.

Picking up my board, I try to psych myself up. I'm scared – scared of being pulled under the water again. The tug in my arm feels much stronger now.

It's as if my entire being is being drawn to the water. What was it Need said about the key? The key is drawn to the energy of the collar and vice versa.

So essentially, it's like having a tracker on your dog's collar – only you're magnetically drawn to it.

Yup, I'm a glorified paranormal dog walker.

Suddenly, the hairs on the back of my neck start to stand. I get the distinct feeling that I'm being watched.

I spin around but can't see anyone. That doesn't mean a whole lot, though. The storm clouds hide the moon, and I can't see very far.

If this is one of the supernatural hotshots coming for me, I don't have time to second-guess my good sense. I spin on my heel and race into the water, broken surfboard in tow.

Cold. Holy cold, cold, cold.

I push through the waves in the shallow area and run for the deeper water. There, I quickly lay on my board and paddle out. I want as much distance between myself and the shoreline on the off chance that someone is watching me.

I'm not as fast as I'd like since I'm diligently keeping my left hand out of the water. I'd rather not be a living homing beacon if someone is on shore.

When I'm far out enough that the shore has disappeared under the cloak of darkness, I scoot further up the board and put my left hand in the water. Sure enough, the blue lights fly out and dance like little strings further off into the water.

I start paddling with my arms now, keeping my eyes on the lights and trying not to think about how deep the water is out here.

The tugging is getting stronger. I'm getting closer. My hand is starting to feel like it's being pulled along rather than the small tugs I was getting before.

I can't place why I feel such an immense need to find what is on the other side of the rope. It isn't just that I need to find the Destroyer. It's as if my very soul sings for it.

The feeling is almost intoxicating, and there's a desperation to it.

A part of me shudders at the thought that this feeling is all because some supernatural creatures decided to give me a magic key and played with my destiny.

I keep paddling until the blue lights extending from my hand no longer lead further into the water. I must have paddled far enough because now, the lights lead down. I stare into the inky black depths, barely illuminated by the blue lights.

I let myself rest for a moment on my board, catching my breath as I try to figure out the best way to get the Destroyer out of the water.

Maybe I'm close enough now that the creature will swim to me.

That hope was quickly squashed when I remember that Need said the creatures are kept in deep sleep when they're not needed.

Well, it would have been helpful if Need bothered to tell me *how* to wake up the Destroyer. But no such luck.

When no creature magically rises out of the water, I concede that I'm going to need to dive down and retrieve it. I know I can't dive with the board, so it will undoubtedly float away and be taken by a wave.

With the way I'm starting to go numb, I have zero chance of swimming back to shore on my own. So, going down there is a one-way trip for me.

Do or die.

I successfully find and awaken the Destroyer, or I drown.

If I make it down to the Destroyer, hopefully, it will have some way to get us back up and out of the water.

I try to find a silver lining before taking the plunge.

If mortals are commonly used to free Destroyers (and mind you, I have no idea if that is true or not), then surely the Council will only store them in places where the Keepers can reach them without dying.

Right?

Taking a deep breath, I jump into the frigid water.

Swimming freely now, I float at the surface but can still feel the tug on my hand coaxing me down.

I can't feel any panic now. All I feel is the burning need to follow the lights.

Again, a small part of me wonders what the hell it is about this bond that makes me feel calm in risking my life for it.

Thunder cracks above me. Despite the cold, my brain is working well enough to remember that thunderstorms and water don't go so well for humans caught in the middle. I'm low on time.

Taking multiple shallow, fast breaths to prepare for the deep dive, I finally take one deep breath and dive down.

I swim deeper into the water, and the pulling on my wrist quickly becomes as strong as a few days ago. The deeper I get, the stronger the tug.

Well, at least there's no chance I'll get lost.

My eyes are open, and I can see the blue wispy lights leading down further than I can see. I keep pressing on, swimming faster, trying to get down to the Destroyer before I run out of air.

I'm not sure how deep I am or how long I can hold my breath. When I start to feel lightheaded, I pause from swimming, my physical instincts telling me I need to turn around.

I fight it and continue swimming further down.

Time, I'm running out of time.

As if the bond can sense my body is struggling, the lights extending from my hand become taut, and I'm pulled down deeper.

My body is going into shock now.

My lungs feel like they are burning with the need to breathe, and my vision is darkening.

I'm not far off from drowning. Soon, I know I'll breathe in lungs full of water – because anything is better than the spasms that are starting to rack my body.

The edges of my vision are darkening, and I'm about to black out.

That's when I see the large sphere of blue light in front of me. Inside is a person – eyes closed, asleep and frozen in time.

I reach out for the light in a desperate attempt as water finally floods my lungs.

Just as my finger touches the light, the person in the sphere opens their eyes, locking them onto mine.

And then, I drown.

CHAPTER 13

I WAKE UP, COUGHING UP LUNGS FULL OF WATER, sprawled out in the sand. My lungs feel like they are on fire, and I think I've been transformed into a popsicle.

Oh, and to top it off, someone has their hands on me.

I shake my head and try to get rid of the small black dots still swimming in my vision. It isn't working, but I sit up anyway, effectively shrugging off whoever was touching me.

Holy smokes, my chest hurts. I sway in my more upright position. The dots in my vision are finally starting to clear.

"You should let me finish getting the water out of your lungs," a voice calls from behind me.

A man's voice. I turn to find the person I saw in the blue orb now crouching behind me. He's looking down at me with concern.

My heart skips a beat. He looks to be in his late twenties, and his hair reaches almost shoulder length, though I can't tell what colour it is from the rain that is still pouring down on us. His eyes are his most striking feature, shining an eerie blue. Even half-drowned, I can appreciate his appeal.

It's amazing the things you notice when you aren't fully drowned.

He must have been giving me CPR.

I shake my head, more than okay with coughing out the rest of the water myself if it means not having the stranger pushing down on my chest again.

He isn't a stranger, though. I recognize him. "I – I know you," I stammer out.

Understanding flashes across his face as he gives me a small smile. "Yes, you do. But you're also hypothermic, and I need to get you dry. Please." He adds the please gently, like he doesn't want to frighten me.

My body is shaking. I didn't notice until now, I was a bit too preoccupied with the burning that still racks my lungs.

I wrap my hands around myself in an attempt to warm up. I'm surprised to feel my bare skin.

Right – I'm still only wearing my bra and a thong. I must really be out of it.

My eyes snap back to the man. Bad idea.

At my own inspection of my near-naked state, he takes a good look too. Heat flashes across his eyes. I'm not in the mood to test his good manners.

Quickly standing up, I keep my arms wrapped around myself as I try to get my bearings and find my clothes. I spot them not far off, still in a heap.

Hurrying, I make for my clothes, eager to cover up. The familiar stranger follows me silently. I can't tell if he's looking at my body, and I'm shivering too much to bother finding out.

I quickly pull the sweater over my head. It's oversized and reaches mid-thigh. "I, uhm, I have an apartment not too far from here. We can go there," I suggest.

Now, looking at the man while he's standing, I realize he's fully naked. Well then, maybe I'm not the exposed one in this scenario after all.

"Here," I say, shoving my soaked sweatpants at him. He cocks an eyebrow but puts on the pants without protest.

I most certainly did NOT notice his body before averting my eyes. The heat that flushes through me is probably just shock.

The stranger breaks through my hypocritical thoughts. "You said you have an apartment here? Can you picture it in your head for me?" He's back to frowning at me like he's concerned.

I'm guessing I probably look as blue as his eerie glowing eyes, though on me, I bet it looks a lot closer to death.

"What? Yes, and yeah, okay, why?" I ask, just as the stranger takes my hand, and we vanish.

Instantly, we're transported back inside of my apartment. I sway as my feet hit solid ground, but the hand holding mine holds me steady.

"I hope you don't mind," he says. "I thought this would be faster than walking."

I nod. I have no idea what to say and settle on letting go of his hand before heading to my closet for dry clothes.

I don't miss the slight look of disappointment that crosses his face when I break the contact between us.

What's weird is that I feel it, too, that pang of loss. The bond that helped me find him hasn't dissipated. It's still here, trying to draw us closer.

I'm a bit miffed that the thing didn't disappear once I freed him from his ocean nap time.

Picking out my largest and most comfy sweatpants, I turn from my closet and throw them at the stranger. He's much taller than me – at least six feet tall. Well – beggars can't be choosers. "They're going to be too short, but it's all I have that will fit you. You can change in the bathroom; I'll change here."

He catches the sweatpants and pauses before following my directions. I make the mistake of making full eye contact. His eyes lock on mine, and he carefully eyes me up and down. The intensity in his gaze is a bit shocking, and my body instantly reacts. I let out a small gasp, my breath catching in my throat.

At my response, he looks satisfied, breaking into a smirk before heading to the bathroom. I'm mostly relieved that he's left my immediate presence.

Mostly.

Did my landlord finally turn on the heat? Because I am feeling really warm all of a sudden, even though my hands are still shaking from the cold.

It's a new kind of heat, one that doesn't leave me entirely unwelcoming of this man's attention.

Snap out of it, Vivian.

I throw on some warm fleece-lined leggings, a long-sleeved shirt, and another sweater. The stranger's voice calls out a moment later, asking if he can come out of the bathroom. At my all-clear, he comes back out.

Immediately, I avert my eyes to anywhere but him. In hindsight, I think I should have given him my only dry sweater. At least it would have covered some of him up.

Now that I'm mostly dry and not drowning, I can take in more of his appearance. The man is devastatingly attractive. Not like the cute fuckboys from the university, kind of hot. This man is an entirely new category unto himself.

He has broad shoulders and is very well-muscled. His chest and arms are covered in spiralling blue tattoos, but they do nothing to hide his well-defined abs. And yeah, I take that all in before gluing my eyes to the rug.

My cheeks flush.

Of course. OF COURSE.

After years of never feeling attracted to anyone, I finally get the hots for someone who just happens to be the paranormal stranger standing across from me in my living room.

I was right – fantasy romance novels ruined me for ordinary men.

I need to break the ice. This is getting a bit awkward. I force myself to ignore my burning cheeks and look back at him. "So, uhm. You aren't a dog."

Why am I like this?

The stranger coughs to conceal a laugh. I'm about to ramble about why I thought he might be a dog, but the stranger stops me before I can make an even bigger fool of myself.

He takes a few steps towards me as if unsure of himself.

"Is it really you?" he asks, his voice a whisper. There's a tenderness in his gaze that warms my soul.

I'm unsure how to answer the question, but the next word from his mouth instantly cools me off. "Cassandra?"

I take a step back, shaking my head. "Uhm, no, sorry. I'm Vivian."

The stranger's eyebrows bunch together. "I, I don't know how this is possible. It's been over ten thousand years, but I would recognize you anywhere. You look exactly like her."

This sparks my memory. "I know you too – I, I've dreamt of you. At a temple, before a battle broke out."

Understanding dawns on the stranger's face. "Of course. So, it is you. They've brought back your soul. They've given you back to me." He moves towards me again but then pauses as if suddenly realizing he might be confusing me.

"Sorry, you – Cassandra was my lover. Long, long ago. But she gave her life when Atlantis fell. The Council must have seen your sacrifice and deemed you worthy to serve them. They brought your soul back and gave you my key. They bound us by destiny itself." His tone is reverent, and he's looking at me like he's just won the lottery.

I frown. So not only am I tasked with dog-walking a crazy-powerful supernatural creature – but he's my ex from my past life. I haven't even dated in this life. I don't know how to deal with exes. This all feels… messy.

"I…" Yeah, I'm at a loss. I cross my arms around myself. "I don't even know your name. Who are you?"

The stranger smiles at me a little sheepishly.

He has a great smile.

"Of course, this must be very strange for you, especially if you don't have much recollection of your past life. My name is Leon, and I am the Destroyer you're bound to."

The adrenaline from my latest near-death experience is finally fading. My shoulders sag, and the chills are starting up again. My wet hair isn't helping, but I don't think I could lift my hair dryer, even if I wanted to. "It's nice to meet you, Leon."

Leon looks amused with my generic conversational skills but plays along. "It's very nice to meet you too, Vivian." He says my name like a caress as he tests it out on his tongue. "You should get warmer," he says, nodding to my bed.

"Oh, uhm" I pause, looking around my tiny apartment. I bite my lips in an attempt to get my teeth to stop chattering. "I'm sorry – I don't have a couch for you to sleep on."

Leon's gaze is locked on my lips as I continue to bite them. I feel it again, the pull between our bond. It's making me want to be closer to him. "I guess you could crash on the bed too – I'll give you your own blankets, though."

Yup, making sound decisions left, right and center. Inviting my paranormal ex-boyfriend into bed with me.

Real smart, Vivian.

This is a terrible idea. From the looks Leon is giving me and the way it makes my body flush, sharing a bed is a dangerous move.

Stranger – he's a stranger.

I'm trying to check myself mentally, but something in my body *knows* him. There's a familiarity, and it hums along the bond that connects us.

Leon eyes the bed and turns back to me. "I have slept for a VERY long time, but if it's alright with you, I'll lay beside you and at least provide some body heat. I'll stay awake and make sure nothing follows us back here. You should get some rest. We can talk more afterwards."

I should probably argue, but I'm starting to sway from the exhaustion. Stupid delayed response to adrenaline.

I move for my bed, sliding under my blankets. Leon outright ignores the blanket I hold out for him and slides under the blankets with me.

Oh no. Oh no, no, no.

I immediately sit up to let him know that he's supposed to have his own blankets because we just met and aren't going to share. But just as I open my mouth to protest, he slips an arm around my waist and pulls me down beside him. I let out a squeak of surprise. He wraps his arm around me and nestles my body into his.

His body runs hot. I am trying to ignore how good this feels.

He explains before I have a chance to let him know this isn't happening. "I'm not trying to be forward. You're still freezing, and I can fix that in a matter of minutes. Let me at least make sure you're well and not cold."

I can feel him harden against my ass. I go very still so as not to give him any kind of friction. Leon must notice and adds, "Don't worry, I won't touch you until you ask me to."

I choke on my own spit.

Yeah, that's attractive.

"That's a bit presumptuous," I answer, trying to sound indignant.

This feels far too intimate. I should move. I don't, though. The heat radiating through my body from his touch is too good to pass up. Besides, his hand stays over my sweater, resting on my waist – this is entirely platonic. His face is pressed against the back of my hair, and I think I feel him smile at my retort.

I'm just nodding off into an exhausted sleep when he whispers, "Not presumptuous, Vivian. You were made for me. It's destiny."

CHAPTER 14

I WAKE UP A FEW HOURS LATER, IMMEDIATELY remembering the events of the night before.

Sure enough, I'm not alone in my bed. Leon is sitting up beside me. Thankfully, he's now on top of the blankets.

As an added bonus to pretending my life is normal, his eyes are no longer glowing.

His hair is dry now, and the dark blonde locks fall in soft curls around his face. He looks perfectly relaxed, lounging on my bed, one leg crossed over the other, in my sweatpants.

I look back up to his face only to see he's already noticed I'm awake. Our eyes meet, and once again, I'm hit with a wave of heat, igniting my body. The bond between us practically vibrates. Leon's eyes darken.

If this bond is a two-way streak, then he's certainly feeling the pull between us, too.

Immediately, I sit up and move to put some space between us. I repeat last night's mantra.

Stranger – he's a stranger.

Now isn't the time to test out this newfound sexual attraction.

Leon's eyes track my every movement like a predator eyeing his prey. I shouldn't like it. But his gaze feels like a caress on my skin, and the energy passing between our bond hums. I feel warmth pooling between my legs, and Leon's eyes shift to that exact spot, like he knows exactly the reaction I'm having.

This isn't going to work, both of us sitting so closely on the bed. There is no way I will get any answers if I sit here a minute longer.

I bolt out of bed.

"I'm going to shower," I exclaim before running to my closet.

Leon grins lasciviously like he knows exactly what I'm up to.

The closet is next to his side of the bed, and I need to squeeze up close to him to get to it. I can feel his closeness. It's like an aura that calls me closer.

Not good.

I grab the first thing I can reach off the hanger before heading into the bathroom. It's a snug, grey cotton dress I usually don't wear because it's sinfully tight.

Not exactly what I had in mind, but I'm not about to turn around and go back for another outfit. I need to cool off.

The shower doesn't do much for the lust, but I feel much cleaner without the saltwater in my hair. I take a bit of extra time to blow dry my hair and pull it into a high ponytail. Some small strands still hang around my face, but at least it's out of my eyes, and I don't need to spend another twenty minutes styling it.

In theory, the dress is modest enough. It's long-sleeved and reaches mid-calf. But there's enough spandex in the fabric that it clings to me everywhere.

I bought it from a thrift store while reading a particularly delicious book last summer. It was so delicious that I was seriously considering finding someone I could try and date. If anything, I just wanted to see if the books were overemphasizing how awesome sex was. But after taking the dress home, I chickened out and shoved it into my closet.

Maybe I can try out the dress today.

The thought gives me pause. Is that really my own desire? I'm still not comfortable with the knowledge that a supernatural bond is at least part of the reason I want Leon.

The man is attractive, there's no denying that, but I wonder if I'd want him nearly as much if there wasn't a paranormal connection that seems determined to take my V card.

This is a new level of interference with my sex life. Now, even the supernatural creatures and 'destiny' want me to get laid.

No pressure.

Exiting the bathroom, I grab my barstool, bringing it over to the bed. Best if we aren't both on the bed again.

I've read enough smut to know precisely where that almost led.

It's too bad I don't own more than one stool. Still, one person on the bed is better than two.

I pause before sitting when I realize Leon is wearing new clothes. He's now sporting brown leather pants and a white shirt. Neither look like they are from a century I recognize. Next to the bed, leaning against my headboard is a sword. And it's an honest-to-goodness sword with a blue gem in the hilt.

"How – where did you get the clothes?" I ask, bewildered. I double-check the oven clock. I've slept in, and the stores in town are open now, but I doubt he could get any of that gear from around here.

Leon is amused. "They're mine. I apparated them from my holdings." He pauses and looks me up and down. Twice. "I like your clothes too." He says the words slowly as he stands up to join me, but I hold up my hand, stopping him.

"Oh no, you don't. I know we have a weird bond-connection thing going on, but I have questions, and we need to talk. And we just met. Literally last night." I'm ready to go on and list more reasons why we should keep our distance when Leon leans back against the wall and holds out a hand, indicating that I should sit.

"Then let's talk," he says, looking relaxed once again.

"I have questions," I repeat, definitely not paying attention to the chest muscles I can see through his very thin shirt.

Leon notices me noticing and smiles. I blush and look down.

"Look all you want, Vivian, we're bound. I will have no other but you." I can feel his eyes on my body again. It's getting very hot, very fast.

I try to catch my train of thought again. The man is blowing away my concentration. "Questions," I breathe.

His voice is low, like a purr. "You have some for me?"

"Yes," I respond, and then spot my grey sweatpants folded on my bed. "Wait – why did you wear my pants last night if you can just magic yourself some clothes?"

Still smiling, he answers, "I didn't want to overwhelm you last night. You'd already been through a lot, and..."

"And?" I press on.

Leon looks mischievous now. "I would never say no to the opportunity of getting in your pants."

Once again, the bond between us lights up.

Oh boy.

"Why does it do that? The bond…" I ask. "Why does it make me..."

"Hot?" he supplies.

"Yes," I answer. I think my face might catch fire from blushing.

"The bond between Destroyers or Creators and their Keepers is meant to keep them close at all costs. It can feel like the bond of siblings, of a cherished friend, and, more rarely, it can take the form of a lover's bond. It all depends on who is chosen to be the Keeper and how their soul reacts to the Destroyer or Creator."

I pause. "Then, do you feel it too? Like I do, I mean?"

Leon looks at me with a burning intensity that leaves no room for second-guessing whether the bond is affecting him, too.

"Vivian," he purrs, putting both hands behind his back as if to stop himself from reaching out for me. "If I had my way, I would have already had you last night, over and over again. I would already have heard you yell my name with your legs wrapped around me while I was deep – very deep inside of you. And then again, this morning, when you opened your eyes and looked at me with innocent wonder, I would have taken you, hard. Until the only thing on your mind was pleasure. And right now. Right now, I would love nothing more than to slide that sinfully delicious dress up your thighs so I could kneel between your legs and taste you. I wouldn't stop until you came on my face, and then..."

"Okay – I think I get the picture," I interrupt. My body feels like it's on fire, and I can feel myself getting wet.

Leon gives me a satisfied smile as if he knows, once again, the reaction I'm having to him. "Just so there's no misunderstanding about what *I* want," he adds.

"There's no way we're going to be able to talk in my apartment alone," I respond. My pulse is thundering, and I feel myself being pulled towards him.

Leon cocks an eyebrow again. "Afraid you won't be able to keep your hands off me?"

I don't think I could blush any more than I already am. "No – I just think being in public would make it easier to ignore this," I pause, looking for the right word.

Leon grins, clearly enjoying my embarrassment. "This what, Vivian?"

"I don't know, I can barely think straight. How do we make it stop?" I answer. It feels like the apartment walls are closing in on us. My body is aching, and I can feel every place his gaze lingers on my body, tingling with electricity, lighting me up.

Is this magic?

It's overwhelming and triggering my claustrophobia. My chest constricts, and my breathing comes faster as the familiar fear settles over me.

At my change in expression, Leon quickly pushes himself off the wall, coming over to me to take my hand. He averts his eyes, and the bond connecting us hums as the burning abates. I take a few calming breaths now that the pressure is easing off.

After a while, Leon lifts his eyes to me, looking concerned now. "Better?" he asks.

I nod. "How did you do that?"

"The bond is here to make sure we stay close to each other, so I got closer," Leon answers, squeezing my hand.

"Oh God, will it do this until I give back the key?" I ask, my face blanching. I don't think I can do this long-term.

Leon's eyes darken, but he quickly schools his expression back to one of nonchalance. "Only in the beginning. It will act up until it's satisfied that we won't leave each other. Then it tones down."

"Okay, good," I breathe, relieved. I need a buffer – something to take this tension away. "Why don't we talk over breakfast?"

Food – food is a good buffer.

Leon nods, letting go of my hand and following me into the kitchen. "I hope you like cereal?" I ask, reaching for two bowls.

"Sure," Leon says. He's careful not to touch me in the tiny kitchen area.

I make each of us a bowl and then scoot around the counter to grab my stool, pulling it up to the opposite side of the counter. A kitchen counter is an even better buffer.

"I have questions," I begin.

Instead of meeting me with the same flirtatious response, Leon looks serious as he responds, "So do I."

"Alright," I answer. "Then we take turns, fair?"

"Fair enough," Leon replies. He is purposefully looking at his bowl, and the bond stays blissfully quiet. "Well, you went last, so I think it's my turn. Why am I here?" His voice has a hard edge as if he is dreading my answer.

I swallow, pausing to try and remember what Need told me. "There's a Council member, Mor- Morgana? She left the Council and stole the key to another Destroyer, the oldest one. And Need thinks Morgana will use the Destroyer to permanently tip the world into darkness."

Leon lowers his head, and his hands grip the countertop edge. His knuckles are going white from the force, and the countertop gives an audible crack.

"Woah – hey!" I reach over and take his hands before he snaps it. I have a damage deposit to reclaim someday. Leon's eyes lift to mine. They're back to shining the same blue as the lights that had come from my wrist.

"Like hell, she will," he growls. The blue light in his eyes spreads down his skin, illuminating his swirling tattoos. My eyes are drawn to the tattoo around his neck, his collar.

Standing, I push aside my cereal bowl and climb onto the counter to kneel before him. "Hey, Leon. Leon, it's okay, come back. It's going to be alright. We're going to stop them."

I take his face in my hands and try to coax him back. I can't be sure, but I have a feeling that his lighting up with power in my tiny kitchen is a bad idea. Bad for the entire building.

"Come back to me, Leon," I repeat, looking into his glowing eyes.

Slowly, the light retreats from his tattoos and back into his body. Finally, Leon's eyes clear as well.

Letting go of his face, I move to ease myself back off the counter and onto my stool, but Leon's hands come around me, gently settling me so I'm sitting in front of him on the counter's edge. I consider pulling away to return to my buffer zone, but Leon is still faintly glowing, and I'm not sure what my prospects are for not getting barbequed.

His hands rest on my outer thighs, and I can feel them on me like a brand.

Swallowing, I continue, "Need doesn't know if there's more corruption in the Council. That's why I was chosen as your Keeper rather than one of them. We're supposed to find Morgana and her Destroyer so that you can kill the other Destroyer."

Leon looks shocked, but a dark smile spreads across his face a moment later. "Perfect."

"Perfect?" I ask, taken aback that he would so happily kill one of his own kind. "Doesn't it bother you? Killing another Destroyer?"

"Gods no," Leon answers, disgust seeping into his tone. "Destroyers are dark creatures; they live to cause pain, loss, and sorrow. They *thrive* off it. To take one down would bring me nothing but the greatest satisfaction."

I pause, frowning at his choice of words. "Don't you mean *we* thrive off it? Aren't you a Destroyer, too?"

Leon's dark look disappears instantly, and he grins up at me. "That's two questions, Vivian. My turn."

I give a slight impatient sigh but nod. "Yes, alright."

"You said earlier that you were going to give back your key. What did you mean by that?" Leon asks. His tone is mild, but his gaze is locked on me, and the unmistakable intensity of it is back.

I glance down at my wrist before answering him. "Need said that if we succeed on this mission, I can give back the key when we're done."

"That –" Leon starts, "I've never heard of that being done before. I didn't even know it was possible. A key is imbued into your very energy. It doesn't leave you until you die."

It's my turn to look confused. "That's what she told me – I just assumed I could hand back the key when we're done."

"Hmm, we'll see about that," Leon answers, his tone once again dark. His hands tighten possessively on my thighs.

My body responds instantly to the touch, a warm heat spreading between my thighs yet again.

If no one has given their key back before, I'm just going to go ahead and assume it's because of this crazy bond.

I won't keep mine, though. I don't want to spend my entire life bound to someone by a magical bond I have no say in.

I glance over at the oven clock to distract myself from Leon's touch when I notice the time. "Oh crap, I have class today. I need to get to campus soon, or I'll be late."

I scoot out of Leon's grip and jump off the counter, quickly moving around the room to grab my things.

Leon stands at the counter, his eyebrow cocked in curiosity. "You have… class?" he asks, a bit confused.

"Yes," I answer, throwing my bag by the door before doubling back for my shoes. "College."

"So, to be clear, you're going to class rather than working on our mission. The mission to stop your world and the universe as we know it from being destroyed." His tone is a tad incredulous, and I'm not too pleased with the slightly mocking tone.

"Yes, Leon," I say, slipping on my shoes. "I have a life to return to when we finish our mission, and if I want it to be a good life, I need to keep up my GPA. Besides, it's my last class before reading week. Then you have my undivided attention for the next ten days."

Conceding, Leon moves from the kitchen and makes his way to the bedroom.

"You'll be okay here?" I ask, grabbing my keys.

Leon emerges from the bedroom with his sword, strapping it to his back. I pause in front of him. "Leon – you can't be thinking of coming with me. This is college, not a medieval castle."

Leon gives me a small, amused smile before answering, "Vivian, I'm not sure you quite understand how this bond works, where you go. I go."

I start to object when he continues, "Don't worry, I can be unseen. Magic, remember? You'll be able to hear me, though."

I pause to consider his words but glance at the time again and agree.

"Alright, let's go then," I say, making my way to the door. I reach for it when I feel Leon's hand on my wrist. His touch is light.

"A moment please, Vivian?" he asks mildly.

I spin to look at him, feeling impatient. I don't like getting to class late and needing to walk in front of the entire class to get to a seat.

However, the expression on Leon's face makes me forget my anxiety in an instant. His look is of pure possessive fire, and desire ignites in my veins as the bond between us flares to life.

I gasp at the heat just as his mouth settles on mine, claiming me.

The kiss is raw, his tongue sweeping into my mouth, electricity flowing between us. I'm passive for a moment before falling into the kiss, wrapping my arms around his neck and touching my tongue to his.

The pleasure is immediate. I moan, pressing my body into his, feeling the pull of our bond urging me to get closer.

Leon's hands sweep over me from my back to my hips, with one finally settling on my ass and the other wrapping into my hair and pulling me even closer to him.

Leon takes full possession of my mouth, exploring me, owning me.

The kiss is consuming, and I want nothing more than to give in to it completely. My body grinds into Leon's, begging for more. But a moment later, he releases me, hands coming to my shoulders to steady me as I stumble forward, dazed.

"What – why did you kiss me?" I ask, working on quieting my racing heartbeat.

Leon's eyes burn into mine. "You've told me three times now that you want to break our bond and give back your key. I just want to ensure you know what you'll be giving up if you do."

I frown but see the time on my oven clock again. "That – shoot, I don't have time for this right now. We need to go." I open the front door, and when I turn to close it, Leon is no longer standing there.

"Leon?" I ask quietly, lest someone come out and think I'm talking to myself.

"Hmm?" he answers, right behind my ear.

My body shivers in response. Leon must notice because he trails a finger down the back of my neck.

"Cut it out," I hiss as I lock the door.

"Alright, I'll behave," he replies, but not before adding in another far-too-close whisper, "for now."

CHAPTER 15

I SOON FIND OUT THAT BEHAVING IS NOT LEON'S strong suit. At least not when it comes to me.

Our trip to the college starts innocently enough. We walk to campus in silence, each lost in our thoughts. I assume Leon is walking with me, even though I can't see him.

My mind is racing, trying to make sense of everything that just happened.

He kissed me, and I kissed him back. I enjoyed the kiss, though 'enjoyed' is probably putting it mildly.

Still, I can't shake the thought that something is off. Leon looked almost wild before he kissed me – like the idea of me breaking our bond was enough to push him over the edge.

How much of his reaction is due to the bond's magic, urging us to stay together, and how much stems from his affection for me in my past life?

Neither of those reasons is comforting.

I'm uncomfortable with the idea that we have a history I know basically nothing about. Leon clearly cares for whoever I once was, but how much of that person am I now?

I dreamt of Cassandra. If that girl was me, I feel no connection to her. In fact, I can't feel more far removed from her. I am practically the antithesis of a warrior.

Even more bothersome, if my dream really was a memory, then parts of it don't sit well with me. If Leon is an all-powerful Destroyer, and he loved Cassandra, why didn't he stay to help fight off the invaders?

I might feel disconnected from my past self, but I can't understand how someone can leave a loved one to die. The more I learn, the more questions I'm left with.

The campus is quiet. I assume many students are getting a head start on their reading week. Typically, the halls are flooded with students who insist on standing in doorways, effectively slowing down every other student who has somewhere to be.

Without the traffic, I make it to my Greek history class, just in time to take a free seat by the front door. Thankfully, there is a second empty seat to my right. This is another auditorium-style class with comfortable couch-like chairs with movable desks attached to their sides, so no one will notice if Leon sits next to me.

As I sit, I glance up at the top of the class and find my friends occupying the top row. Sarah waves to me and looks at the full seats beside her, giving an exaggerated pout before pointing to her phone. Picking up my phone, I see three texts from her.

Sarah: You coming today? We saved you a seat.

Sarah: Rise and shine sleepy head!

Sarah: I'm just going to assume you're still sleeping. SLACKER!

I look up from my phone and mouth 'Sorry' before giving Sarah an apologetic smile.

That's when I notice Conner sitting beside Sarah, eyeing me intently.

Oh crap.

Conner asked me out last night.

In all the events that followed my friend's declaration of interest, I completely forgot about it. But Conner evidently hasn't. His eyes roam appreciatively over me.

Quickly, I turn around and pretend to be busy with my notebook as the teacher quiets the class.

Apparently, I'm not the only one who noticed Conner's attention.

Leon's voice comes as a bare whisper right over my ear. "Not that it will matter, but I should probably pretend to be courteous and ask if you're already... involved with someone."

My arms erupt in goosebumps. I answer by giving the slightest shake of my head, keeping my eyes on the professor, and trying hard not to react to the heat that his words stir within me.

Leon's voice comes again, this time with a more amused tone, "Interesting. Does the boy know you aren't involved with him?"

I pull my pen from my notebook, scribbling a small note in the corner.

'*He will.*'

"Ahh," Leon whispers again. "I could let him know for you." His tone is deceptively calm, but I can almost taste the underlying menace.

An all-powerful supernatural creature letting Conner know I'm not interested is NOT something I think would go over well. Not with the possessive streak I'm already feeling from Leon. I scribble in the corner of my paper again.

'*No. He's a friend.*'

My concentration is already shot, and I scribble underneath.

'*Now let me focus.*'

Leon must be satisfied with my answer because he doesn't press further. I do my best to focus on the lecture.

Greek history is one of my favourite classes, even if the professor refuses to post his slides. The Greeks got up to all kinds of fun and trouble.

Today, the lecture centers on the famous scientists of ancient Greece. The professor starts with the mathematician Archimedes and how he used science to defend the city of Syracuse against Roman invaders.

The professor brings the story to life, evidently also a fan of this particular tale. He tells us how legends state that Archimedes used a giant mirror to focus the sun and set Roman ships ablaze. I'm completely invested in learning more.

Leon's voice comes again as a faint whisper against my ear. "That's a lie, there weren't any mirrors."

I ignore him. The last thing I need is to encourage Leon to stand up and give the lecture himself. I imagine someone as old as he is has probably experienced this all firsthand. And as much as I would love to learn the material from someone who lived it, I'm not ready for the absolute mayhem that will occur if Leon decides to go fully visible again and terrify everyone here.

I've had years to come to terms with the supernatural activity that invaded my life. My friends and other students – not so much.

Despite Leon's corrections to the professor, I take diligent notes, ensuring I remember the professor's accountings correctly for my exams later in the year.

Leon isn't in the mood to keep quiet. His whisper comes again, just behind my ear, "Actually, it wasn't even Archimedes who had all those brilliant ideas. He had an assistant; she was the true genius. But as a woman, she wasn't allowed to take credit, and Archimedes went on to be immortalized in your lessons, and she was left to be forgotten by the passage of time. She was a friend of mine."

I can feel his body heat, and it makes my skin tingle. The now-familiar warmth of our bond spreads through me. He must be trying to distract me on purpose. I steadfastly continue to try and ignore him.

The professor has moved on now to Hipparchus, the founder of trigonometry. Leon doesn't have much to say about Hipparchus but keeps messing with my concentration.

His voice comes again, "Do you always study so diligently? Such precise notes."

I crouch forward on my desk, trying to put some distance between us. If this man ever went to school, he was definitely the naughty student who distracted the class for attention. I scribble again in the corner of my notebook.

'*Yes. Because I pay attention to the prof, now knock it off.*'

Leon takes the hint and stops talking.

That doesn't mean he behaves.

I feel his hand on the back of my neck, his fingers coming around to brush lightly against my throat. Instantly, the warmth I've been feeling from his whispers becomes a full-on bolt of heat that travels right to my core. I try not to gasp and instantly sit straight up.

Now he's gone and done it. The bond between us flares fully to life. I try to be discrete as I cross my legs, squirming a bit in my seat.

My discretion is lost on Leon, who immediately changes his focus, moving to trail one hand up my thigh. My eyes widen as his hand reaches further up.

I move to write him another note, but in my haste, I drop my pen. A couple of students look my way, but I give them a tight smile as I bend under my chair to retrieve it.

I should have abandoned the damn pen.

While I'm leaning over, Leon takes the opportunity to sit back and place his arm where I was sitting. As I lean back again, I feel his arm around my lower back, stopping me from leaning back in my seat.

Doing my best to look completely normal to the few people who give me quizzical looks –I sit ramrod straight, not letting my back rest against Leon's arm. Yet again, I try to focus and figure out which scientist we're on now.

183

I should have stayed home today.

Finally, catching up with where the professor is, I continue to try to take notes.

Seeing that I'm once again focused on my work, Leon sets about completely shattering my focus.

His arm curls around my back, and his hand settles on my stomach, his fingers grazing against the bottom of my breasts. I try not to whimper at the heavy feeling it causes and inhale slightly to increase his touch.

Leon's hand freezes at the movement, only to realize what I'm doing. At that, he gives a slight growl before continuing, his thumb coming up to tease my nipple.

I'm breathing hard now, my legs once again crossing. I force myself not to show any obvious reaction that might draw more attention to me.

All powerful or not, I'm going to kill this Destroyer for the games he's playing.

Leon's second hand once again starts its path up my thigh, reaching the junction where I've crossed my legs. My dress is thin and doesn't provide much of a barrier as he slips his fingers into the crease of my legs, allowing them to graze across the innermost part of my thighs.

My folded-over desk is on my left side, shielding me enough that no one can see the crease Leon's hand is leaving.

I quickly let my right hand drop to grab Leon's. I continue to take notes, thankful to be left-handed in this moment. I squirm a bit in my seat again, trying to put a stop to the heat that is building even further now.

I tug on Leon's hand, trying to move it from my thighs. That would be easy to do if we were alone, but in a room full of people, I try to look as though I'm only stretching as I twist my back to add to this illusion.

Leon doesn't stop.

His fingers slide directly over my pussy, and even with the fabric of my dress, an explosion of pleasure courses through me. My grip on Leon's hand loosens, and he slowly starts rubbing small circles directly over my clit.

My eyes dart around the room, ensuring no one can see what's happening.

"Such a good student. Let me see you take notes while I make you come on my fingers. I want you to come undone with everyone here watching."

My breaths come fast, and I have a death grip on my pen. Leon's other hand grabs my thigh to uncross them before coming back to play with my breasts.

I spread my legs as far as the spandex of my dress will allow me, the bond between us humming and giving a static electricity feel to every place Leon touches me.

Leon pinches my nipple, and I bite my lip so hard I think it might bleed.

"Focus, little student. Write your notes like a good girl."

Holy fuck.

I shouldn't like this.

It feels so good, though. Pressure builds within me as Leon's fingers keep playing with my clit, over my dress. Every one of my muscles is tightening, and I feel like I might explode.

I try to keep writing my notes, but my left hand is shaking. My other hand hasn't let go of Leon's as he continues to drive me crazy. Only now, I'm not trying to push his hand away. I'm pushing it down onto myself, silently begging for more.

Leon's fingers work faster, and I feel like I might snap. His whisper comes again, tickling my neck, "Good girl, now come for me."

I shatter.

The orgasm rips through me, and just as I gasp, Leon's hand covers my mouth. His other hand holds me down as wave after wave of pleasure courses through me.

Once my breathing starts to slow, Leon painstakingly slowly removes his hands from my mouth and thighs. Spent and still trying not to squirm from the aftershocks of my orgasm, I let myself lean back into his arms. One of his hands is wrapped around my shoulders, while the other stays draped over my thigh.

Leon must be satisfied with the closeness because he finally shuts up and stops messing with me.

So, he only tries to drive me crazy when I move away from him. Lesson learned.

The bond between us hums quietly at our closeness, causing a flood of endorphins to wash over me.

A small part of that still bothers me, but when I try to lock onto what exactly is nagging at me, my thoughts feel muddled, like that night Sarah and I discovered peach schnapps.

Letting go of the fleeting discomfort, I let myself relax a bit into Leon's arm as I finally focus on the lecture and take the notes I need.

Once the professor is done, I hustle to gather my things. Just as I'm closing my bag, my friends come up to stand in front of me. "What happened to you this morning?" Sarah asks. "I know you like to sleep in, but jeez, girl, you just about got here late."

Sarah is very much aware of my aversion to arriving to class late. She was a firsthand witness when I left my paid-for but unmade coffee at the campus's coffee shop because any extra time spent waiting would have resulted in arriving to class late.

The take-home message? I don't do late.

Standing very close to Sarah, Isaac chimes in before I can answer, "She's probably exhausted from the partying she did with the ghosts last night." He wags his eyebrows suggestively at me.

I laugh. "If only. Sorry, no. I just slept through my alarm and then lost track of time."

The other students quickly leave class when Isaac asks, "We're going to the library to work on our modern history term papers before fall break. You in?"

I give him an embarrassed smile. "Actually, I'm kind of already done that one."

"Always so efficient," Leon's voice purrs behind me silently enough that only I hear him.

Oh boy.

I'd better get out of here quickly before he starts acting out again.

Sarah laughs, "Of course, you're already done. And I'm just going to pretend you were busy with a man all night, and that's what kept you today."

I try not to blush, and Conner chokes on the coffee he's just taken a swig of. "You keep telling yourself that," I answer with a laugh I hope isn't too panicked.

"Your friend is very perceptive. I like her," Leon whispers.

The heat hits again, radiating down my bones.

Damn it.

Wasn't once enough? How much will it take for this bond to calm the fuck down?

"Well, uhm, I'd better go. I've got some stuff I need to get done at home today," I say quickly, trying to get out of the classroom before Leon fully triggers the bond again.

I almost make it.

"Wait!" Sarah calls. I stop just next to the door and force a smile. "We have no more classes together today, and I leave early tomorrow for home."

That's right, I realize. Fall break starts this Friday, and my friends also have Thursdays off. Since I have no more classes scheduled today, my break effectively begins now. "We won't see each other for another week and a half," Sarah finishes with a pout.

"Oh gosh, that's true. I hope you have an amazing trip," I respond, genuinely smiling now.

My throat gets itchy as I choke up a bit. I really hope I'll survive whatever adventure is waiting for me. Otherwise, I'll miss my friends.

Of course, that's assuming you can still miss people while you're dead. I lower my bag back down. I'm not leaving without saying a proper goodbye.

"Thanks!" Sarah answers brightly, her smile cutting through my intrusive thoughts. "I hope you have a great break too! I'll see you when we get back. Please get into a lot of trouble while I'm gone!" she calls as she heads out of the door.

Isaac follows close behind her, waving at me. "Later, Vivs!" He calls as he leaves the class.

Conner holds back, looking at me expectantly. He's in dark jeans and a snug white T-shirt, the living embodiment of a fuckboy.

I give him my full attention, knowing that this conversation needs to happen. I don't want to lead him on, and I'd rather rip off the band-aid now rather than let him get his hopes up over fall break. If I bruise his ego, he'll have over a week to bolster it again with other women.

"I, uh, I like your dress. You look great in it," Conner starts, eyeing me appreciatively and much more closely now that he's directly in front of me.

I give him a small smile when Leon's voice comes again, directly behind me, his breath tickling the hairs at the back of my neck. "Not the word I'd use. I think you look delicious."

I blush.

Crap.

I don't want Conner to think I'm blushing at him.

"Thanks," I answer as I shuffle one foot back, trying to step on one of Leon's feet. No luck.

"Look, uh..." Conner starts.

"You missed," Leon whispers again.

I feel my pulse starting to race.

Damn it, Leon.

The man cannot keep his mouth shut.

Conner continues, oblivious to my discomfort, "I was just wondering if you'd given any thought to what I said last night. Whether you'll give me a shot?"

Leon's voice comes again, only this time it's less playful, "What did he say to you last night, Vivian?"

He speaks my name like a caress, but I can still hear the possessiveness in it.

Leon isn't touching me, but I'd bet my next semester's worth of student loans that he's less than a hair's breadth away from me.

I refocus my attention on Conner.

"I did, yeah," I start, trying to let him down easy. Conner looks so full of hope, and I feel guilty for rejecting him. "Look, I really adore you, but honestly, it's as a friend. You nailed it last night when you said I'd been through some stuff. I…" I pause for a moment, trying to find the right words but not reveal too much about my past.

"I'm damaged, Conner. I don't really think of you that way, or anyone for that matter. I'm broken," I finish with a small smile, hoping Conner won't press any further.

"Don't think about anyone that way? Hmm…." Leon whispers as he lets one of his hands trail a line down my spine. My knees go weak.

"Liar," he whispers again, undoubtedly feeling my reaction to him as our bond flares up again.

I shift, this time nailing one of Leon's feet under my heel.

Conner's look of hope has vanished. Instead, he's frowning, but in understanding, not anger. "I'm really sorry that you've been through some stuff, Viv. I'd be lying if I said I wasn't disappointed, but I get it. Or at least as much as I can from the outside. I'm here for you if you ever want to talk about what happened to you, okay?" he finishes.

I can see he's completely earnest. I'm yet again shocked at how amazing my new friends are. I didn't realize how terrified I was that this conversation would end our friendship. But Conner offers me his goofy smile and continues, "Well, I've got to finish this term paper today, so I'd better get going. I hope you have a great break, Viv," he finishes, readjusting his bag onto his shoulder.

"Thank you, Conner, truly," I answer, and I mean it. "Have a great break, too," I call as I wave him off.

Once I'm sure we're alone, I turn to where I think Leon is standing and whisper, "What the hell was all of that about?"

Leon's voice reeks of false innocence. "I haven't the foggiest clue what you're talking about."

I roll my eyes. "I think you like making me uncomfortable."

"I wouldn't dream of making you uncomfortable, Vivian. I just find I cannot quite stop myself from making you blush. I like the way your body reacts to me. It's..." Leon pauses as if trying to choose the right word, "intoxicating."

From the heat that radiates from him, I know that if I shift my posture slightly, I'll be enveloped by him. Leon must sense where my thoughts are headed through the bond because he becomes fully visible as he pushes me up against the wall.

I gasp at his sudden appearance and at the feel of his body pressing into mine. The leather of his pants creates some very well-placed friction against my dress, especially since I'm still overly sensitive from the orgasm he just gave me.

Leon presses both his hands against the wall on either side of me, caging me in. His stare is hungry as he takes me in, he looks at me as if he has me exactly where he wants me.

"Such a nice little life you've built for yourself here, Vivian." His voice is soft, but his gaze has that feral edge again. "And so damn eager to return to it," he continues as he lowers one of his hands to grip my ass, pulling me even closer to him.

My body responds instantly — the overwhelming need to be as humanly close to him as possible courses through the bond. I start to burn with the need for it, and the only thing that stops me from acting on my desire is the very public place we're currently standing in.

At this point, I should know Leon doesn't share my reservations about public demonstrations of affection.

He lifts me so that my pussy grinds against his hard length, kissing a trail up the side of my neck. "Leon," I whisper, trying to remember how to breathe. "This is a public place. Someone could come inside."

I try to slip out from under his arms.

Leon growls at my attempt to shake him off and responds by grabbing my hands and pinning them above my head with one of his own. "Let them watch. I want them to know who you belong to."

His eyes drink me in a moment longer before his mouth settles on mine in absolute possession. His tongue plunges into my mouth, demanding and rough.

I go lightheaded as the bond reacts, sending bolts of heat and pleasure through me. I grind my body against him as I kiss him back.

Leon uses his free hand to lift the hem of my dress up my legs until it only reaches my upper thighs. I gasp at the feel of the cool wall behind me, pressing against the exposed lower curve of my ass.

"Tell me you don't want this, Vivian. Tell me to stop." Leon stops kissing me to whisper against my neck.

I can't answer. At that moment, his hand slips under my dress, making its way up my inner thigh. In my hurry this morning to grab clothes from my closet, I didn't pause at my underwear drawer. Not wanting to wear the same underwear I slept in, I went without.

Leon growls at my lack of immediate answer, letting go of my hands to wrap his around my throat. My hands immediately grab his arm, trying to free myself.

Leon ignores my pushback and continues his trail up my thighs. "If you aren't going to answer me when I ask you a question, then I'll make it so you *can't* answer, Vivian." His voice is domineering.

When his fingers graze my bare centre, Leon groans. He releases my neck just enough for me to gasp and let out a small moan. Without hesitation at the slickness he feels, his mouth descends on me for another bruising kiss just as his fingers plunge inside of me.

Letting go of my neck, Leon grips my thigh, pulling it around him. I moan into his mouth, wrapping my other leg around him and hanging on to him for dear life.

His fingers feel like a brand as they move tortuously slow, in and out of me. I try to remember why I was trying to avoid this, but my mind is foggy, and I'm already close to coming undone yet again.

Tightening my legs around him, I'm about to reach for his clothes just as I hear voices outside the class and see the door opening.

CHAPTER 16

MY EYES WIDEN IN HORROR. LEON ONLY GRINS, and the next second, I feel the familiar stretching sensation as we disappear from the class and reappear in my living room.

My dress is hiked around my waist, and I'm still wrapped around Leon.

Cheeks burning, I uncurl my legs from around him. Leon is looking far too pleased with himself as he reluctantly lets go of my ass.

I think it would be really neat if the Earth could swallow me whole right now.

I rearrange my dress, shaking my head at the fog that still clings to my mind whenever Leon gets close to me. I cross my arms across and frown up at him. "You're doing an awful lot of touching for someone who said that he wouldn't touch me until I asked them to."

I'm frustrated with my lack of control and double frustrated that this seemingly all-powerful creature is in no mood to control his baser urges. Leon watches my every step. I take a step back, not sure I'm ready for another close encounter with this very attractive Destroyer.

Frowning at the distance I put between us, Leon stalks my retreating figure across the room as he answers, "That was before I knew you wanted to give back your key and break our bond."

My back bumps against the kitchen counter, blocking me from backing up any further. Leon takes full advantage, his hands coming to my waist and picking me up to sit on the edge. His gaze is once again intense as he continues, "Now that I know of your intentions, I am *very* invested in convincing you otherwise."

His hands reach for my dress, lifting the hem before quickly spreading my legs, forcing my dress to rise all the way up as he presses himself against me again. I gasp at the feeling of being fully exposed, feeling his clothes brush up against my clit.

"You can try and pretend you don't want this, but I can feel you aching for me. Every time you think about me sliding into you, I feel it through the bond. You might not be ready to fully accept our connection yet, but I know you burn for this." He emphasizes his point by grinding his hard length against me.

"Leon," I moan, the fog in my head coming back in full force. My body just proves him right by once again burning with desire.

Leon grins, giving me a bit more friction before pulling away. "But since you brought it up, I can oblige. I'll keep my hands to myself a little while longer," and with that, he turns and heads to the bedroom.

I stay on the counter unmoving, a bit shell-shocked. My pulse is thundering, and my body feels like it's on the brink of shattering from the tension Leon has been building in me.

This mission will be very difficult if I keep fighting the bond. As it stands, I haven't even made it 24 hours without being ready to sleep with this guy.

Closing my legs and adjusting my dress, I jump off the counter as Leon returns to the kitchen. He's taken off his sword but is still wearing his clothes from this morning. I try not to stare at his sinfully tight leather pants.

Leon cocks an eyebrow at me. "Looking for something?" he asks.

I snap my gaze back to his face, cheeks burning as I answer, "Yes, I am."

Leon misunderstands, his gaze darkening.

I quickly clarify, "Answers Leon. I have a lot of questions about this world I was just pulled into, and I think we still have a lot to discuss about what we're going to do."

Slightly disappointed, Leon leans against the wall and motions for me to take the bar stool. "Ask away, Vivian. I believe it's your turn."

I take a seat and eye him carefully as I ask my question. "Earlier, when you spoke about Destroyers, you talked about them as if you aren't one of them. Why?"

Leon frowns at my mention of Destroyers. "I don't include myself as a Destroyer because I didn't start as one.

I was a Creator. I was made to build up civilizations, to nurture them and grow them into greatness."

I want to press about how he went from Creator to Destroyer when Leon asks his question. "You told the boy – Conner, that you're damaged. What did you mean by that?"

I frown at the question. I don't like to talk about this, so rather than immediately answering, I stand up and head into the kitchen, pulling out two microwavable meals. Once I have them cooking in the microwave, I look back at Leon, determined to be at least as honest and forthcoming as he's been.

"I – some friends of mine got hurt a few years ago. My best friend's twin brother died, and I was blamed for his death. My best friend and the other kids in my town decided to get their revenge, and they hurt me. I have a lot of trouble trusting people because of it."

Leon frowns as he thinks over something. "Is that – last night when you woke me, you weren't wearing much. Did they give you the scars?"

I look away from him, ashamed that he saw me like that. "Yeah. They did."

Before Leon has a chance to show me any sympathy, I ask him, "How did you become a Destroyer?"

Just then, our food dings and the questioning is put on hold for dinner. We both eat standing at the kitchen counter.

I really need to invest in a second bar stool.

We eat our microwave pasta in silence, letting the answers we've just given hang in the air. I hope Leon won't ask me more about my past. I want to forget it had ever happened, and up until a few days ago, I thought I was doing an excellent job.

I look up at Leon and see that he's looking equally troubled. Are there parts of him that he's loath to share as well?

I think back to my dream and how he left me, or not actually me, but Cassandra, to die. I don't have the nerve to ask him more about that life.

Leon turns to me when we finish eating and clearing up. "Did you want to get comfortable?"

I do, but I'm also wary about getting into my bed with him again. After today's events, I don't think it's a good idea to be in my bed together for any length of time. Not when there is a magic bond between us that makes me want to climb him like a tree. At this point, I'm not sure I have the willpower to keep trying to fight the bond. I can still feel the desire from earlier wound up inside of me.

I mean, it's just sex.

I'm sure lots of girls have had sex with someone far less meaningful than their supernatural ex-boyfriend bound to them by destiny itself. What am I fighting for?

The fog in my head still muddles my thoughts whenever I think about why I should fight the bond. I feel a pang of anxiety, but it's quickly lost to the fog.

Leon grins back at me knowingly. "Afraid you won't be able to keep your hands off me?"

That comment has its intended reaction as I huff back, "By my count, you're the one who can't keep *your* hands off me. So, I think the question is, can you behave?"

Leon gives his best impression of an innocent man. "Of course! Like I said, I'll be good and wait until you ask."

I roll my eyes at his cockiness. "I've heard that before. So good luck with that."

Leon only smirks at my sass, but his gaze is intense. "It's not luck, Vivian. It's destiny. Our bond is wound into every fibre of your being. Your very soul sings for me. You're fighting the inevitable."

My cheeks flush at his admission. Again, something scrapes at the back of my mind when Leon mentions our being together is inevitable.

I have no say in this.

But just as the thought enters my mind, the fog grows thicker, obscuring it from existence.

"I'm getting changed first."

If I'm going to be sitting in bed with him, I can at least be wearing underwear. Leon has made it clear this morning and throughout the day what he wants to do to me in this dress.

Mentally shaking myself, I turn away from Leon and head for my dresser. As I walk to the bedroom, I feel the bond give a quick pulse. Either the bond doesn't like me going to the other side of the small apartment, or Leon is thinking about me in a less-than-platonic way.

I look over my shoulder at him as I turn towards my dresser, my ponytail swishing. His eyes are locked on me, and I catch his scorching look before he schools himself back into a casual smile.

Oh boy.

I pull out black leggings and a pale pink long-sleeved shirt from my dresser. I pause at my underwear drawer. It isn't that I don't have anything to choose from. I have a thing for matching lacey bras and underwear. As such, I don't own anything that *isn't* suggestive. Not the message

I'm trying to convey, but without other options, I settle on a black lace bralette and matching thong.

I roll them up in my leggings before closing my drawer. I purposefully don't meet Leon's gaze as I head to the bathroom to change.

I'm out shortly thereafter and notice Leon is back in my grey sweatpants. He's sitting in my bed, looking relaxed, with his hands resting behind his head. His chest is bare, and I can't stop myself from looking him up and down. The man is built like a god. When I look back up at his face, he's watching me with a very satisfied expression.

Blushing, I look away as I climb onto the far bottom corner of the bed so I can sit diagonally from Leon and avoid touching him. A smile twitches over his face. He knows exactly what I'm doing.

I sit up straight and ask him again, "How did you become a Destroyer?"

With that, Leon's smile vanishes, and he doesn't answer immediately. He closes his eyes, taking a deep breath as if trying to bring himself back to another moment. "When you lived in Atlantis, I was also living in the city. I was tasked to help bring the city into a new era. Atlantis was one of my favourite civilizations, and meeting you there made it all the more dear to me. You were a priestess, and I watched over the city, helping it grow. We fell in love, and I'd never been more content. But…"

He pauses, sorrow creeping into his voice. "It can never be allowed to last. A Destroyer will always be called when a civilization becomes too far advanced. It's necessary to hold the balance, but watching as they tear down every beautiful thing you build is sickening. To watch the very people that you nurtured into greatness fall to greed and ruin."

Leon's eyes are open now, but he looks like he's in a very faraway place.

"The Council – they try to keep their Creators happy when possible. I was allowed to remain in the city to take you to safety so long as I didn't interfere with the Destroyer's work. Not that I could have done much to interfere. A Creator's power is limited to creation. When you refused to leave with me, I left, thinking I couldn't bear to watch you die. As the battle wore on, I could still feel you living. I knew you hadn't fallen. So, I returned, hopeful that you'd let me take you away once your city had fallen."

His expression becomes crestfallen. "I was making my way through the city when I looked up to the temple and saw you – Cassandra. My sweet, innocent priestess – and you were slaying them. A group of fully trained, seasoned soldiers, and you cut them down like they were made of clay. I have no idea where Cassandra learned to do that. All I wanted was to apparate to you, to take you to safety, but my oath to the Council was binding. Now that you were engaged with the invaders, it would have been considered interfering to whisk you away in the midst of battle. And so, I watched, holding my breath, waiting for a moment when I could get to you. As you cut down the last soldier, I saw you run to the rope they'd used to climb up to the temple. I was coming for you. And then you – you crumpled. Two arrows and you fell from the cliff."

Leon stares at his hands now, where he'd folded them on his lap. He doesn't look back up when he continues,

"After that, I felt a rage surge through me that I never knew possible. My collar," he stops again, struggling for words. "It fell to the ground, and I murdered every last defiler that invaded Atlantis. The Council, of course, found out, and I was given a new collar. Creators cannot destroy things, and I tainted the Creator power by going against the natural order. The Council banished me into the role of Destroyer. They have only ever given me tasks since then of destroying other civilizations. It's my punishment for breaking my oath and acting of my own accord." He continues to look down at his hands after he finishes.

I don't know how to respond. I wrap my hands around myself, suddenly cold. Leon finally looks up at me, a searching look on his face.

I feel bad for him. Being forced to do something you hate for thousands of years as a punishment sounds atrocious. He went against orders, but to punish someone for thousands of years – that's a bit excessive.

"I'm so sorry you've had to destroy things for the Council," I say softly, climbing up the bed to slip into the covers by his side. My empathy overrides my caution to keep my distance.

Leon seems relieved that I'm not judging him and answers, a bitter smile on his face now. "It's what I am now, Vivian. I'm a Destroyer."

I lean against my headboard, considering his words. "I wish I knew more about our history together," I admit.

It's true. I hate that he harbours so much feeling for someone I have no recollection of. I'm constantly missing pieces of the puzzle as I try to work out my new reality.

Leon shifts against the headboard, and our arms rest comfortably against each other. "You were absolute perfection to me." He starts, once again closing his eyes as if watching a memory unfold in his mind.

I relax against him, wanting to hear more. "You were a priestess at the moon temple. The priestesses were pacifists sworn to light and life. We met in a field on the outer borders of Atlantis. You were picking flowers, and as I saw the sun shining down on you, I already knew I was going to love you for eternity. We talked for hours and would take long walks around the city, but we always ended up at the water's edge. It was your favourite place. You were kind to all and loved to smile and laugh. You had an undeniable light to you, which drew me closer by the moment. When I finally told you what I was and showed you some of my power, you didn't cower or show any fear. From that day forward, you were mine, just as I was yours." He finishes, opening his eyes to look down at me.

I'm slightly uncomfortable seeing how deeply he feels for me when I'm no longer that person. Perhaps if I had all of Cassandra's memories, this would all be easier, and I could accept this magical pull. It feels like a long shot, but I might as well try. "Is there a way that I can remember? To regain my memories as Cassandra?"

At this, it's Leon's turn to look uncomfortable as he pauses, considering my question. "I don't think so," he answers. "I could break the walls that hold the memories of Cassandra, but in doing so, your mind would be flooded with every thought, emotion, and memory of that lifetime. The force of those memories entering your consciousness might break your mind."

I blanch at the thought of losing my mind. "Never mind then," I quickly answer. "It's your turn for a question."

Leon considers what he wants to ask.

"Why are you fighting it?" His gaze bores into me with renewed intensity, and there's no reason for me to pretend I don't know what he's asking.

I break eye contact and stare at my own hands as I answer, "The bond worries me. I don't like the idea that some magical force is making me want someone. I worry that it isn't my desire but just what the bond wants. If I wait until the bond is broken, I can see whether this is real."

I glance up at Leon in time to see his gaze darken again at my mention of breaking the bond.

Rather than acting on his possessives like he did this morning, Leon sits up off the headboard and turns to face me fully.

His voice is soft as he answers, but the intensity isn't lost. "Have you considered that perhaps our bond is not some unnatural magical force? It was put there by the fates themselves, just like every other choice you've made in your life, every preference you have, every taste, colour, and person you've loved. By going against your destiny and breaking the bond, you'd be breaking a piece of yourself."

I've gone back to staring at my hands, focused on processing his words, when Leon pauses to place his hand on my chin, lifting it so our eyes meet again.

"I have loved you for lifetimes, have grieved you and shattered myself over the loss of you. To have you here now, returned to me, and bound to me – it is the greatest gift I will ever receive. You're fighting against your own nature, rebelling against emotions you have yet to let yourself even feel. There's a reason the Council brought you back to me. We are made for each other, Vivian. The only reason the bond takes the form it has is because it recognizes that."

I search Leon's eyes, considering his declaration. Maybe he has a point. Perhaps if I give into the bond, the mental fog will clear, and I can be fully happy. Still, that scratching at the back of my mind doesn't let up.

"I'll think about it," I answer, smiling softly at him.

Leon's hand falls from my face as he looks at me with tenderness. "Thank you," he answers earnestly. "I believe it is your turn."

His tenderness is stirring our bond to life, and I need to change the subject. I focus on our mission and what we're getting ourselves into. "Tell me more about the other Destroyers."

Leon's tone shifts instantly, the disgust leaching into his voice. "They are despicable creatures. Their very existence is sustained by darkness and pain. Just like a Creator can only create, the entirety of a Destroyer's power is used to destroy. Every horrible thing you can think of that has ever happened to your planet, famine, plague, war, natural disasters, every last one of them has been caused by a Destroyer using a drop of their power."

I'm a bit confused. "Leon, if the Destroyers are acting on the Council's instructions, then is your hate really well placed? It sounds like they don't have much choice in their actions."

Leon scoffs, "They love it, Vivian. Just as Creators are chosen for the light within them, the Destroyers are chosen for their darkness. There are two of them that were originally made as Destroyers. Irena is pestilence brought to life. She spreads illness and sweeps through civilizations, killing all without conscience. The other is Sin. They say he was chosen because he can bend minds to his will, making people commit all kinds of atrocities with only a thought, even before his Destroyer powers were granted. He ends civilizations by corrupting others with greed, anger, and whatever other vile thoughts he wants to play around with. Like a puppet master, he controls them and revels in the destruction they cause. These creatures cannot change their nature. Their darkness permeates their very souls."

I don't respond. The Destroyers are dark creatures, but the Council gave them this power, harnessing their darkness for their own means. If someone is acting despicably, then the true puppet masters should at least be held accountable.

At this thought, the bond flares to life, only this time, it brings me a world of pain. White hot light momentarily blinds my vision, searing my thoughts.

When my vision returns, my eyes lock onto Leon's. My mind is blank as if all my thoughts were burned away and replaced with an excruciating need for him.

My leggings suddenly feel itchy, and any fabric on my skin is unbearable. I shift in bed, pulling off the blankets. I'm overheating, and even though Leon is only inches from me, the bond isn't letting up. Instead, it snaps even tighter so that even the hairs on my arms seem to be reaching for him.

Leon watches my every movement but doesn't move for me. I try to focus on anything other than the heat that courses through my body and the pulling sensation to the very attractive and willing man across the bed.

My clothes are giving me major claustrophobia, and taking off the blankets hasn't helped. I frown at Leon. "How do you look so comfortable?" My tone is accusatory.

Leon smirks, leaning back to cross his arms behind his head, looking thoroughly at ease. "I'm not trying to fight the bond, Vivian. You are. The idea of being separated from you is already unbearable to me. And in terms of soothing the bond – I will touch and taste every inch of you when I have your permission."

I try to gasp for air, unable to catch my breath. "I – I need to make it stop, Leon; I can't breathe."

I don't know what set off the bond this time, but it isn't letting me go. The usual feeling of heat between us has become an unquenchable inferno.

At my pleading, Leon moves to kneel in front of me but doesn't touch me. The force between our bodies is magnetic, and I whimper. I lean closer to him, trying to ease the burning, but to no avail.

My nipples scratch against the lacey material of my bralette and harden against it. Leon's eyes move down to my chest, and he groans, digging his hands into the blankets as if to stop himself from reaching for me. I can feel myself getting wet as his eyes rake over my body once again, the hunger evident in his stare.

"Tell me you want me to touch you, Vivian," Leon growls, his voice low.

I feel lightheaded as if I might be consumed by the burning that lights up my every nerve ending.

"Please," I breathe, closing my eyes as my body screams in anticipation of the relief his touch will bring. But no touch comes.

When he doesn't touch me, I open my eyes to look at him pleadingly, my body molten hot. Leon moves forward, and his mouth is just a hair's breadth from touching my neck when he stops and whispers, "I want you to say it, Vivian. Tell me you want me to touch you."

I lean into him, but he pulls back, his gaze predatory.

My body must appreciate that look because, once again, pleasure courses through me. I want to rip off my clothes to try and rid myself of this heat that pulses under my veins.

"Leon, please. I want you to touch me," I manage to whisper, my voice coming out as a strangled moan.

He's on me in an instant, crushing his mouth to mine, pressing my body back into the bed as his body covers mine.

I gasp, and he takes that opportunity to plunge his tongue into my mouth. I moan into his mouth, wrapping my fingers into his hair.

The kiss is carnal. Leon is thorough as he ravages me.

I arch my body into him, trying to get even closer, and I can feel his arousal through his pants, pressing into me. I grind my core up against it.

Leon growls in response and pauses from kissing me long enough to pull my shirt over my head. He looks at the thin lace bralette that now covers my chest and groans before lowering his head back down to mine. "I want to take this slow for you, but gods, Vivian. You make it hard."

I can tell he's struggling, and the thought gives me immense satisfaction. It's the first time I feel like I might have some power in this.

Emboldened by Leon's words and the way he's looking at me, I arch my back again, loving the sensation of his chest against my bare skin. Every part of our exposed bodies that touches crackles with electricity, sending pleasure directly into my very core.

Craving more, I start pulling down my leggings. Leon notices and quickly takes over the job, running his hands along my bare legs as he removes them.

I now lay on the bed, exposed, in nothing but my thin lace bra and thong, and he eyes me like he's just caught his next meal before descending on me once again for another heart-thundering kiss.

I wrap my legs around his waist, and Leon's hands move under my bralette to caress my nipples. I gasp at the pleasure, and Leon gives me a wicked grin before tearing off my bralette and lowering his head to take a nipple in his mouth.

I moan as he sucks, and his second hand comes to my other breast, pinching my nipple. I gasp at the pain, feeling it blend into the pleasure he's still causing.

Leon looks up at me as he takes the pinched nipple into his mouth. My eyes roll back when he sucks it, his hands now roaming lower to the hem of my thong. I feel his hand slip beneath the fabric, and I spread my legs, not sure of what he will do but aching for his touch.

"Leon," I breathe against his hair.

Leon responds by lifting his head from my breasts and once again crushing his lips to mine, devouring me. As his tongue plunges into my mouth, his fingers seek out my soaked entrance. He moans when he feels how slick I am.

"So wet," he growls as he continues to make love to me with his tongue. His thumb starts rubbing circles on my clit.

Moaning at the touch, I roll my hips into his hand. Leon takes that moment to plunge a finger into my pussy.

Despite his earlier teasing, I feel my walls stretching at the new invasion. I gasp before closing my eyes, lost in the feeling of pleasure.

Leon uses his free hand to rip off my thong before wrapping his fingers around my hair and pulling my head back to look at him. My eyes fly open at the feeling of my hair being pulled, and I lock eyes with Leon, who stares down at me with complete possession.

"Oh no, Vivian. You don't get to close your eyes. I want you to see who makes you come undone. Who will make you scream and beg for more."

My eyes stay locked on his as he adds another finger, still rubbing slow circles around my clit. The pace is torturous, and I've never experienced pleasure this intense.

As he continues to finger me, I run my hands down his arms, his back, his thighs, anywhere to feel more of him. Soon, the pressure building within me feels like it might explode, and I know I'm close.

Leon doesn't stop watching me as my body tightens.

My legs start to shake, and I buck my hips against him, begging for more. My hand finds the hem of his sweatpants, and I slip underneath them to stroke his cock.

Leon responds to my touch by thrusting his hips against my hand, fingering me even harder. I squeeze him tighter, and he groans in pleasure.

"Fuck, Vivian," he growls as he starts thrusting his cock into my hand. His fingers mimic the sensation, and the action sends more flares of the bond's energy throughout me.

"Do you want to come?" he asks, knowing I'm on the edge of oblivion.

His fingers never stop their sweet torture, and I try to focus on his words. The pleasure he's giving me makes it almost impossible to think straight. The bond wraps around us like an elastic band.

"Please, Leon," I breathe, trying to answer him.

Leon's eyes look wild as he stares down at me. "Tell me you're mine, Vivian."

His fingers work even faster now, and he grows even harder in my hand.

I moan at the new pace.

I pull at his hair, trying to get his body to press into mine. I'm so close.

"Leon!" I shout through another moan, but still, he doesn't give me what I need.

Instead, his fingers slow, and his thumb runs a delicate caress against my clit. Once again, I arch in response, trying to ride his hand, begging without words for more of him.

"Say it, Vivian, tell me you belong to me." His voice urges as his fingers continue their slow pace, in and out of me, driving me crazy.

"Leon, I don't," I start, but at my words, Leon uncurls his hand from my hair to rip off his pants. In an instant, he plunges his hard length into me, his hand gripping my throat, cutting off my scream.

My eyes widen, trying to come to terms with not breathing and the sharp pain between my legs as I feel myself stretched further than ever before.

Leon gives me no time to grow accustomed to him but instead pushes himself even deeper inside of me, not stopping until he's fully sheathed. Only at that point does he loosen his grip on my neck, letting me have one life-saving breath.

I gasp, and then his hand is back around my neck as he pulls his hips back and thrusts inside of me. My eyes roll into the back of my head with both pain and ecstasy.

Leon doesn't stop but starts thrusting faster, his free hand back on my breast, pinching my nipple.

I grasp at his arm, desperate for air, to let out the screams building inside of me as he pounds into me, harder with each passing second.

He isn't gentle, as he purposefully drags his length across my entrance to increase the friction.

My legs start to tremble, and my vision darkens at the edges. I lift my hips now to meet his thrusts, blind to the pain, only wanting release. Leon's pace is bruising, and I'm teetering over the edge.

"Mine, Vivian," Leon growls as he releases my breast, using his free hand to grip my hip, angling them up so he can slam into me even deeper.

I wrap my legs around him, my vision going almost entirely dark. Leon isn't having it. He eases his grip on my throat just enough to give me another hit of oxygen.

"Eyes on me, Vivian," he commands.

Once my eyes lock on him, I see they're glowing with the same eery blue.

"We are bound, and you belong to me." He punctuates every word with another punishing thrust, and his grip on my throat tightens even further.

I come undone, and my entire body feels as though it's being shocked by waves of electric energy that course through me.

At my orgasm, Leon releases my neck before thrusting hard into me again, spilling his seed deep within me. I cling to him, and Leon moves to lightly stroke my clit, coaxing every aftershock from my body.

When I finally come down from my orgasm, Leon turns me so my ass is cradled against him and wraps his arms around me. He lays there holding me but doesn't say a word, evidently very content with simply holding me now.

I think of what I should say, if anything.

I don't know how to feel right now. I only feel the heat of him envelop me. I don't want it to go away because I know that as soon as it does, the crushing emptiness clinging to the edges of my mind will take me.

Just as I drift off into sleep, Leon's hands tighten possessively around me, and I hear him whisper, "Mine."

CHAPTER 17

I WAKE TO THE FEELING OF LEON LIGHTLY shaking my shoulder. My eyes open and I immediately realize his hand is pressed against my mouth.

Still half asleep, I frown at his hand before looking up at him, confused.

Leon signals me to be quiet before removing his hand. He looks grave as he whispers, "We have company. Get dressed and stay away from the windows."

Fear pierces through my sleep haze as I scramble out of bed and look for my leggings and top. They're in a heap, crumpled on the floor. Throwing on my clothes, I see Leon is fully dressed in his fighting garb, his sword strapped to his back.

I remember Need's warning that my signal to the Otherworld would be overheard by many. I probably should have thought to mention that to Leon.

Stupid.

I throw on a sweater and shoes, still mentally kicking myself.

"Who is it?" I whisper.

"Forsaken," Leon says as he stands in front of me, watching the windows without letting me become a target. "They're Morgana's spies, come to kill you. No doubt they're hoping you haven't found me yet. They will want to make sure you never do."

I hear a scraping sound against my window as one of the creatures crawls across it.

They're searching the building for me. I quickly jump to get closer to the wall with no windows.

"What do we do?" I ask. My heart is hammering, and my palms start to sweat. I take calming breaths to keep the fear paralysis at bay.

"Take off my collar, Vivian. I'll make short work of them," Leon orders as he turns towards me. He has a sinister smile like he's eager to use his power against the creatures.

I balk at his demand. Despite his aversion to the title, Leon is a creature of infinite destructive power, capable of destroying entire civilizations with just a thought.

I'm rather fond of my small town and even more concerning, we're currently standing in a small apartment surrounded by innocents. Infinite destructive power and apartments full of innocents can't go well together.

Slowly, I shake my head at him.

Leon looks at me as if I've grown a second head.

Frowning now, he growls at me, "Vivian, this is *why* we are paired together, so that when a threat arises – I can defend us. This is a threat, and I need my power to make sure you're safe." His hands fist and unfist in annoyance at his sides, and he thinks to add, "Please."

"No, Leon," I answer. My voice is shaking a bit – I don't do conflict, but I'm not going to bend on this. "I won't unleash you here. There are too many innocents in this town. This is an apartment complex. A Destroyer's power around this many people? Not a good idea."

Leon's eyes widen at my defiance, and then immediately narrow. "This isn't how the Destroyer-Keeper relationship works, Vivian. You obey me. I protect you. I can't do that with the collar. *Free* me," he urges, approaching me and crowding me against the wall.

The alluring pull of his heat sweeps over me, but I ignore it, lifting my chin. In doing so, I see the shadows gathering outside my windows through the blinds. They're accompanied by what sounds like claws on the outside walls.

Pulling my gaze back to Leon, I stand firm. "I won't risk all the people that live here," I answer, not backing down from the ancient and very powerful being I've just infuriated.

He won't hurt me, will he?

He wouldn't – he loved me once.

"Then you are signing your death," Leon spits back, hand reaching for his sword.

My heart skips at the motion, reminding myself I'm not in danger from him.

I'm not one to lay down and accept death. There must be another way. "Why can't we do the disappearing thing?" I ask.

Leon turns away from me to face the windows as he answers me, "Because Vivian –" he spits my name like a curse now. "The bad guys can apparate too. And they will follow your energy signature from here, to wherever they feel us apparate to. Oh – and if they catch us midway through apparating, they can just divert our energy to wherever they please. That magic will only leave us more vulnerable."

My shoulders slump and I ignore his mocking tone while I consider other possibilities.

We need to get out of here fast.

Fast.

I can do fast.

"I have a way out of here!" I exclaim, in excited urgency.

Leon turns to me, now very agitated. "They have swarmed the outside perimeter, Vivian. We can't outrun them. FREE ME," he urges again, this time raising his voice.

I flinch.

The automatic response to his voice only further pisses me off, and my blood boils as I answer, "I have a fucking car, Leon. Parked underneath the building. If we can get to it, then I'm guessing I can out-drive them."

Leon pauses a moment before nodding. "The forsaken can't hurt me. I'll distract them and lead them away from the building. Once you're out, I'll find you."

I nod, running for my car keys. They're in my bag. I look around for it, momentarily confused.

My bag isn't here.

Shit.

I must have left it on the floor of my class when Leon apparated us out.

Good thing I'm used to misplacing things. I dash for my spares, kept on a hook in my medicine cabinet.

Wrenching my apartment door open, I scan the hallways for any sign of whatever the hell is outside. Not seeing anything, I run for the stairs that lead five floors down to the underground parking garage.

Just as I open the stairwell door, I hear glass shattering behind me, followed by an unearthly screech.

There's no time for caution now. I tear down the stairs as fast as my feet carry me, taking the steps two at a time. I frantically look around as I hit every bend in the stairs, expecting that each will bring me face to face with a monster.

Luck must be on my side because as I round the last bend in the stairs, I can see the door to the parking garage. I let myself be hopeful that not meeting any creatures in the stairwell means they haven't found the parking garage yet.

I slow my steps as I reach the door, pressing my ear to it while being as quiet as possible.

The door is solid metal, and there's no way to look inside the garage before opening it. Hearing nothing, I turn the handle painstakingly slowly, trying to avoid any potential creak or click that the door might make.

I've never taken the time to pay attention to how noisy the doors are in the building. I make a mental note to be more aware of my surroundings in the future.

Assuming, of course, my future extends past the next five minutes.

The door to the parking garage makes the slightest creek when I open it, just wide enough to poke my head through.

Soft light from the stairwell floods the garage in a bright triangle. I hold my breath as I scan the parking garage. It's dimly lit by soft overhead lights on a few outer edges.

The garage is relatively small, fitting less than fifty cars. I have about forty feet between me and my vehicle, which is parked midway through.

Scanning as far as my eyes can see in the dim light, I don't see any sign of movement.

Creeping now, I step from the stairwell area and enter the garage, closing the door behind me just as quietly as I opened it.

I stand in front of the door, again waiting to make sure there's no sign of movement. I could make a break for my car and reach it quickly, but instead, I try to be as quiet as possible.

When Leon told me to run to my car alone, I didn't think it wise to mention that the parking garage has no actual garage door and is open to the outside air.

So, in case the creatures are still prowling around the building, I'm guessing my best chance is to be as stealthy as possible until I'm inside my vehicle.

My steps are measured, and I strain to listen for the slightest sound. My heart is hammering wildly, and I have no idea how people in survival situations ever hear anything beyond the thundering of their pulse.

Five steps from the door now, and still, I see no sign of movement. Of course, I could never be that lucky.

White plaster powder trickles down on me from the ceiling. Realization hits like a bitch.

I made a critical error.

Up.

I didn't bother to look for movement on the ceiling.

Dreading what I'm about to see, I freeze and slowly raise my eyes to see what made the plaster fall on me. There, directly atop me, is what I can confidently assume is a forsaken.

It has the same unearthly glow as the faceless creatures I'm used to and shares the same smooth skin that mars most of its features. This creature looks like a terrifying second cousin of the faceless. Its skin is a dark, leathery grey, and it has no eyes I can see. Its hands and feet are also elongated but end in sharp claws that it now uses to dig into the ceiling plaster.

Perhaps the most terrifying part of the forsaken is its mouth. Stretching wide like its jaw has been permanently unhinged, it doesn't hold a black void but is filled with thousands of needle-sharp teeth.

The creature clings to the ceiling with its hands and feet, and its back is arched. Its neck also arches so it can watch me as I stand directly below it.

I take a slow step back, unsure how well the creature can see if it has no eyes. The creature twists its head at an impossible angle, watching my movement.

No such luck.

The creature makes a few clicking sounds from the back of its throat as it skitters across the ceiling to circle me, like a predator stalking its prey.

My mouth goes dry, and I feel myself starting to become flooded by the fear paralysis. The creature begins advancing on me, moving slowly as it snaps its jaws at me.

Staring at the creature's teeth, I get struck with the realization that if death is taking me today, I'm not going to stand here and wait for it to happen.

Without waiting for another breath, I run for my car. The creature responds by letting out a few high-pitched, clipped shrieks. I hear some answering shrieks from somewhere outside. My face blanches as I realize what the creature is doing.

It's calling for its friends.

Clever girl.

I'm only a few feet from my car when it darts across the ceiling and jumps onto the car directly in front of me.

The faceless creatures in the woods are creepy when they move, blinking in and out of existence.

These forsaken creatures are utterly terrifying. It moves abhorrently fast, running across the ceiling like one of those impossibly fast spiders that dart across your wall only to then jump on your face.

I screech to a stop, now face to face with the forsaken.

If I want to get to my car, I have to run by this creature, and at the speed at which it's moving, there's no way it won't catch me. The creature takes a measured step on the crushed hood of the car towards me, once again making a trilling, clicking noise.

I take an equal, measured step backwards, and it snaps its teeth at me.

I pause, trying not to piss it off. Maybe this thing is a like a cougar or bear. Aren't you not supposed to run from those? You need to look bigger.

Or maybe you need to look small and less threatening, and then they'll leave you alone. I'm thinking I already look small and less threatening compared to this thing, and it hasn't left me alone, so I go for option A.

Standing straight, I shove my fear down to the box deep inside of me where I keep emotions and feelings that I'm not prepared to deal with. Sex with Leon is in there, too. I'm in no way ready to process that.

My body calms, aided by years of experience in dealing with the faceless. I take a step towards the creature, fully prepared to tell it to get the fuck out of here. But as I look at it without fear, I'm surprised to feel a familiar pain emanating from it. The feeling is almost exactly what I feel from the faceless.

Well, shit.

I think this might be another trapped soul. It's either that or this creature has huge problems with projecting its negativity.

Keeping my breathing even, I let the pain of the creature flood through me. Despair, shame, and so much anger radiate from it. The creature is now deathly still as I step forward, slowly extending my shaking hand toward it.

There are a lot of teeth. No amount of self-soothing techniques will make those teeth less of a threat.

I can hear the creatures outside now, getting closer to us. There are claws scraping against the roof and walls of the parking garage. Everything is happening fast, but my mind feels like running in slow motion.

Unsure of whether it will work, I mentally search for whatever is binding the forsaken to the earth. As I do so, the same warm silver energy rises through my chest and out my arms, feeling like goosebumps erupting over my skin. My energy reaches for the forsaken that is now only a foot away from me.

Still, it makes no move to attack me as light envelopes it. While I can't understand the creature, I can feel for it. It's pitiful that something has lived trapped in those negative emotions.

Other forsaken are now entering the garage, scrambling up walls and along the ceiling. I block them all out.

My silvery light fully encompasses the forsaken now, blocking out its shape. I hold my breath, hoping this will work.

As the energy dissipates, the forsaken is replaced by what looks like a warrior. He is massive and wears leather and metal armour, akin to something I've only seen in movies. He's holding a large battle axe.

Just like the faceless I've freed, he still holds a slight unearthly glow. I don't have time to take in much else because the warrior looks around at the forsaken that are now swarming into the building and mouths, '*Run.*'

The sound of the forsaken's claws digging into cement and plaster is a steady scratching sound. Breaking my eyes from the warrior, I see them pouring into the garage, skittering across the walls and other cars, moving like a swarm of insects.

I don't need to be told twice and run the last couple of steps towards my car.

Throwing myself inside of it, I can hear the creatures running and jumping for me, but instead of feeling pain, I hear their pained shrieks as the warrior attacks them, buying me some time.

Turning my keys in the ignition, I slam my foot onto the gas. I hear a thump just as claws pierce the passenger side of my car as I speed for the open door. The forsaken slams a clawed hand through the passenger window, trying to reach for me.

I scream and twist the wheel so that as I tear through the parking garage exit, I pinch the creature between the garage wall and my car — the forsaken screeches in pain before it's effectively dislodged.

My car emerges from the parking garage, and I can see more of them through the thin fog that coats the outside air.

I swerve my car to try and avoid them as I speed through my building's outer parking lot, heading for the road. All the while, I scan the area, looking for Leon.

He said the creatures can't hurt him, so I hope that means he's well and alive.

Spinning my car onto the road, I see him running towards me from another side of the building. His eyes glow that same vivid blue, making it easy to spot him. I fishtail my car around, turning to pick him up.

Behind me now, a swarm of forsaken tears out of the parking garage, running towards us, the soft glow of the warrior nowhere in sight. Without slowing, I speed towards Leon and only slam the brakes once I reach him.

As Leon jumps into the car, he looks up to see the forsaken still coming out of the parking garage in droves. I say nothing at his shocked expression as he puts two and two together, realizing that is where I just came from. Instead, I step on the gas, speeding as quickly as my car can take us to get anywhere that isn't here.

CHAPTER 18

WE'VE BEEN DRIVING FOR A QUARTER OF AN hour without any sign of being followed when I finally ease off the gas pedal, and offer Leon a weak smile. "See? Plan B totally worked."

Leon's jaw twitches as he slowly turns to look at me. He still looks furious. "Worked? Your plan worked?" he whispers.

I frown back at him. "Well, yeah, we got out of the apartment without blowing up the town during some epic supernatural fight. I think that counts as a win."

I'm just going to pretend his barely contained fury doesn't exist. That way, it can't hurt me. Right?

Leon narrows his eyes. "I don't think you understand what is at stake here. This is bigger than just one insignificant town. The universe, Vivian. If we allow

Morgana to release her Destroyer, the entire universe could be ended in a heartbeat."

He snaps his fingers for effect.

I fume but bite my tongue. The voice inside my head is screaming, even though I don't let her out. I never let her out.

Seeing the entrance to a major highway, I take the onramp. I don't have a particular destination in mind, but the highway is the fastest way to distance us from my apartment.

Leon isn't finished. "Now the forsaken have seen you, and they know you are with me. Because you didn't let me un-exist them all, they will report that information to Morgana. So not only can they tell their mistress that we are reunited, but they have your scent and know exactly who you are. They will not stop coming for you now, Vivian. They will come in armies. They will rip apart the very fabric of your realm to get to you. And if you won't release me from my bindings. I cannot stop them from doing so. So please, Vivian. When I make the order to be released, I expect you to obey without question."

I keep my eyes on the road. Fury simmers somewhere deep inside of me. It spreads across me like a molten liquid.

Insignificant.

I rage over the word. He called my home, my safe place, insignificant and would undoubtedly destroy it without a moment's hesitation to serve the greater good.

Leon takes my silence as remorse and nods before turning back to the road.

My hands tighten on the steering wheel, and I refuse to look at him. Ahead of us, storm clouds gather on the horizon.

I'm furious that otherworldly creatures have invaded my life, my world, and that they're playing with our very fates. I rage over the fact that innocent human lives are too insignificant to be considered in the scope of the troubles that plague the supernatural world. Troubles that *they* created.

I will not accept their rules.

I will not step aside and turn a blind eye to the injustice.

I will not enable the destruction.

The bond within me flares to life, once again searing me with a shock of pain.

I push against it, fighting the fog that gathers in my mind.

My thoughts will not be erased.

Not again.

Leon is oblivious to my fury and pain, focusing on the storm ahead. He watches as silver lightning streaks across the sky, jumping from cloud to cloud. There are hundreds of bolts.

He quickly turns to me, eyes widening in surprise. "Vivian – you need to pull over. Now."

My vision is darkening from the pain as I mutely continue to fight the fog. Relenting, I pull over onto the side of the highway. My hands keep their death grip on the steering wheel.

Something is trying to cloud my thoughts again, and I am beyond livid.

I don't want to be complacent.

I don't want to sit silently and take whatever fate others throw at me.

Stones, fog, no more.

Leon jumps from the car's passenger side and wrenches open my door. The storm is getting bigger now, massive clouds circling overhead.

"Vivian," he calls to me when I don't look at him. His voice is urgent - worried. I ignore him, not ready to tell him where he can shove his supernatural superiority complex.

The lightning is starting to strike the ocean that borders the highway.

I'm still fighting the blinding pain that scalds me through the bond. The pain of it consumes me, and I latch onto my rage, refusing to let it fade into the nothingness that the fog threatens.

Whatever is hurting me through the bond evidently isn't touching Leon. He stands at my door, not looking at all discomforted other than looking worried.

At my lack of response, he tries a new tactic, reaching around to unclip my belt and gently prying my fingers from the steering wheel. Turning my body so that I'm facing him now, he calls out to me again.

Still, I'm unwilling to break and back down. I ignore him, holding on to the anger for dear life.

Leon cups my cheek with one hand, tilting my face so I'm looking at him. The bond reacts to his gentle touch, and a haze of pleasure joins the fog that wants to steal my thoughts.

My ears are ringing, and it feels like fire is licking at every corner of my brain.

Leon's voice is gentle, speaking to me as if I'm a wounded animal. "Vivian, you need to stop. Whatever it is you're doing, you have to let it go before you kill someone."

I frown through the haze that surrounds me, wondering what he means. Overhead, thunder booms. My gaze focuses on Leon, who is looking very concerned. My eyes travel further behind him, and I see the lightning lighting up all corners of the bay. Eyes widening, I snap my gaze back to him.

Seeing my confusion, Leon continues in his soft tone, "Breathe, Vivian. Deep breaths and try to calm down." His other hand takes one of mine, and his thumb gently strokes across it.

I listen, taking deep, calming breaths, distracted enough by the massive storm to let my rage simmer down. As soon as my concentration begins to fade, the fog presses in, and I feel myself fully calm, my anger no longer existing.

Somewhere inside me, a small voice weeps, but the storm dissipates around us, turning into a gentle rain. Leon still faces me, but his concern is replaced by a very troubled expression.

I pull back from his hand, and he doesn't oppose me. Instead, he looks around us warily before turning back to me. "Do you know someplace we can go for the night? Just so we can make sure we aren't being followed?"

Wordlessly, I nod, still trying to figure out what on earth that storm was and why Leon seemed to think I was causing it.

Perhaps he felt my pain through the bond, and his power was affected by it. He did say his collar fell off once before. Maybe my pain was enough to set him off. I shudder at the thought.

Leon leaves me to get back into the passenger seat.

"You're okay?" he asks as I put my seatbelt back on.

"Yeah," I answer, only half truthfully. If Leon is about to blow through a second collar, that can't be a good thing for anyone nearby. "You?" I ask, now very worried.

Leon sits back. "Yeah."

I nod again and pull the car back onto the highway, starting for the destination I have in mind. Neither of us speaks as I drive another hour.

We come off the highway, following a road that skirts around the bay's edge, hugging the coast. We stay the course for another half hour, until we reach our destination. We're now on a peninsula that juts out from one side of the bay, at its very tip, where the road ends, facing the open ocean.

We passed a ferry a quarter of an hour ago, but I continued driving until I reached the end. There is a small parking lot directly beside the road, where a few lookout binoculars are stationed. Behind us, there are a few dilapidated houses, all of them looking abandoned. A small pier sits adjacent to the houses, where a few larger boats are tied off.

I explain my plan before Leon can ask, "These are tourist cottages. People from out of province or country bought them up, and only come down for a few weeks in the summer. They come to do some fishing, eat the seafood, and then leave. There's an island not far from here. It has an abandoned fishing village on it. There's no power, but it's remote. The ferry runs to it during the on-season when the tourists want to explore. Some locals rent them out during the summer, but it's fully deserted the rest of the year."

I came here last summer with Sarah, Conner and Isaac. We went whale watching and got hammered on the island, making bonfires on the beach and eating clams we dug up. I smile at the memory.

Leon dubiously eyes the boats and then looks at the ocean before us. The storm is entirely dissipated, and the water seems calm enough. "So, you want to steal one of their boats?"

I laugh at the thought. "God, no. Those are very expensive, and I imagine the cottage owners are paying someone to keep an eye on them. Hell, they might even be outfitted with some kind of alarm system."

I turn away from Leon and walk towards the cottages, beckoning him to follow.

Leon follows, prodding further, "So, you want to go to the abandoned island, but not with the boats." He continues before I can further explain, "If I apparate us there, Vivian, there's a good chance one of the creatures will pick up on the energy if it comes over here. I like the idea of going to an island, though. That will make it difficult for them to follow your scent over the water."

We walk through high, unkept grass around the back of the cottages. It's still dark out, only about four o'clock in the morning, according to the last time I looked at the time in my car. I'm thankful there's no one around. The moon is half full, and without clouds, we have decent light to see everything around us.

I scan the area as I further explain my plan, "One of these cottages will undoubtedly have a light boat stored out back. People tend to leave them lying around since they're so common out here. Generally, you take them out of the water after the on season before the ocean starts to freeze and tears them to pieces."

I've seen them scattered around so many houses, and I've never seen a lock on one. I'm confident there will be at least one behind these cottages.

Leon, again, seems dubious. "And you want to row to the island?"

I ignore his lack of confidence in me. "I can probably find a motor. And if for some reason I can't, we can try to hotwire one of the bigger boats. But let's hope it doesn't come to that."

I've never tried to hotwire something before, and if I had my bag in my apartment, I could have grabbed my phone while running for my life. Phones are infinitely helpful when it comes to finding how-to videos. As it stands, my only experience with hotwiring is from watching movies. I hope the directors at least did their research if I end up leaning on that experience.

My legs are soaked through from walking through the grass. After scanning the entirety of the overgrown yard behind cottage one, I move to cottage two.

Taking notice that I'm so far unsuccessful, Leon interjects, "If you remove my collar, I can just apparate us there and take care of whatever tries to follow us, Vivian."

His voice holds a slight hard edge. He's evidently not over the whole, not listening to him thing.

I just keep walking. If Leon thinks his snarky comments will change my mind, he's in for a world of disappointment. You don't get through an entire childhood of bullying without building a thick skin.

Sticks and stones may break my bones and whatnot.

Albeit, the stones hurt like a bitch.

It takes no time for me to find a small aluminum boat, flipped over and shoved underneath the back deck. "Bingo," I say, finally smiling. "Now for a motor."

Moving away from the deck, I walk to one of the small sheds in the cottage's backyard. The door has a deadbolt locking it. I start fishing around on the upper rim of the door.

Leon stands beside me, arms crossed. "So, what are you doing now?" he asks, clearly still not on board with the idea that I have this covered.

Fighting the urge to roll my eyes, I finally feel what I'm looking for on the upper rim of the shed. I pull down the key and work on opening the lock.

"Like I said, most of these tourists are only here a few weeks of the year. But often, they let their friends and family come and stay when they aren't around. I highly doubt someone who owns a new higher tech boat would let inexperienced friends and family take it out on their own. So, instead, they keep the motors to their smaller, easier-to-manage boats in the shed and leave the key out so their friends and family can use them whenever they come down. I'd be willing to bet the house keys are also hidden around the doors."

I'm pulling the lock off the door and opening it as I finish my perfectly logical explanation.

Leon only arches an eyebrow, looking less than impressed as we peer inside the shed, seeing it's empty except for a few cans of paint and a couple of kayaks. I mentally log the kayaks as another fallback plan, and I shut the door and re-lock it before replacing the key.

I head for the next shed down the line of cottages as Leon interjects, "You're a bit more polished at this whole breaking and entering thing than I expected. I find I am a bit at odds with this aspect of you. It very drastically contrasts what I know of you."

His eyebrows are furrowed as if he's frustrated with this development.

I scoff at his words, "No kidding, Leon. I'm not Cassandra. We are separated by thousands of years and have been shaped by completely different life experiences. That's what I mean when I say the bond might not be real. This love that you've felt. It isn't for me. I'm a different person. Only breaking the bond will let us know for sure."

Leon's eyes darken at my statement. "You're wrong." He pulls my arm and stops my walking, turning me to face him. "I don't care what life has shaped you into. Your soul, your spirit, is the same. Nothing can change that love, and no matter how little you believe it, to your core, you are the same."

He pauses now, his eyes taking on their feral look again. "Breaking our bond won't give you clarity, Vivian. It will shatter you. Will shatter us. I thought I made it abundantly clear last night. You are *mine*. No matter what you believe about the magic that draws us together. No matter how badly you fight it, there is no beating it. It's already written into our destinies. You. Will. Always. Be. Mine."

His tone is vicious as he spits each of his last words, punctuating them by wrapping his fingers into my hair and jerking me towards him before crushing his mouth to mine.

I feel momentary shock before the bond springs back to life, enveloping me with the same heat. It's like a drug, the haze that pours over me, making it difficult to think a straight thought and always leaving me craving more.

Leon's mouth claims mine, and he holds me so tightly, I'm sure I'll have bruises on my arm where one of his hands still holds me. His grip on my hair is no less punishing, and I feel some of my hair being pulled out.

I go limp in his arms as my body gives in to the heat that the bond commands, not daring to fight it. As soon as he feels me relax into him, Leon loosens his grip. He softens the kiss until he finally releases me.

I'm quiet, feeling on edge. Rather than facing him, I turn and continue for the shed ahead of us.

This one has no key on the ledge, but I find it a few minutes later, underneath a well-placed rock, leaning up against the back of the shed. If the owners took extra care to hide this key, it has potential. Coming around to the shed door where Leon waits, I don't bother showing him I've found the key. Clearly, the man is not happy with my excellent critical thinking skills.

Instead, I unlock the door, swinging it open to find a small motor hanging from a stand on the back wall. There's a can of gasoline next to it. I motion for Leon, and he comes in, wordlessly picking up the motor. I grab the gas can and think to also grab a coiled length of rope hanging on one of the walls. Together, we return to the pier, setting them down.

Still, in silence, we make a second trip, carrying the aluminum boat. Tying off the boat, I step inside and wordlessly try to figure out how to latch on the motor once Leon hands it down to me. My experience with boats and motors is severely lacking. Still, I figure it out, finding the small clamps on one side and securing the motor as tightly as possible.

Unsure what to do next, I spot the pull cord. I yank it, hoping something will happen. No luck. Leon gets on board now.

I turn to him. "Have you got any experience with motors?"

Again, Leon lets the skepticism bleed from him, "No, I haven't had the occasion to be around them."

I turn away from him. I'm not going to take the bait from his tone. I eye the motor again, and then spot what I thought was an empty flat gas can in the back corner of the boat. Looking at it more closely, I see a small line extending from it. I can't help but smile at solving another bit of the puzzle. I connect the small line to the motor.

Fuel.

Fuel probably helps the boat do the whole *go* thing.

Leon calls from behind me, sounding impatient now as the sun is starting to rise. "Just unlock my collar, Vivian. Let me take care of things."

Once again, I ignore him, not entirely sure I even like him right now.

I can do this.

The bond gives a slight tug at my irritation, and I pay no attention to it. The bond is strong, but I'm stubborn. Besides, I'm rapidly developing a long list of reasons not to want to give into the bond anymore.

I add some gas from the small can we brought along. It takes me a few more minutes of tinkering before I get the engine to roar to life. Silently, I reach over to the dock and untie us. It isn't the best boat driving you've ever seen, but I do my best to navigate the small waves.

Evidently still in an unhelpful and foul mood, Leon asks, "So, how are you going to find the island? Have you got any experience navigating?"

Again, that underlying skepticism grates at me. I take a deep breath to stamp down my newfound temper and answer patiently, "I took the ferry last summer when I visited the island. Once I see the ferry, I'll have a reference point. The island is a straight fifteen minute boat ride from the ferry."

I remember the path because my friends and I were the only ones on the ferry the last time I was on these waters. Conner charmed the summer student who was monitoring the cars. She let us exit Sarah's car and go onto the second level, where we could watch humpback whales feeding around us.

East Coasters often looked at rules as more of a set of general guidelines. Their salty attitudes gained them a reputation for their rebellious natures. Maybe that rebellious nature has grown on me. This boat does mark my second theft in under a week.

I'm well on my way to getting my own Netflix true crime special.

After a few minutes of driving along the coast, I spot the ferry, though it looks tiny from where we are now. I don't expect to see too many fishing boats on the water, as the major fishing season has yet to start, but I don't want to take a chance. Besides, Leon said it would be harder for the forsaken to track me across the water, so best to stay as far from the mainland as possible.

Turning from the ferry and facing the open ocean, we drive through the water for well over fifteen minutes without seeing anything that looks like land ahead. Leon sits at the front of the boat, facing me rather than helping me look for land. His expression is schooled into boredom, but I see his smug look grow with every passing minute.

My cheeks flush.

Death at sea.

I might very well be willing to choose death at sea before giving in to Leon's solution at this point. The bond flares at my irritation again, sending heat through me.

Taking a deep inhale, I keep my eyes locked on the horizon. Leon cocks his eyebrow at me, no doubt sensing the bond trying to pull us closer again. He doesn't make a move for me but smiles with the same stupid smug smile, knowing that some part of me is craving him.

Thankfully, before my temper can ignite at his expression, which would undoubtedly trigger the bond again, I spot land on the horizon.

CHAPTER 19

THE ISLAND IS SMALL, AND IT TAKES NO TIME for me to find the same beach I visited the last time I was here. The tide is up, so I drive the boat as far up the sandy beach as possible. The boat doesn't weigh much, so I get us pretty close to shore. There's only a couple of feet of water below us now.

I'm impressed with myself, but Mr. Broody Pants doesn't say a word.

Jumping off the boat, Leon and I wordlessly pull it into shore. We hide it behind some tall grass.

I'm still not in the mood to speak to him, but I'm feeling guilty over all the bickering we've been doing. Is Leon irked because I refuse to uncollar him? Or is it because I keep making decisions without him?

"Did you want to pick the house?" I ask.

I was heading for the same house my friends and I stayed at, but I'm trying to extend the olive branch. Leon and I need to work together, bond or no bond, and I want us to succeed. No good can come out of constantly being at odds. Not when there's so much at stake.

I make a mental note to be more – I struggle to find a word that doesn't make my stomach hurt.

Submissive.

Meek.

Leon eyes the houses that dot the rocky shores. Many are dilapidated with broken windows and caved-in roofs, but others have been somewhat maintained to keep the tourist dollars flowing. He nods to a house at the island's far end, situated on a large outcrop that looks to the water.

"That one," he notes.

I consider his choice as we make our way towards it. The house is surrounded by water on three sides, with steep rocky cliffs that lead to the open ocean.

I can see the appeal from Leon's perspective. We'll be able to see almost the entire island from here, but if we're found, there's nowhere to run. After Leon's repeated comments about uncollaring him, maybe that's the point. Still, I say nothing and follow him up to the house.

The house is in decent shape. The interior is locked in the 1970's and shag rugs dot the worn wood floors. Kerosine lamps are spread around the house, and in one corner sits temptation incarnate – a wood stove.

I would love a fire right now. My lower half is still soaked from pulling the boat into shore. But a fire means smoke, and the last thing I want to do is draw attention to the island.

Leon walks around the house, scanning the windows and looking at every door before returning to the kitchen. "We can stay here for the day until I'm sure no one has followed us. Afterwards, I'll apparate us to my holdings. We'll be vulnerable there for a short while. I'll need to re-establish the wards around it."

I frown, a bit confused. "What are wards?"

Leon pulls a chair from the small dining nook and takes a seat. "Wards are protections. I haven't lived in my home for thousands of years. It's in the Otherworld, and I'll be able to re-establish the wards even while wearing this."

His jaw ticks as he indicates to his collar. "It takes me a bit of time, so we have to make sure we are nowhere near where the forsaken can follow your energy signature when we do apparate there."

I nod, leaning against the bright pink kitchen countertops. I'm just grateful his plan doesn't include unleashed destructive power. That's a nice change of pace.

Leon continues, "Once we're at my holdings and you're warded, the forsaken won't be able to get to you. They won't even be able to trace that your energy was ever near it. You'll be safe there."

A small knot uncurls inside of my stomach.

Safe.

After the week I've had, the word has a really nice ring to it. Not to mention how much of a relief it will be to get as far away from innocent people as possible.

Taking a deep inhale, my body finally starts to come down from the adrenaline and hypervigilance of the evening.

Leon sees me fading. "You should get some sleep," he notes. "There's a bedroom down the hallway to the right. I'm going to stay here and keep watch."

Wordlessly, I nod and head into the bedroom, ignoring the pull of the bond as I close the door behind me. I need to be alone for a while, and I hope Leon takes the hint and doesn't follow me.

I strip from my soaked leggings and hang them on a chair to dry out before crawling into the small single bed. Now that I'm not running for my life, I notice the pain between my legs when I move to climb into the bed.

I guess some soreness is to be expected when you have your virginity taken so… enthusiastically.

The bed is covered in a few fleece blankets and a moth-eaten quilt, but it's warm. I get cozy, but my mind reels as I slowly work through the thoughts that I've been continuously shoving into the dark place inside my mind.

For a moment last night, I stopped fighting the bond and gave in to Leon. I always wondered how it would feel to finally be intimate with someone.

This feels hollow.

Is it supposed to feel hollow? If so, romance novels have been leading me on for years now.

Sex was definitely pleasurable, and I can't say I didn't enjoy it. The mind-shattering orgasm was proof enough of that. But Leon's possessiveness and the dominance – those are troubling.

I shudder at the memory.

He might preach an undying love between us, but unless the bond is firing up, I'm less than sure about it, especially after tonight. The man yelled at me, demanded blind obedience, and then showed blatant disregard for human life.

Swallowing, I push the thoughts back down as I feel the bond start to hum at the direction my thoughts are headed. The bond is feeling more and more like a mental leash, set on making sure I go along with destiny's plan. Any time I don't obey blindly, I get hit with lust, brain fog or pain. If this is what destiny feels like, I'm not a fan.

It's my last coherent thought as the fog clouds my mind again. I give into the haze and drift off into a dreamless sleep.

CHAPTER 20

WHEN I WAKE UP SOMETIME LATER, I'M completely disoriented. The sun is still up, but without my phone or any clocks around, I have no idea what time of day it is. Quickly, I put on my now only slightly damp pants and head out of the room to find Leon.

He's standing outside, looking over the town that sits below us. As soon as I close the cottage door and take a step towards him, he turns to me. Our bond crackles to life as we make eye contact, evidently displeased at our being separated by a couple dozen feet for so long.

I make my way over to him but take my time since my knees are wobbling from the lust the bond is pumping into me.

I ignore the desire and give no hint that I'm being affected by the bond.

Leon is evidently irritated by yet another one of my attempts to brush off the pull between us. Taking in my forced, nonchalant look, he narrows his eyes at me before scooping me up off the ground, wrapping my legs around him and kissing me soundly.

You'd think I would have learned my lesson in class yesterday about not paying attention to the pull between us and how Leon reacts to being ignored. His body demands I pay attention to the heat that flows between us.

My arms come around his neck to steady myself as his hands grip my ass, holding me wrapped against him. The bond burns even hotter, sending surges of pleasure through me, and an instant later, I sigh into his mouth, kissing him back.

After completely ravaging me, Leon ends the kiss and settles me back onto the ground. He looks very satisfied with himself. "We're going to head over to my holdings now. There are no signs we've been followed."

Before I can nod, we're wrenched from my world.

We reappear next to a castle, surrounded by lush green fields on three sides and what looks like another ocean on the other. The place is completely deserted, and I'm in awe of the honest-to-goodness castle before us. It isn't huge, maybe the size of one of the larger churches in my town, but there's no mistaking the turrets.

Leon beckons me towards it, pride evident in his face. "This belonged to my family long ago, before I was ever chosen to be a Creator. Once our mission is complete, we'll bring in a full staff again. But for now, we'll be on our own since Morgana's spies can be anywhere."

I notice the word *we* when he notes we'll bring in staff after the mission is completed.

Again, it seems presumptuous of him to assume I'm going to be staying with him, especially given I've made it very clear I have a life to return to. But I don't push the point.

Maybe we will end up staying here together after the mission. Crazier things have happened. For example, just a couple of days ago, I became in charge of the fate of humanity. So, I'm not quick to discount the impossible.

Besides, part of me worries he's right. Maybe I am being crazy to continuously fight against something as unstoppable as fate. The insecurity winds around me, and won't relent.

How would I even know what love is supposed to feel like?

Whatever is between us is probably better than I can ever expect to find. I need to stop being so obstinate. The man loves me more than anyone else ever has.

Maybe I'm just self-sabotaging.

Leon continues, oblivious to my spiralling, "I'll build the wards if you want to go inside."

Looking up at the castle, I only feel more unsure of myself. I don't belong in a castle. I don't deserve riches or power. "Could I watch?" I ask instead as I look back towards him.

Leon grins, genuinely pleased at my interest. "Sure."

He takes my hand and together, we walk further out from the castle. Letting me go, Leon starts muttering a few words, and a white light comes from his hands, pouring into the ground. I follow as he starts to circle the property.

I can't help but notice the energy isn't his signature blue colour. "Leon…" I whisper, unsure of if I'm supposed to talk.

"Yes?" he answers, still slowly walking.

"How can you still use your energy, even with your collar on?" I ask.

Leon smiles again. "The collar binds my Destroyer's energy. This power has been in my family for as long as I can remember. It's enhanced by the Destroyer power, but the collar doesn't stop it since it isn't destruction. It's the same reason I can apparate. It's still magic, but not Destroyer magic."

Interesting, so magic is potentially more common in this realm. Either that or Leon comes from a family of wizards. I glance up at the sky, hopeful to see an owl or two carrying letters.

No such luck.

Shame.

Still, my curiosity is at an all-time high. "Could you tell me more about them? Your family. You keep saying you were chosen to be a Creator. How does that work?"

Leon turns back to the wards he's building but doesn't seem offset by my question. "My family were once wealthy nobles of Otherworld. My father was an architect to the Council and had been tasked with helping design and build whatever it was they desired. When I came of age, I joined him, and we worked together for years. I was good at my job. I loved the ability to make new things, to build them bigger, stronger, and more beautiful than before. Need had tasked my family with a particular project, and I was the lead designer. I helped build an entirely new city, and Need was impressed with my abilities. She told my family that the Council had taken notice of me and that they'd chosen me to be their Creator. It was an honour to be selected for such a task. My family's status was elevated, and they were able to live out their lives in riches."

"Didn't you miss them?" I ask softly, frowning.

Leon shakes his head, still smiling at the memories. "The rules that hold Destroyers are a bit different than those that hold Creators. Because I was already loyal to the Council and a force of good, light energy, I was no threat to them so long as I remained collared between assignments. I was able to live alongside my family until the end of their lives. It's the same reason I was able to stay in Atlantis after I finished my duty of bringing it to greatness. The only times I was put to sleep as a Creator was when I asked to be. It wears you down over time. Seeing those you care about pass on. Even in the Otherworld, though lives are much longer than humans, many are not immortal."

I'm about to ask why the rules are so different for the Destroyers, but we've come full circle around the castle, and Leon stops his warding energy.

"Come on," he says, once again taking my hand. "I want to show you our home."

Walking through the castle doors, I look around, still in awe. Tapestries and paintings line the walls, and lush rugs cover the dark-stained floors. Overhead, stained-glass windows of every colour imaginable blend the sunlight, scattering it about the room. The colours from the stained glass amplify the beauty of every surface it touches.

Even though Leon says no one has been here in thousands of years, there's no telltale musty odour or dust covering the surfaces. Everything still looks pristine, as if it was newly built.

A large table sits directly in front of us, and there's a hearth to the right, with some comfortable-looking chairs stationed before it. To my left, a staircase curves to a second floor.

The main hall looks more like a cathedral, its ceiling spanning at least three stories in height. "It's beautiful," I breathe, taking in the grandeur.

Leon grins down at me, practically glowing, seeing that I like the space. His pride is evident as he answers, "Like I said, designing buildings has been a family trade for a long time."

Still holding my hand, he leads me to the table, motioning for me to take a seat as he pulls a chair in front of me.

Sitting, I look up at Leon as he takes his seat. I'm about to ask another question when he starts talking, "Not that I don't much prefer the close quarters of your bedroom, but as you noted, talking might be better served if it happens elsewhere."

My cheeks heat at the memory. The last time we sat on a bed together, the bond was triggered by something unknown, and I asked him to touch me. The thought causes the same heat to spread throughout me, and when I lock eyes with Leon, I can see the same intensity as he looks at me.

Clearing my throat, I try to change the subject, "Talking. Yes. I still have so many questions."

Leon interjects, "I believe after our walk around the property that it's my turn, though." His tone is mild.

"Of course. Ask away."

Leon eyes me closely as he asks, "How did you escape the forsaken in the parking garage? I saw them, Vivian. And don't think I didn't see the hole in your car's window. No mortal should have ever been able to come out of there alive."

His gaze on me is scrutinizing, as if he's looking for the slightest hint that I'm keeping something.

The memory of Leon's shocked expression at seeing the forsaken spilling out of the garage after me quickly comes to mind.

I consider my answer carefully before starting. Leon hasn't made any mention of my ability to free trapped souls or to see ghosts. And the more he refers to me as a powerless mortal, the more I get the sinking suspicion that what I can do isn't tied to my role as a Keeper.

I should tell him.

We're on the same side.

But Leon has made it abundantly clear he's loyal to the Council, to the point of leaving my past self to die. I have to assume anything I tell him will make its way back to the Council. The more I learn about the Council's beliefs, the less I want to be on their radar.

"I…" I start, "I got very, very lucky. My car wasn't far from the door, and I was able to get inside before most of the forsaken ever even noticed me."

It isn't an outright lie, but hopefully, it will satisfy him.

I lay it on a bit thicker with a small smile. "I almost didn't make it out though. One of the creatures got a hold of my car, and well, you saw the damage. I drove my car against the edge of the garage door to knock the creature off."

I'm staring at my nails and force myself to make eye contact.

Leon definitely knows I'm omitting some information. His eyebrows knit together, but he doesn't press me for more details.

I ask my question before he changes his mind, "What are they? The forsaken, I mean."

"They're broken souls," Leon says.

Nailed it!

A small wave of triumph glows within me.

Leon continues, "Some forsaken are powerful Otherworld beings that have been disgraced in death, either at a fight they lost, or they died asleep in their beds. These souls are broken by humiliation and dishonour. Morgana is the lady of the shadows and the only creature known to any realm who can communicate with and control them. She can direct their fury. They're bloodthirsty creatures, twisted by hate and darkness."

At the mention of Morgana, Leon's eyes get the faint blue glow again. He pauses to take a deep inhale before he continues, "The souls in the Otherworld are not like the souls of your realm. Our souls can move about in the physical world despite losing their bodies. They can still pick up objects and complete tasks. You'll even be able to see them here, so try not to be too alarmed. Most of the souls can't do you any harm. But the forsaken are an exception. They can murder the living. Something no other soul can do."

I frown at his explanation. So, the ghosts here are visible, which is less of a shock than he might imagine, but there's one point that bothers me.

"I don't understand. Why aren't the souls just freed and allowed to pass on?"

Leon starts laughing as if my question is absurd. "The forsaken? Because their disgrace bars them from serving as any other soul. Any soul that doesn't live their life in the light or passes on in a dark way becomes a forsaken. Souls that live in the light and pass on naturally become servants to the Council, helping to run the entirety of the Otherworld."

My jaw drops. "Wait – so no one's soul is free in death? They become those twisted creatures, or they become servants?"

Leon just shrugs. "The forsaken have made their bed. Besides, there's nowhere else for spirits to go."

"That's barbaric," I exclaim.

I want to ask him what he means by the souls having nowhere to go, but Leon continues, ready to move on to more important topics, "We need to discuss the mission. I had time to think about a plan while you slept today. I need to know where Morgana is hiding. There's little doubt that wherever she is, Sin will be."

At this, I swallow. "The Destroyer Morgana has is the one that can control minds?"

That thought puts a thread of fear inside of me. I'm already wary of having magical forces in my head.

Leon nods. "Yes. And I am going to kill him before he can ever touch you, Vivian." He says the words fervently. "If it's any consolation, I can do it too – control minds to some degree. All three of us are unlimited in our abilities, but we all have our… talents."

I gulp. That isn't a consolation.

"Morgana used to work for the Council. During her time there, she amassed countless spies. That's where we'll start trying to root out where she's holed up."

"Sounds good," I answer quickly, happy we have a solid direction for our mission.

As we both stand, my stomach growls, drawing Leon's attention.

I haven't eaten anything since our small microwavable dinner almost 24 hours ago.

Leon pauses, giving me an apologetic smile. "Sorry – first we feed you. Then we go to the Council's castle."

CHAPTER 21

IF I THOUGHT LEON'S CASTLE WAS GRAND, I have no choice but to call the Council's castle breathtaking. It's massive, likely larger than my entire college campus.

The castle stands in the center of the massive city atop a tall hill. Despite being so central to the city, the castle is far removed, with the hill surrounded by sprawling, immaculately manicured gardens and forests.

Every facet of the building oozes excess and wealth. The windows are crested in gold, and the architecture looks like something out of a fantasy movie. There are tall towers, ornate arches, and more stained glass. Despite the beauty, the castle seems imposing, looming over the city below.

I guess some things never change. The elite love to look down on normal people, no matter what realm they're from.

Leon is eyeing me, waiting for my reaction to the beautiful scene. I look up at him and smile. "It's beautiful," I say, knowing it's what he wants to hear.

If Leon grew up here as a wealthy noble, I don't want to accidentally insult his heritage with my opinions of upper-class snobbery.

Leon grins back, pleased with my reaction. He's apparated us just on the outer edges of the castle grounds, partway up the hill so that I can see the city and castle. He explained that it's impossible to apparate within the castle grounds due to the vigorous shields and wards. As an added precaution, the castle wards also block out all Creator and Destroyer power.

Leon lets me marvel at the sight a moment longer before taking my hand into his and heading up the main path that leads to the massive castle doors. I hurry beside him; suddenly feeling thankful that Leon took the time to loan me a beautiful long dress. He warned me that it's likely out of season since it's been sitting in his castle for millennia, but it will have to do.

The dress looks like something from out of a fairy tale, out of season or not. The soft pink chiffon skirts swish with my every step. The bust of the dress is corseted with a modest square neckline, and the sleeves end in sharp points just above each of my wrists. Chiffon butterflies and flowers are sewn into a large V at the bottom of the dress and travel all the way up the bust before disappearing at one side of my neck. I wasn't sure what to do with my hair, so I settled on letting it fall into loose waves around my shoulders.

The dress looks like a fairy tale wedding gown; it's so fluffy.

I outright ignored the long underwear that came with it. Admittedly, that decision was a gamble. I didn't have a chance to grab any underwear when I left my apartment, especially given the fact that Leon had shredded the ones that I'd had on that night.

Here's to hoping no strong gust of wind comes around.

Leon must have some idea of how to act here because as we approach the castle, I see other people just exiting the doors and some in a garden nearby. Looking at what they're wearing, we will fit right in.

It looks like Cinderella's ball is the daily standard for attire here. Leon is dressed up, too, abandoning his leather pants and white shirt for a more elegant royal blue outfit. His jacket has a high collar and twin gold buttons coming down the front. It fits him snugly, giving him a regal look. The colour matches his eyes perfectly.

Leon leans down and whispers to me as we approach the castle doors, "Stay close to me at all times. You have no allies here. Trust no one except myself and Need."

I nod, not needing to be reminded of the corruption in this place.

I'm not saying this place has the same vibe as a white van with the words 'free candy' spray painted on the outside, but we're in that same wheelhouse of foreboding.

Reaching the grand doors now, Leon inclines his head to the guards as he moves to open it. One of the guards puts out a hand, blocking Leon's passage. Leon steps back, annoyance flashing across his face.

"Business here?" The guard asks. He's wearing metal armour that looks similar to what knights wear in movies. His head isn't covered, though. His hair is thin and dark and hangs around his face. His eyes are narrowed, and he eyes Leon in obvious contempt.

Leon holds his temper. "We're on official business for Need. Above your pay grade, so I suggest you step aside and let us in." His voice is coated in obvious threat.

The guard balks a moment, considering his choice. Moving aside, he murmurs, "Not a good time to be a Destroyer. I heard the Council wants to put you all down. The humane option for rabid animals."

Leon bristles but ignores the guard, wrenching open the door and walking inside.

I start to follow behind him but pause, meaning to give the guard a good, solid frown. At the contemptuous look on his face, I can't help myself as I let my mouth get away from me. "You didn't hear it from me, but you're right. The Destroyers are being put out of business." I whisper, looking around conspiringly. "But the Council is planning a special event where all low-ranking guards will be forced to fight them for sport. It's how Need wants to clear house. A fresh start to rid the castle of stale guards."

As I finish, I look at him with a worried expression. "I wish you the best of luck."

It's official. Hanging out with Sarah has definitely removed some of my inhibitions. I'm not sure whether it's for the better or the worse.

The rude guard blanches, obviously believing my story. I turn from him, smirking, meaning to enter the castle, but before I do, I catch the younger guard biting his lips, trying not to laugh at my little ruse. He holds the door for me now as he tries to school himself into a bored expression. "Madam," he notes, slightly bowing his head.

I nod to him as I head inside, hurrying to catch up to Leon, who is already halfway down the grand entryway.

When I reach him, Leon barely spares me a glance. "Close, Vivian. I asked you to stay close."

I mentally kick myself. "Sorry," I mutter.

The grand entryway is empty but opens to a hall filled with people moving this way and that. The first thing that stands out is that not everyone here is human. There are tall, elegant-looking fairies, their glittering wingtips reaching at least nine feet in the air. They move with an ethereal grace about the hall. Others are massive bear-looking creatures, but they seem to be able to speak without issue. And on the diversity goes. There are some kind of water-dwelling people, something that might be a leprechaun or a gnome, and there's an honest-to-goodness human-sized cat lady.

It would be rude to scratch her ears.

Right?

After the initial shock of seeing so many new creatures in one place, the next glaring thing in the palace is the abundance of ghosts. Unlike in the human world, as Leon mentioned, these ghosts can move things in the physical realm, bringing people their drinks, serving food, and down the hall, I can see others cleaning. As Leon leads us through the throng of people, I can't stop myself from asking, "Leon, why are all the ghosts servants?"

Leon keeps his eyes ahead as he answers, "Like I said earlier, they have nowhere else to go. The Council puts them to work, serving the physical realm."

We exit the busy hall without drawing any attention. Evidently, this is a busy place, used to lots of people coming and going. Two more ghosts are working in the halls here, dusting the curtains, and I swear I see the ghosts of children scrubbing at a floor as we pass a room. "How are they compensated?"

Leon scoffs at my question, "They're servants, Vivian. They aren't compensated. They aren't even people anymore."

Bile rises in my throat at his words. I want to argue that this is abhorrent, but Leon must sense my discomfort.

He stops walking and cups my face with his hands. His tone is soothing. "Vivian, you mustn't judge an entire realm after only being here for such a short time. I'm positive there are parts of your realm that are even worse than what you are seeing here."

Thinking of all the horrors that are committed by humans and the depths of depravity that some hold, I slowly nod, gulping down my disgust. "I'll try to be less judgemental," I add softly.

Smiling at my agreement, Leon kisses my forehead before letting go of my cheeks and continuing down the labyrinth within the castle walls. Every now and again, we pass other people, and I can't help but notice the looks of disdain some throw at Leon.

I can practically feel Leon's mounting fury with each passing sneer.

"Where are we going?" I ask, hoping to take his mind off the passerby's.

Leon answers, not looking at me, "I know of a few people that were close to Morgana. Some worked here. I will speak to the head of the guard to inquire about their whereabouts."

I don't bother nodding as I continue to follow him. He wouldn't see me anyway. Leon is walking at a fast clip, and I keep getting distracted by new sights. There's a room with what looks like thousands of rows of glowing jars and another with small, fluffy creatures that bounce about as a woman chases them, yelling at them to get back into their cage. The little creatures look like fluffy snowballs, and I can't see any legs on them. I want to see more, but Leon is getting further and further ahead.

Running again to catch up to Leon, I see a room that makes me skid to a stop and do a double-take. It's a library. I can't just pass this room by. The large double doors are a turquoise blue, carved with leaves and woodland scenes. They're propped open, and as I step inside, I can see bookshelves running all the way down the massive room. You could have fit an entire football stadium into here; it's so grand.

Stepping further inside, I see that there are multiple floors to the library, with spiral staircases that lead up to them scattered about the room. Overhead, the cathedral-like ceiling is lined with carved arches, and each arch is separated by stained glass, showing more beautiful nature scenes. The light that flows into the room is dappled along the surfaces as if I'm walking under the canopy of a forest on a sunlit afternoon.

This is it. I've found my paradise.

As I walk further into the library, the bond gives a slight tug. For some reason, it's less annoying this afternoon. Ignoring the tug, I continue to explore the library.

If I'm on what is likely a sure-death mission, then seeing this library is my final wish. To experience this room and smell the pages as I get lost in their magic is worth the trouble I'll likely be in for venturing off.

Walking along one of the shelves, I let my hands trail along the books. Some of them shudder beneath my fingers as if they're alive. My eyes widen, and I move to open one when I hear voices from further inside of the library.

"How is the mission going? Have you imbued her yet?" It's a man's voice. I turn to leave but pause when I hear the voice that answers him.

"Yes, of course I have. And it's going exactly to plan. The mortal has no idea."

I know that voice. It's Need. Are they talking about me? How many mortals do they know?

"And you're sure she won't find out until it's too late? This is a risky plan; I don't like it. Too much can go wrong." The male's voice sounds concerned.

The voices are starting to make their way towards the exit. They're coming my way.

As silently as possible, I inch down the shelf and spot a staircase ahead. It's made of a solid white stone that looks like quartz. I hope my sneakers will be quiet as I quickly climb the steps. Not making a sound, I'm grateful I went without the pointed shoes Leon gave me. We're on a mission. Sneakers are much more suited to missions.

I hear Need's voice again just as I reach the next floor, throwing myself against it and pulling my skirts down so they lay flat.

"She's distracted, Rydon. We've ensured she is not able to piece it together. The prophecy will come to light, and she will work for us."

Peeking over the edge, I watch them make their way to the doors. Need is speaking to a guard. I can only see the back of his head, but he has long black hair tied in a low ponytail. They're just leaving now, but I can still hear their voices echoing through the hallway as I slowly descend the steps.

"And if you fail?" the man – Need called him Rydon, asks.

"We cannot." Need's voice is harsh.

I press myself against the wall next to the door, straining to hear the last echoes.

"*Everything* hinges on this. We cannot let her loose from our control. It would…" Need's voice finally tapers off.

My chest sinks at not hearing the rest. I wait a few more moments, ensuring there's no one around to see me emerge from the library after Need, and then hurry out, headed in the direction that Leon was walking. Arriving at a split in the hall, I pause, wondering which way to go.

Leon saves me from making the wrong choice by turning a corner on my right and heading towards me. He looks irritated.

"Vivian," he breathes when he reaches me. "Have you not heard me each time I've told you to stay close? I've been searching every room I passed, looking for you."

He eyes me up and down as if to reassure himself that I'm safe.

Guilt blossoms within me for worrying him. I give him a small smile and answer with my best half-truth. "I'm so sorry." I try to sound contrite. "I got distracted by the rooms. There were fluffy creatures bouncing about and other rooms, too, all containing things I've never seen before. I got distracted, and when I went to keep up with you, I couldn't see you anymore. So, I walked until I found this break in the hallway. I didn't know which way to go, so I waited for you."

Finishing my explanation, I look at Leon with what I hope is an earnest expression. I don't want to tell him about what I overheard. It's very possible that Need was discussing me, and I don't want anyone to know I heard them. Not when Need made it clear that keeping their mortal in the dark is a high priority. I have no idea what they're talking about, but I'm beginning to come to terms with the fact that eavesdropping may be one of the only ways I'm going to figure out exactly what's going on here.

It's time to go full super spy on this realm.

I'm a terrible candidate for a spy.

Leon smiles at me, understanding coming across his face. "Of course, you were distracted. I keep forgetting that this entire world is new to you. You need to stay close, though. You're vulnerable, Vivian. Only I can protect you."

I smile gratefully at Leon. "Thank you. I appreciate having you here to look out for me."

Again, not actually a lie. I have no intention of being caught alone in a room with other supernatural creatures that may or may not have my best interests at heart.

Leon seems placated by my appreciation. Taking my hand, he notes, "I'm happy to see the bond is settling down."

I look at him, surprised he's noticed. "How do you know it's settled?"

Leon beams at me. "You couldn't have gotten more than thirty feet away from me and stayed conscious if it hadn't. The pain alone would have taken you out."

My eye twitches. "Please tell me why that is something you look giddy about."

Leon pulls my hand as he starts down the hall again, now laughing at my retort. "Because it means you're accepting our bond. You're accepting us."

I don't respond and only feel myself swallow loudly.

Is that what I'm doing?

I've been trying to get along better with Leon and trying not to set him off as much. Is that me accepting us?

I don't feel overwhelming happiness at the thought.

I need to change the subject. "When was the last time you were here?"

Leon's gaze darkens. "Just shortly after you died. I was brought back here to be stripped of my power and imbued with Destroyer energy. Destroyers are not allotted the same freedoms because their nature is much darker and dangerous. Since I was changed, I've been locked up and asleep unless I was called to act on behalf of the Council."

There's the guilt again, clawing through me. I keep being distrustful of uncollaring Leon. But being constantly controlled by a Council or collar for thousands of years can't be a good life.

Then again, Leon called my town insignificant. Maybe keeping him under lock and key unless absolutely necessary isn't such a bad idea.

"I'm sorry you lost so much," I answer, unsure of what else I can say. Leon's thumb brushes against my hand in a gentle motion.

"It's all been for a higher purpose. We're reunited now. Destiny has served us well, no matter the cost."

I'm not going down the fervent destiny speeches again. The bond gives another tug, but it doesn't come from me this time. Leon is eyeing me as we exit into a courtyard, heading for a smaller building up ahead. A hunger in his expression sends a pooling heat through me.

My breath catches in my throat as I try to think of something to say to distract me from the bond lighting up again. "The people here. They don't seem very welcoming of you. Why is that?"

Way to go, Vivian. Why not find other elephants in the room to call out?

Leon slows as we approach the smaller building. It sits in the centre of the courtyard, and the ground is covered in dirt and sand rather than grass.

"As a Creator, I was welcomed, worshiped even. But when I fell from greatness and became a Destroyer, I was tainted in the eyes of the Otherworld. I have not been forgiven."

We stop not far from the small building, and Leon lets go of my hand, turning to face me. "I need to speak to the captain of the guard. Wait here for me, and don't go anywhere."

I want to come inside, but the soldier must have heard us approaching. A man opens the front door before Leon reaches it.

"I assumed you'd be by soon," he says, eyeing Leon.

His hair is long and black, tied behind his head. His skin is olive-coloured, and he has dark brown eyes. I've seen him before. Very recently.

I hope my face doesn't give anything away when Leon greets him. "Rydon, just the man I've been looking for. We need to talk." And without another word or bothering to introduce me, Leon walks into the cabin and shuts the door.

I probably would feel a little more insulted, except my anxiety is now skyrocketing. There's no way Rydon could know I overheard his conversation with Need. But creatures here are supernatural. What if Rydon has a crazy smelling ability?

Taking a deep breath, I mentally talk myself down. It will be fine. Surely, he and Need wouldn't have continued their conversation if he'd sensed me in the library.

It's fine. Totally fine.

My heart always thunders this fast.

Trying to distract myself, I spin around to get a better look at where we've ended up. I keep saying I need to be more aware of my surroundings – so here we go. It's a beautiful day, like a warm summer back on Earth. This part of the castle courtyard is deserted but looks like a training area for soldiers.

The sun is beating down on me, and I'm starting to overheat in the tight corset of the dress. A tree just a hundred feet away beckons me. The shade below it looks very inviting. Still, I don't move. Leon keeps asking me not to stray, and this time, I'm determined to listen — teamwork at its finest.

Maybe if I earn Leon's trust, he'll be less wary of my judgment.

Of course, climbing up the window to the commander's hut to listen in on their conversation probably doesn't count as staying put. I'm getting more irked by the moment at Leon's high-handed attitude in excluding me from their conversation.

How am I supposed to figure anything out if I can't hear anything? I'm not a fan of being treated like a schoolbag. Something to drag around and drop whenever convenient. Or, in Leon's case, to leave in a college, without considering that maybe the schoolbag's owner was attached to its contents.

At my rising frustration, the bond begins to burn again, and my body flushes with even more heat, my dress now uncomfortably tight.

Of course.

How dare I have a single negative thought about the man?

My body is starting to react further to the bond as I grow more bitter with each passing wave of heat. Taking deep breaths, I try to replay the sound of a yoga video I often watched from memory.

I'm saved from having to start the visualizing exercise when Leon opens the door and exits, taking my hand without saying a word as we leave the courtyard. Rydon is nowhere in sight and doesn't come out to give a farewell.

Leon looks excited. I wait a few breaths, but when he says nothing, I cave and ask, "What has you in such a good mood? Do you know where Morgana is?"

Leon grins as he keeps walking forward. "Not yet, but I know someone who just might."

CHAPTER 22

LEON LEADS ME BACK INTO THE CASTLE, AND I'm once again lost in the labyrinth of halls. I can't be certain, but I don't think this looks like the way we came from. I'm terrible with directions. Yet another reason my life is a hazard.

"That's great!" I respond to Leon.

The less time Morgana spends with the proverbial red button to a universal nuke is a win in my books. At this rate, I'm hoping I might even be able to get back home before the end of my fall break.

The thought of my apartment gives me another pang of sadness. There is likely a ton of damage from the forsaken. I'm so getting evicted. Before the sadness can swallow me, I remind myself to be present. To focus on what I can control.

"So where are we going?" I prod when Leon doesn't volunteer any extra information.

We exit out one of the castle doors and enter a large garden. Leon pauses, giving me a chance to take in the utopia we've ventured into. There are ornamental trees and beautiful flowers scattered throughout, and further ahead, there's a massive wall of hedges covered in a rainbow of flowering vines.

The hedges must be thirty feet tall, and though I can't tell how far they extend since their height blocks out much of what lies beyond, I can see an upper canopy of forest hundreds of feet beyond it.

I gasp at the beauty of it. The flowers are unlike any kind I've ever seen in my world; the blooms are the size of basketballs. A small rocky stream winds through parts of the garden, providing the ambient sounds of a soothing brook. It's uncannily familiar to the sounds I've heard in sound machines when I've had difficulty sleeping.

Leon smiles down at me as I take it all in and then pulls me along as we make our way down the marble garden path.

"Morgana used to have countless spies that worked in the Council," he explains. "She was one of the most esteemed members of the Council and even trusted with the key to a Destroyer because he was so dangerous, and she is very powerful. Her loyalty had never once been questioned. It wasn't until the fall of Atlantis that the Council became aware of her treachery."

I frown up at him, surprised that the timing coincided with my previous life. The threads of this tangled web continue to grow.

Leon continues, "It was discovered that Morgana had been secretly planning to overthrow the Council for millennia. The Council is naturally made of both light and dark creatures. Need has only ever wanted balance and insisted on representation from either side. But Morgana is not content with the balance. She wants to tip the realms into pure darkness."

Shivering at the thought, I pause at an inconsistency in Leon's story. "Leon, if Morgana is the Keeper of the dangerous Destroyer, then hasn't she held his key for thousands of years? Why is she a problem only now?"

I replay my conversation with Need in my mind. I'm sure Need made it sound as though Morgana had only just attained the key. With that thought, though, my mind starts to fill with that same drunken fog. I try my best to hold onto my thoughts, a part of me knowing that it's important.

Something isn't adding up.

The more I fight the fog, the more my body fights back. My ears start to ring, and a blinding flash of light sears my brain, burning away the thought before I can mull it over any further.

Slowly, I blink up at Leon, trying to remember what it was we were discussing, but Leon is preoccupied. We've reached the hedges, and he looks like he's searching for something. A moment later, he reaches into the hedge and catches a small, green creature. It looks like a cross between a squirrel and a gnome if gnomes had prominent front teeth and a bushy tail. The creature wiggles furiously, trying to escape Leon's grip. My eyes widen at his treatment of it.

"Leon, I think you're hurting it," I exclaim, worried.

Leon laughs at my concern. "Don't worry so much, Vivian. This is garden vermin, but they do have one particular skill I'd like to make use of."

He looks down at the creature and squeezes it a little harder so that it stops struggling. The creature looks up at him with small, terrified eyes.

"Open the door," he commands it. "And then take your friends with you. I want no one to enter while we are here. Understood?"

Again, his fist flexes and the creature's eyes bug out even further. I immediately reach over to his hand to try to free it.

"Leon, stop." My voice is urgent, pleading.

Leon only rolls his eyes and releases it. The creature dashes back into the branches, and magically, some branches in front of us twist and move away, opening into a door. Leon takes my hand again and pulls me along as we enter. Behind us, the branches close again.

I can hear the creature scrambling away, chittering to others. Once again, I feel irritated with Leon for his piss-poor attitude, but the bond hums through me, fogging over my thoughts yet again.

My body gives an involuntary twitch at the wave of heat that comes through the bond, and my hand squeezes Leon's. The connection makes the bond between us almost purr with pleasure. The thoughts of the green creature aren't forgotten but feel muddled. Like I'm trying to hear my thinking underwater.

Trying to shake off the brain fog, I take deep breaths and look around to see where Leon is leading us. Monolithic hedges surround us, and I can see their corridors extending in all directions. It's also deathly silent in here. The sound of the brook isn't penetrating through, even though we are only a few steps away from the garden.

"Is this..." I pause, trying to see around the corners where the paths turn. "Is this a hedge maze?"

I want to be amused that something as silly as a hedge maze exists within the Council walls, but there's an aura about this place, something that tells me this is more than just a maze. There's a sinister feel to these walls.

Leon brings my hand to his mouth, kissing my fingers before starting down one of the paths. "Somewhat. This maze is one of the tests of mental strength for only the most powerful soldiers. When you enter the maze, you become completely incapable of remembering your sense of direction and become lost. You could wander the maze for eternity, never finding your way out. The only way to leave is if someone who already knows the way comes to get you."

I frown, suddenly feeling very keen to turn back around. "Then how are the soldiers supposed to get out? The test sounds impossible. Also, why are we in here if this place is impossible to leave?"

I dig my heels into the ground, ready to pull Leon back towards the door. I turn, only to remember it closed once we entered and is now impenetrable.

Leon laughs at my rising panic. "Only impossible to leave if you don't already know the way," he repeats, tugging me along through one of the turns ahead, choosing a path that leads deeper into the maze.

"I designed it, Vivian. Back when I was still a Creator. Building things was one of my specialties. This is one of my creations." He beams at me.

I'm not impressed. "But Leon, why would you build an impossible maze? And don't the soldiers just find each other? What's to stop them from climbing the hedges to get a better vantage?"

Again, Leon grins as if excited to show off his wit. He walks me over to the hedge directly next to us and makes to place a hand on a branch. Immediately, three-inch-long thorns erupt from the branches, threateningly aimed at his hand.

"These can penetrate even metal armour. There is no escaping. The soldiers never find each other because if they get close, the maze re-routes them. They are truly and completely alone."

"But why?" I ask. None of this sounds like any fun, and I can't imagine why anyone would build a place like this.

"Rydon, the guard captain, wants his elite soldiers to be unbreakable. For even impossible situations to unfaze them. They need to remain calm and focused, even after days of searching for an exit. Most of the soldiers go mad after just half a day. Those are the ones that fail the test. But after three days, any soldier who is still searching and hasn't lost their mind is allowed to join the elite forces of Rydon's guard."

Still, I don't see how it makes any sense. "Don't the soldiers just speak to each other? And tell the others the secret."

Leon gives a dark laugh. "Any soldier who passes the test has their memory altered. They are convinced that they found the exit on their own and have no memory of being retrieved by one of the few who already know the path. It is worn as a badge of honour to have escaped the maze."

I hum softly at his explanation. It's well thought out, I admit, but the mention of altering memories rubs me the wrong way. It sets off the same grating sensation at the back of my mind like someone is scratching at my brain with a fingernail.

Remembering why we're here, I warily look around. "Is the person who might know where Morgana is trapped in the maze?"

"No," Leon answers, laughing again at my hesitation. "Rydon said that after Morgana went on the run, they spent centuries removing her spies from the castle and the Council. Though there's likely still corruption within the Council members, none have ties to Morgana. They're likely up to their own nefarious plans. Morgana has no more influence here. Rydon mentioned that while his men have been hunting down all those with ties to Morgana, he's convinced that she still has allies in the black market."

I want to ask what the Otherworld version of a black market is, but Leon continues, anticipating the question, "The black market exists at the city's outer edges, near the water's edge on the south side. It's a sect of the city entirely populated by dark creatures, and they are self-policed. The Council doesn't interfere with their affairs so long as their doings don't have consequences that reach back to them. Mostly, they trade in illegal goods, but merchants from all the magical realms frequent it."

The word 'all' catches me by surprise. I've tallied three realms now. My own, the Otherworld, and the Shadow realm. How complex can the universe be?

We're deep inside the maze now, and it's still deathly quiet. "Are we headed to the black market now?"

Maybe the maze is a shortcut.

Leon grins as we turn another corner. There, hidden in an alcove of the hedges, is a small bench.

"The black market won't be active until past dark," he says as he walks us over to the bench but makes no move to sit. "In the meanwhile, I believe you have earned yourself a reward." His tone is back to being low and predatory.

I only have a chance to gasp as the bond between us flares to light, letting me know precisely where Leon's mind is. The burning need floods through my body as Leon's hand wraps itself in my hair, pulling me forward as his mouth descends on mine.

He ravages my mouth, and once again, my mind is muddled with a hazy fog, and the bond pulses through us, filling me with an aching warmth. Before I'm entirely overtaken with desire, I only think to ask, "Reward for what?"

Leon's mouth leaves mine as he places scorching kisses down my neck. "Because," he starts to answer as he pulls my dress up. As his hands find my bare thighs, he hooks his hands around them, and in one fluid motion, he pulls me up off the ground, wrapping my legs around his waist. My hands come around his neck, and he kisses me soundly again.

With my legs wrapped securely around him, he lets his hands roam hungrily, grabbing my ass and teasing at the junction of my thighs, just close enough to my center to make me moan. Releasing my lips again, Leon slowly sets me down so that I'm sitting on the bench.

Goosebumps erupt on my legs from the cool marble that presses directly against my sensitive, exposed skin.

Leon lowers himself even further so that he's kneeling between my legs. His eyes stay locked on mine as he once again lifts my skirts until I'm fully exposed to him. His eyes darken, noticing that I didn't bother with underwear.

"I gave you an order earlier. And you *finally*," he pauses, punctuating his words as his hands come to my bare ass. He pulls me forward on the bench, lifting my thighs to rest on his shoulders.

I grab at the edges of the bench to keep from falling backwards as my balance shifts.

"*Fucking*," his fingers find my center, already soaked with need for him. "*Listened*," he spits out the last word, and his mouth descends on my pussy, his tongue sweeping in to taste me.

Pleasure sweeps through me as Leon's tongue begins its exquisite torture. He starts slowly, tasting every part of me. His tongue rubs circles around my clit, and I arch on the bench.

Feeling me respond to him, Leon repeats the motion before descending further and licking at the edges of my slit.

"Leon," I gasp at the new sensation. His tongue pushes inside of me, and I almost come off the bench. One of Leon's hands grabs my thigh to hold me in place.

I squirm more, and Leon responds by increasing his pressure on my pussy, his mouth now coming up to suck at my clit.

"Leon!" I demand. I don't know what I want. What he's doing feels good, but I'm quickly becoming overwhelmed by how my body is responding. The bond between us is still burning hot, and suddenly, Leon's tongue feels like it's not enough. I need more.

Leon growls against my center, not ready to stop. Still holding me firmly in place on the bench, he uses his other hand to start fingering me while he sucks and licks at my clit.

"Such a good girl," he says, nipping at my clit. "Your pretty pussy is fucking drenched for me, Vivian."

Again, I arch into his touch, now tightening my legs around his head. When Leon inserts a second finger, pumping them in and out of my soaked slit, I let my head tilt backwards, allowing myself to get lost in the ecstasy.

"That's right, baby," he says as he works me even faster now, "give in and ride my hand like the good little slut you are."

My hips start to buck against his mouth as I meet the thrusts of his fingers.

Still, Leon wants more from me. Wrenching his mouth from my center, he hooks a hand around my waist, lifting me and bending me over so that I'm standing with my hands on the bench. His hand doesn't release me, and I'm grateful, feeling my thighs shake beneath me. My body trembles for release. Leon shuffles behind me, and after a moment, I feel his bare length against my slit.

He teases his hard cock at my entrance, and I push back against him, the burning that consumes me, begging for all of him. Still, he teases, and I moan as he slightly pulls away when I try to ease him into me.

"Mine, Vivian," Leon's voice comes, his tone possessive.

"Say it," he commands, again teasing at my slit with his cock as his other hand comes around me to circle my clit.

I almost cry. "Please, Leon," I beg, as my body is consumed with more trembles.

"Fucking say it, Vivian. Who the fuck do you belong to?" His voice is harsh now, and he impatiently spits the words.

Leon's fingers continue to circle my clit, and I come undone, my orgasm tearing through me, with Leon's cock still teasing at my entrance.

Feeling me come against him, Leon growls, releases my clit, and slams his hard length inside of me. I scream as his thrusts come hard and fast, not giving my body time to adjust to his size. His fingers come up to wrap around my hair, and he pulls at it as he relentlessly pumps deep inside of me, pushing me to orgasm yet again. The pain and pleasure blur together, and I see stars as my body comes apart a second time.

"Leon!" I scream his name.

In response, Leon only fucks me harder, his thrusts coming even faster.

"You. Are. Fucking. Mine," he spits again through his punishing pace.

He yanks back on my hair, and my head comes up with it, tears blurring my eyes. Releasing my hair, he instead wraps his hand around my throat, his grip tightening and cutting off all my oxygen.

I can't make a sound, and I feel myself tremble underneath him, my body coming completely undone.

Still, Leon doesn't stop. "You fucking breathe for me, Vivian. I own every inhale, every thought."

His other hand, still holding me steady, releases me to rub at my clit once again. Already hyper-sensitive from my first two orgasms, my body trembles even harder, and the waves of my third orgasm crash over me.

Feeling me come undone a third time, Leon pushes himself deep inside of me, spilling his seed. He loosens his grip on my neck as his thrusts slow, pulling the aftershocks of my orgasm.

Leon's hands wrap around me as my body finally comes down from the high. He lifts me into his arms before settling himself on the ground, his back against the bench, cradling me against him. He kisses my forehead as he softly exclaims, "So, fucking beautiful. Fucking love seeing you filled with my seed."

Despite the exhaustion that quickly settles over my bones, I almost choke. "Just so you know, I have an IUD. You can't get me pregnant."

Sarah and I got the IUD six months ago. I was going with her for moral support, but after hearing it could help manage my period symptoms, I figured it was worth a try.

Leon only squeezes me tighter as he growls, "Don't forget what I am, Vivian. You might have something to stop you from bearing my children now – but the second my collar comes off, I will un-exist it. I fucking can't wait to see you round with my child."

His hand settles possessively against my stomach.

If I didn't have a reason to be wary of releasing Leon before, you can bet your ass I'm feeling fucking terrified now. The fog takes the thought before I can react, and I let the exhaustion win as I drift off in his arms.

CHAPTER 23

WAKING UP IN UNFAMILIAR PLACES IS STARTING to get old.

Leon is shaking my shoulder, and I peak my eyes open to demand more sleep when I realize I'm not in my bed. Hell, I'm not even in a bed. I'm curled up on soft grass.

I must be more out of it than I thought.

The only other places I'm used to dozing off in are my morning classes. And even then – I usually wake up in complete panic only seconds after my eyes close.

As I rub the sleep from my eyes, my mind struggles to catch up with me. I get flashbacks of the maze and what Leon did to me on the bench.

My body shudders.

I can't tell if it's from pleasure or fear at the memory.

Things between us are moving quickly, and I don't want them to. I want the bond to fuck off so I can think clearly, if only for a minute. But just as the thoughts entered my mind, the same fog seeps in. Once again, I'm left grasping for my thoughts as they're lost to the haze.

Leon is crouching in front of me. "It's dusk now. We should be going." He stands and starts walking down one of the corridors.

There's grass clinging to the chiffon of my dress, and I quickly try to brush it off as I pick myself up and run to catch up. I'm pretty sure I have grass in my hair, but hey, who am I trying to impress? "Where are we going?"

The fog in my mind is still making it difficult to piece together my memories of whatever happened between me and Leon before I fell asleep.

"The black market, remember? We're going to follow a lead." Leon looks over his shoulder at me. He takes my hand and starts to lead me out of the maze.

I hurry to keep up with him. Leon likes to walk fast, and with his considerably longer legs, that means I need to hustle. "Of course."

Idiot. How can you forget the critical part of the mission?

But the fog still presses in on my thoughts, and all I can put together are small bits of my day. If the feeling is supposed to inspire panic, I can't feel it.

Leon navigates the twists and turns of the maze. I look around and can't imagine how he's keeping track. I'm trying to keep track of our turns for fun, but we've spun in what feels like at least twenty circles. Finally, he brings us to an outer wall of the maze. I look for a door and am shocked when, once again, Leon reaches into the hedges.

He pulls out the same small, squirrel-gnome creature that let us in. He squeezes it so its eyes bug out of its head, and the creature scrambles frantically to try and escape.

"Leon, stop!" I yell.

I pull his fingers from the creature, letting it sit in my hands. It's shivering in fear. Leon allows me to take it, his brow furrowing in response.

I glare up at him. The bond tightens at my annoyance, and my knees go weak. Still, I don't return the creature to Leon. Instead, I speak to it in a soft, soothing tone, "You're okay. He won't touch you again."

I don't chance stroking its fur in case the contact will frighten it even further. Without looking at Leon, I reach into the bushes, careful to avoid the razor-sharp thorns that edge at me. The creature hops off my hand and scrambles up a branch. I can still see it, watching us from about ten feet up. "Will you please let us out?"

Leon grumbles, "It's going to take ages for it to come down again so I can make it open the door."

I ignore him, looking at the creature imploringly. A second later, the hedges before us unravel and open. I thank the creature before walking through the exit, not bothering to look back at Leon.

Once the wall closes behind us, Leon sighs and grabs my hand again, pulling me back to face him. He looks like he's trying to figure out how to explain something to a child. "Vivian – you're being a hypocrite. The garden sprite is vermin. The equivalent of a rat in your world. Are you seriously going to tell me you've never used a rat trap, or would condemn those who do? Really?"

His voice has that same mocking undertone, and I grind my teeth at it.

Still, the fog from the bond grows thicker, and the heat between us pulls me to him. My frustration is ebbing away by the second, the void it leaves behind replaced with desire for him. Stepping into his arms, I kiss his cheek. "I'm sorry."

Maybe I am being judgemental. The bond hums, and my body fills with heat at our closeness. Leon huffs at my apology and wraps an arm around my waist.

"We are going to get nothing done tonight if you send those thoughts down the bond," he tells me, his gaze darkening.

I step back at his words. I want to work through the mission.

I need to finish this so I can be free.

The thought is a whisper, somewhere far off in my mind.

Leon watches me step away, looking at me like he's considering whether to pull me back into the maze again. Instead, he grabs my hand and pulls me into the forest that lies less than a dozen feet ahead.

As soon as we break into the tree line, my feet leave the ground as Leon apparates us out. We land in an empty alley.

I wobble for a second. I think I'm getting better at this whole supernatural teleportation thing.

Our new destination does not disappoint. I mean, if you're going to house something as seedy as a black market, there are expectations to be met. The roads are cobbled stones, chipped with sharp edges extending up from them.

I'm thinking there are no cars in the Othcrworld. There's no way in hell my vehicle would ever make it through here without getting a flat. On either side of the narrow alley, there are dilapidated buildings, all in various stages of decay – the stench of rot clings to the air.

Do people actually live here?

As if on cue, there's a noise above us, and someone slams a set of shutters shut.

Okay. I guess people do live here. Evidently, though, they aren't much for paint and flower boxes. The dingy grey and brown colours cling to every surface. Whether from grime or a colour palate preference, I can't tell.

Leon pulls me closely into his side. "You do not leave my side. You speak to no one. Understood?" His tone is stern, leaving no room for argument.

Looking around us, I'm quick to agree, despite the whole ordering me around thing. "You got it. No getting distracted by new things."

Satisfied with my quick agreement, Leon pulls me along to the mouth of the alley we apparated into. There are faint lights and crowds of people not far ahead of us on the right side. Leon pulls my arm, and we start towards the populated side of the road.

I stay silent as we enter the bustling street. There are hundreds of people, and I try not to gape at the stark contrast between the folks here and the people in the Council's castle. Most people on this street are dressed in rags, and many are armed with swords, daggers, and axes.

Someone is spinning a morning star as if it's a freaking fidget spinner.

Pirates. They all look like honest-to-goodness pirates. Or should it be dishonest-to-no-goodness? I guess we're about to find out.

There's a dangerous air about the people here – like anyone on this street can murder for the right price. The threat looms, and everyone looks like they're on edge.

Stalls line each side of the road, and as Leon leads me through throngs of people, I see merchants selling weapons, potions, and something that might be food. Notably, all of that is child's play compared to the next stall we pass. A small, thin man operates the stand. He's dressed in dirty, stained, grey robes. He pauses what he's doing to grin at me, showing off his blackened, stained teeth. Looking at my dress, I imagine he thinks I have a lot of money to spend. "Interested in some new staff, my lady?" he asks as he steps aside.

Bile rises in my throat. Behind him is a group of souls. All of them are women chained together. Their heads are bowed, and they look terrified.

"They're fresh. Harvested them myself, so they'll last a good long while before decaying," the thin man says, taking my pause as interest.

Leon continues to pull me forward as he calls back behind him, "Not interested."

I think I might throw up. I shouldn't be surprised, given the state of soul slavery I saw in the Council's castle. But there is something the merchant said that did surprise me. "What did he mean by decaying?"

Leon keeps his eyes on our surroundings, his body language indicating that he's on guard. Still, he answers me, "Souls do not last indefinitely. Eventually, they break down, their energy leaching from them into the earth. They go mad and are sent to Morgana's realm, so they can't do any damage here."

"What does she do to them?" I ask, horrified.

Leon searches ahead and then starts walking with more purpose. I drag behind him.

"No one knows. And it doesn't matter. They've served their purpose, and they're her problem afterwards."

I want to argue, but Leon squeezes my hand, warning me quietly. "This isn't the time or place to discuss this. And there's our lead." He motions ahead at a small hut and beelines for it before stopping directly in front of the merchant.

I snap my mouth shut at Leon's warning. He's standing directly in front of me, so I try to peek around him. There's a table lined with various weapons. I wiggle a bit from Leon's hold to see who we're here to speak to. I'm expecting more of the same blackened teeth, super creepy-looking types.

I could not be more wrong.

The man is stunningly beautiful. He's slightly shorter than Leon, with strikingly chiselled features. His skin is dark, and his face is framed by luscious dark curls, both of which only accentuate his vivid emerald green eyes.

"Magnus," Leon greets, his tone dripping with hostility.

"Leon. What a pleasant surprise." The man's tone, on the other hand, oozes charm and charisma.

Leon isn't in the mood for idle chatter. "I've gotten word that you might know where we can find Morgana. I want that information." Again, his voice is threatening.

I'm still stuck peeking behind him, trying very hard to be patient and not intervene. Leon likes me better when I play damsel and let him control situations.

My teeth grind against each other.

I can be a damsel. If Leon thinks threatening people is the best way to get information, then I should stay silent.

He probably has way more experience than me. Still, his high-handed attitude seems like a stupid way to approach the situation.

My teeth might be ground smooth by the time we finish this mission.

Magnus is apparently unfazed by Leon's tone. "I may very well have that information. But..." he starts, opening his arms as if to obviously indicate our whereabouts, "I am a businessman, Leon. Information does not come without a price."

Leon growls in response, taking a step forward as he quietly answers Magnus, "Your payment is that I will not unleash my power upon you and all those around you this instant, you miserable leach."

Magnus only smiles back, his tone now becoming threatening, "And how would Need and the Council feel when those actions are reported back to them? I wonder. I doubt she'd be pleased to hear that her disgraced Destroyer let loose his power in their very own city. I'd tread carefully if I were you, Destroyer. In this political scene, some restraint may do you some good."

As Magnus finishes his threat, Leon takes another threatening step forward.

Well, if I needed a cue that I'm not fit to be a damsel, this is it.

Enough is enough. We need a testosterone break in this exchange.

If part of this mission requires people skills, then it looks like I'm better suited to handle that part than Mr. Growly Pants.

Stepping around Leon, I come face to face with Magnus. I hold his stare, refusing to show any kind of intimidation.

Because quite honestly, years of freeing the faceless have taught me how to bluff.

My tone is blunt when I ask him, "What is it you're after as payment?"

At seeing me, Magnus' face morphs into pure delight. Eyeing me with an intense curiosity, he takes a step closer as if to inspect me further. Leon's hand goes to the hilt of his sword, and Magnus stops himself, clearly thinking better. His eyes return to me, once again turning on the charisma. "My apologies for being so forward, madam. But I am struck by your aura. Why is it that you taste so different?"

He cocks his head, looking genuinely puzzled.

Again, Leon's voice comes in a threatening growl, "Mind your own fucking business, shifter."

The shifter doesn't even spare him a look as he keeps his eyes fixed on me. "I have information on Morgana's whereabouts. My price is the answer to my question. Why does your aura taste unlike anything I've ever met?"

"Vivian," Leon's voice is low, still full of threat. It seems he doesn't want me talking to Magnus.

I pause as I consider Magnus's question. Even though Leon isn't too pleased, I don't see how giving Magnus this information will tell him anything that isn't going to be common knowledge soon anyway, especially after our visit to the Council. "I'm from the mortal realm and I'm Leon's Keeper," I answer.

Magnus considers me, and his eyes narrow to slits. I realize at this moment that they're very serpentine-looking eyes. "No, mortal. I've tasted both of those energies in the past. This…" His tongue flicks into the air, a distinct fork at the tip. "This is new."

I pause again. "I'm sorry – I don't know what else I could be." I frown, unsure of what else he could be looking for, for an answer. I could mention the ghosts, but that might go over very poorly.

Only tell him things that are common knowledge.

At my response, Magnus nods, but I can't tell if he accepts my words as truth. "Fair enough mortal, but still not the information I have asked for." He inclines his head, looking me up and down again. "Perhaps we can shift our trade then. I will tell you what I know for a taste of you."

Again, Leon growls behind me, his hand once again going for his sword. I reach a hand behind me to squeeze his arm reassuringly.

The man needs to take a chill pill.

Turning my attention back to Magnus, I arch an eyebrow, trying to give him my best unimpressed expression. "I'm in no mood to be devoured, Magnus. I happen to be quite fond of all my body parts."

Magnus laughs at my answer, "I assure you, Vivian? Was it? My methods are not nearly as brash. Just a taste of your skin will do just fine. Even a bead of sweat can tell me more about your energies than what I can discern from the air around you."

His eyes are glowing a brighter green now, and I can clearly see they're no longer human eyes. The pupils have grown to narrow vertical slits, just like a snake.

I chew my bottom lip for a moment before answering. I'm curious about what he might find from my energies. I've wanted to know more about what I am for years now.

I'm just not entirely sure I want that information broadcasted to strangers. Or to anyone at this point.

"And you're certain the information you have on Morgana is accurate and will lead us to her whereabouts?" I ask, looking at him suspiciously.

I am not about to make my first supernatural deal only to be duped.

"I swear it," the shifter answers earnestly. "I will certainly make this worth your while."

Magnus' tone holds a slightly provocative undertone, and Leon moves to pull me back as his voice comes clipped and angry, "You will not let him touch you, Vivian. There are other ways to extract information from people."

Pulling myself from Leon's grip, I stand in front of Magnus. Leon must be fuming. I can sense the bond pulling tight, and my body is starting to flush.

"You have a deal," I answer Magnus before the bond tries to force me back into submission.

Quick as a coiled snake strikes its prey, Magnus's arm darts towards me, pulling my neck to his mouth as he licks at my pulse. Before he releases me, he pauses, shuddering, as he remarks softly into my ear, "I've never tasted anything quite so exquisite." He sounds in awe. "I wonder what it is you could be, Vivian."

This is Leon's breaking point. His hand comes over me as he grabs the shifter by the neck, lifting him off me. Magnus hangs in the air as Leon holds him, squeezing his throat harder. His tone is menacing. "If you ever touch what is mine again, I will hunt down and kill every snake shifter to have ever slithered their miserable existence through the realms."

I'm shocked at Leon's actions, and my voice comes out louder than I expected. "Leon, put him down."

Leon ignores me, the shifter now turning a shade of blue. I want to yell again, but I need to talk him down, not make him angrier. I try to change my tone.

"Leon?" I keep my voice small and soft. Leon's eyes shift towards me, but he doesn't let go of Magnus. His eyes glow the same blue they do when he gets furious.

"I consented to the trade. He did nothing wrong," I remind him, my hand gently coming down on Leon's arm to try and get him to lower Magnus.

Leon's eyes take on the same feral gleam. Evidently, my words are having the opposite of their intended effect.

"He *touched* you." Again, his voice is murderous.

I stand in front of him, demanding his full attention as my other hand rests on his face. "Yes," I answer softly. "And if you don't let him go, he will die, and then we will have no lead to our true enemy."

At my words, Leon pauses, not responding as if at war with himself. "Please, Leon," I add. "He did nothing wrong. I let him touch me. Be angry with me." I try not to show the slight waver in my tone.

The words finally have their desired effect. Leon's eyes are locked on mine, his murderous intent well and shifted. He drops Magnus, who crumples into a heap on the ground. Magnus shakes himself as he gets back up, and I don't dare go to him to help him up, lest it piss off Leon even more.

Magnus' voice comes low and fast. Evidently, he's now in a hurry to be rid of us. "Morgana freed the Destroyer millennia ago. They've been mostly silent until recently when they started looking for someone. I don't know who they're searching for, though."

Leon answers, his voice still dripping with malice, "Location shifter. You promised a location."

"I'm getting to that," Magnus snaps. "Whoever they've been looking for, they've been looking for them in the mortal realm the most often, so if you're looking for Morgana, that would be a good place to start."

CHAPTER 24

LEON DOESN'T SAY ANOTHER WORD TO MAGNUS and instead grabs my arm with a grip that is sure to leave bruises as he drags me down another alleyway.

"Where are we going?" I breathe, running to keep up with him. Adrenaline floods my system. I'm still very much aware that I'm now the focus of Leon's rage.

"We're finishing this," Leon huffs, stopping at the dead end.

There are a few boarded-up doors on either side of us, and I can smell what I'm pretty sure are human feces.

Classy.

Leon still holds the blue glow to him, his anger still simmering very close to the surface. He turns to face me, and I can see the blue tattoos extend through his neck, his collar on full display. My pulse thunders and I remind myself again that this man of infinite violence probably won't hurt me.

Probably.

He probably doesn't even know he's hurting my arm right now.

"Leon..." I start, trying to find a way to mend this fracture between us.

Why has everything been so hard? Why does a bond that's supposed to be my destiny feel like this? Either I'm being drugged, I'm a sex-crazed maniac, or I feel like there's a hot poker being stabbed into my brain.

I'm tired.

So fucking tired.

Is this what fighting your destiny feels like?

I feel small. The broken fragments of myself I've barely pieced together over the years are crumbling.

I'm the problem.

I've always been a problem. Not outgoing enough, not pretty enough, or social enough. I've kept secrets, and all it's ever done is hurt those I love. I've fought my whole life to keep my head above water, but I'm drowning.

There's finally someone who loves me. Who wants me. And I'm turning my nose up at him like I have a higher moral ground.

I'm worthless. I'm a murderer.

Leon doesn't answer me, but his hand comes around to grab my middle, and my feet leave the ground. The familiar stretching sensation hits and we apparate back in front of Leon's castle.

When our feet are firmly planted on the ground, he lets me go and stalks off into the darkness outside without a word. The bond pulls at me uncomfortably as I watch him fade into the darkness.

Despite the discomfort from the bond, I'm relieved to be alone. It's like a cramp – just sharp enough to make it impossible to get comfortable. Still, the pain doesn't get worse, and considering the amount of brain fog I've had today, I'm assuming that the lack of pain is due to Leon not straying far rather than the bond settling down.

I wait outside the door for a few breaths. Would it be rude to just let myself in? What's the worst that will happen? Leon might not invite me back.

Fat chance of that.

I snort out loud at the thought.

At least I can still find humour in the craziest moments of my life. That helps.

Pulling open the castle doors, I head to the room where I left my clothes earlier this afternoon. The dress I'm wearing is stunning. It makes me feel like a princess.

I can't wait not to be wearing it anymore.

Princess activities should be limited to short, hour-long durations. Anything greater than that borders on torture. While all bras suck, corsets bite into ALL the ribs and are never happening again. I'm categorizing them with long underwear – the no-thank-you list.

I ignore the bruises that are starting to form on my neck and arm as I grab my own clothes. My black leggings call to me, even though they're salt-stained from my jumping into the ocean the other night. I can't even piece together how many nights ago that was now. Two? One? Everything is starting to meld together, and my sleep schedule is fully confused.

Is there a time difference when you jump between realms? Perhaps my exhaustion and time confusion are the result of inter-realm jet lag.

Happily back into the comfort of my clothes, I head downstairs. The cramping feeling in my stomach eased a moment ago, and I know that Leon is back from his walk or general moody staring off into the darkness. I don't know him well enough to be sure which he prefers.

He's sitting at the head of the large wooden table in the centre of the grand hall. The fire is lit, casting a warm glow about the room. The stained-glass windows above us let in the slightest hint of starlight.

Once again, I'm struck by the mastery that went into designing a place with such care.

Leon's eyes catch mine as I make my way down the stairs, not leaving me as he tracks me across the room. They aren't shining blue anymore. I'm taking that as a good sign that he's calmed down.

Neither of us speaks as I walk over to the table. The table is massive, and rather than awkwardly sit at opposing ends and needing to yell, I sit adjacent to him, turning my chair so that we're facing each other.

Is he still mad? Or was he using that time to think about our next plan of attack? Either way, I'm not keen to mention how angry he was with me, so I keep my mouth shut.

This doesn't feel like being called to the principal's office. I'm a grown woman.

AND I came here of my own accord.

That anxious pit in my stomach has always been there.

I try to school my feelings into meek compliance. It's what he wants. I can give him that, even if the man is remarkable at rubbing me the wrong way. Not that I'll mention his rubbing me in any way, lest he get any more ideas.

When Leon finally speaks, I almost let my shoulders slump in disappointment.

Almost.

He's still pissed about the whole Magnus thing. I try not to sigh.

Leon's voice is deceptively mild. "I thought we had an understanding tonight when we arrived at the market. You wouldn't wander off, and you would speak to no one."

I want to argue, to let him know I did what I did for the mission. I bite the inside of my cheek instead, allowing him to continue. His hands rest on the table. His muscles are tense, and he is in no way relaxed.

Bummer.

"Once again, I find myself struck by how little you seem to grasp how this relationship works. I lead, Vivian. I lead, and you follow. I protect you, and you obey me. When I give you a command, I expect you to follow it, regardless of whether you see the logic in it. It is your duty to obey."

Leon's words feel like nails on a chalkboard across my mind. Something about the word 'obey' makes my blood boil. I'm not well suited to it. I open my mouth to speak, but Leon shushes me, refusing to give me room to defend my actions.

Again, my blood boils, and the fog starts to trickle into the edges of my mind. Heat from the bond is already beginning to spread through me at the anger Leon's words spark in me. I push against it and focus on Leon's words.

"I am going to give you details of our plan moving forward, Vivian. Not because I am looking for your permission but because I feel that you need time to come to grips with my decision so you are prepared to do your part. Because you *will* obey me. We have no other choice."

I tense. There's no way I'm going to like what he has to say.

"I believe Morgana is looking to form an alliance with me. I've considered the attacks, and how the forsaken came for you, even after seeing I was already awakened. Morgana is searching the human world for someone. If her first order of business is to kill me, the forsaken would have immediately reported back to her that I was awake, and Sin would have come to try and end me. It's clear that they have some kind of agenda that they want to discuss."

My eyes widen at his conclusions. "Leon, that's great news. If they want to talk, we can try and work out a way to end this peacefully, without a fight to the death between two Destroyers." My body relaxes, feeling weak with relief.

The relief is short-lived.

"There will be no talking, Vivian," Leon answers like he's explaining the most obvious thing in the world. "There can be no peace with Morgana. She has been wicked for millennia and can never be trusted. She and her Destroyer must fall, or we forever risk the end of the realms."

I frown at his explanation. "Then what do you want to do, if they just want to talk?"

Leon leans back in his chair, crossing his arms as a malicious grin spreads across his face. He looks hungry for what's coming next. "We use their temporary peace to our advantage."

I'm about to ask how, but Leon continues, once again ignoring how I opened my mouth to speak. His eagerness to give me a breakdown of his masterful plan is evidently more important than anything I could ever add.

"We are going to be returning to the mortal realm. We will need to go back to somewhere that has a lot of your energy imbued into it. Perhaps your apartment or school. That will make it easier for Morgana's forsaken to track you down. Once we've arrived, we will wait. Morgana will come to us. It's doubtful she will show up without her Destroyer. Not if she has an iota of self-preservation. She's made it this long on the run from the Council, so we can bet she won't be unprotected."

My stomach sours. I hate where this is going. And still, Leon continues, "We will act as though we want to hear them out, that we are open to a possible truce. Then, the moment I see the Destroyer, I will annihilate him before either he or Morgana ever has a chance to speak. I'll end them once and for all."

I sit still, gobsmacked by Leon's plan. I'm utterly speechless at the insanity he's proposing.

Leon takes my temporary stunned silence as compliance. He shifts back from his chair, standing as he continues, "We'll leave for the mortal realm shortly – the sooner we end this, the better. You need to unlock my collar now, Vivian. So that we are prepared to strike at the first chance. If what Magnus says is true, then Sin is already completely free to obliterate the realms. We can't afford to hesitate."

His soft tone is long gone now. He speaks with urgency like he's ready to apparate us out in the next two minutes.

Still incredulous, I finally find my voice. I'm using all my willpower to stamp down the anger rising within me. I can't activate the bond any further. This is too important, and I won't be backing down. Instead, I try to approach the situation logically in hopes that I can sway Leon into changing his plans. He needs to see reason.

"Leon…" I begin.

I keep my voice soft and my eyes downcast. Submissive. I need to act as submissive as possible. The man wants obedience, and there's no way he'll listen to a word I say if I start yelling my thoughts at him. "Surely, you understand that having two Destroyers set to fight to the death so close to humanity can't be safe. You're asking me to put my entire town – my entire realm at risk here."

Leon sighs at my argument, leaning forward again to rest his arms on the table as he looks at me closely. "Vivian – you need to think about this logically. Sin could obliterate all the realms without a moment's notice. Putting one realm, one coastline in the line of danger is a minimal price to pay for the guaranteed safety of every other living being." The mockery is back in his voice.

I try to ignore his tone. At least he doesn't seem angry. If we can keep things rational rather than emotionally charged, then we might actually get somewhere.

"But Leon, Sin has been free for millennia and hasn't destroyed anything. I think it's safe to say that we have time. We can lead them somewhere else if you'd like. To a place where there are no other living beings. We can even invite them to talk."

Leon's hands fist on the table, and his eyes narrow. It looks like trying to calmly argue my point is starting to grate on him. His body language isn't promising.

"They'll see through it, Vivian. We need to go somewhere they don't expect a trap from us. We need to be in your realm. Around mortals. That's the only way they'll let down their guard. I've already considered every alternative you're going to have, Vivian. I've been doing this for millennia. Unlock my collar. Do your job, and let me do mine."

More fog in the corners of my mind now.

Deep breaths – sooth the anger.

Rational. Not emotionally charged.

"Leon, you can't expect me to put my realm, those I love, at risk. I can't do that." I look at him earnestly, pleading with him to see reason. To understand why I can't do what he's asking of me.

It doesn't work.

"You need to look at this from the bigger picture, Vivian. A sliver of humanity is nothing – nothing compared to the survival of all the realms."

Oh boy.

My vision starts to go red. My mind fogs further, and I dig my nails into my palms to stop my concentration from breaking. The bond is lighting up, the heat between us now magnetizing. The pull strengthens, trying to draw me closer to Leon. Still, I fight it, refusing to leave my chair. Sweat breaks out at my temple from the effort.

Leon continues, still trying to sway me, "It isn't even your realm anymore. You need to let that foolish notion go. You belong with me. Here. Think of it. The moment the Council hears that we have succeeded in our mission,

I'll be redeemed in their eyes. It's likely they will grant you immortality for your services to them and allow us to remain bonded together for eternity. This is our second chance, Vivian. Stop being irrational and unlock my collar – now."

That does it.

Standing abruptly in my chair, I ignore my trembling legs as my body fights against the bond. The fog and heat in my brain are urging me to forget this argument and do whatever it is he wants. Fury grounds me, and I hold onto it with a vengeance.

"No, Leon. You're delusional. I am not going to live here with you. I am not going to keep our bond. And I will NOT be uncollaring you so you can go obliterate MY home!"

I might be a murderer with no worth. This might be the only person who will ever love me. But if that love comes at the cost of the people I love, then I will burn this relationship to the ground. No one gets to hurt my friends. I want to live, but I will gladly die for them.

Leon responds with a low growl, letting go of the table to tower in front of me. He's eyeing me like I'm his target rather than Sin or Morgana. I sway, but I'm determined to hold my ground or blackout trying. Leon watches me struggle, tilting his head at me. He can undoubtedly feel the impossibly tight snapping of the bond as I fight against it with everything I've got.

His voice is low and threatening, "You cannot break the bond. You cannot run from our destiny. Stop thinking you have a choice in this."

I'm almost delirious now from the throbbing in my head, and I can feel blood oozing down my hands as my nails bite into my palms even further. "I won't." My voice breaks, and my words come out as a strangled choke.

Leon steps closer to me now, his gaze taking on the same feral look he gets whenever I bring up breaking our bond. The pull of him makes me sway, and I bite harder on the inside of my cheek. The pain in my head is becoming in ear-splitting ringing.

My realm. My home. My friends.

I keep repeating the words as a mantra, trying to ground myself.

I won't break. I can't.

Leon's feral look is accompanied by a wicked smirk as he takes in the state I'm in. Rather than helping, he moves to stand behind me so our bodies are only a hair's breadth apart.

"Look at you," he whispers, his voice coming low, just at the sensitive spot below my ear. I shudder.

"Fighting an impossible fight, just like Cassandra did." His hand comes around me to stroke a path from my jaw to my chest. My body leans into his touch, feeling as though I'm being branded with pleasure.

His whisper returns at the same spot behind my ear, "Our destiny has been written long before you were ever born Vivian. Need explained it to me. Cassandra had to fall so that you could be born, and together, we could bring a new age. You couldn't fight your destiny then, and you certainly can't fight it now. You are mine. Every breath you have, you breathe for me. Every thought you think, you will think of me. Every touch on your body, it will come from me. No one else."

I frown at his words. It's like I'm trying to hear underwater again. I want to piece together what he's saying. I know he's telling me something new. But Leon's hand now strokes a path down my side, coming to rest on my outer thigh. My body goes limp, and the ringing is getting worse. The heat envelops me so thoroughly I feel its claustrophobic vice on me, making my pulse race even more wildly.

"I know you feel it. The desire and the pain from fighting it. It will not stop," Leon continues, his hand continuing its gentle toying with me. "And I will *never* let you go."

With those words, he grabs my hair, yanking my head back as he spins me to face him. I gasp at the pain, and he takes that opportunity to claim my mouth.

My body burns for him. I will shatter if he stops. The bond is molten fire as it strips away every thought I have. Every thought I've ever had. There's only Leon.

Leon throws me onto the table before descending over me to claim my mouth for another devouring kiss. My head comes off the hard surface, making it hurt even more. He wrenches up my shirt to cup my breasts, and my body responds, oblivious to the pain.

Leon growls as I respond to his touch. I wrap my arms around his neck, kissing him as passionately as he kisses me. He pinches at my nipple hard. I press myself into him, moaning at his touch.

I wrap my legs around his waist to pull him even closer. Leon uses that opportunity to stop kissing me and grabs my hair again. Wrenching my head back to expose my neck, he places hot kisses down the exposed column of my throat. The hand that is toying with my nipple releases me momentarily to rip off my bra so that I'm fully bared to him. He takes my nipple into his mouth, sucking and licking at it.

I'm caught in a haze of pain and pleasure. I can't remember why we're here or what we've been talking about. I can only feel, and right now, I feel like I'm going mad with pleasure.

Leon's hand trails back to my stomach, slipping below my leggings. He takes full advantage of the fact that my legs are still spread open on either side of him. His fingers tease along my slit, already soaked for him.

Leon's mouth releases my nipple, but he keeps a firm grip on my hair so I can't see him. His other hand still only teases at my entrance and his palm glances over my clit. I writhe, trying to get him to give me more.

"Say it, Vivian," he whispers in my ear. Again, his finger teases.

I arch my hips to try and find relief from the burning he's building within me.

"I want you to tell me who you belong to," his voice purrs now. His finger lightly flicks inside of me for the briefest moment.

I can barely hear him now; my body feels like it's in serious danger of spontaneous combustion if he doesn't touch more of me soon. I moan and yell in frustration, "Leon!"

At my answer, Leon uses his hold on my hair to lift my head back up so I'm now looking directly into his eyes. There's a dark smile on his face as he wrenches my pants down. His own pants are discarded a moment later.

He teases the tip of his cock against my slit. I try to inch forward to take him inside of me, but his grip on my hair only increases, and his other hand clamps down on my thigh, gripping me in a bruising hold, ensuring I can't move.

"Take off my collar, Vivian," he demands, and he lightly pushes his hips forward so only an inch of him is inside of me.

I try to push against his hand to feel more of him. At that, Leon, pulls my head even further back, exposing the entire column of my throat and bites down on my neck, just over my collarbone. Hard. I scream, the sharp edges of his teeth searing white hot pleasure and pain through me simultaneously and bleeding together. My body wants to writhe, but he holds me firm.

"Take off my collar, Vivian, and I'll give you what you want," he croons as he licks at the spot he just bit, trailing hot kisses up to my ear.

"Leon, please," I beg, my body screaming for release.

Leon pushes a little deeper inside of me, and I moan loudly before he completely withdraws again. He releases my hair to pull my left arm from his neck, kissing my wrist before holding it in front of me. "The key, Vivian. Use your key."

His hard length is still lightly pressed against my slit, and every time I angle my hips to try and take more of him, he moves back, denying me the pleasure I so desperately crave.

I frown at him, trying to figure out what he's asking me to do. The brain fog makes it almost impossible to focus.

Again, Leon presses himself only an inch inside of me before stopping. "You need to use your key, Vivian. Use your key to unlock my collar so that I can fuck you into oblivion." He speaks to me slowly, like he knows I'm having difficulty thinking clearly.

Slowly, I nod at his words. That makes sense. He can't give me what I want because of the collar. If I unlock it, he can finally give me release. Lifting my hand, I try to figure out how to get the key out.

No instructions.

But as I have the thought, the weight of the key appears in my hand. It's heavier than I expected. Though my eyes feel like they're glazed, I hold it up, considering what to do next.

"Yes." Leon's voice comes as a hushed and excited whisper. "Such a good girl."

My eyes lock on his, confusion still clouding my mind. I need to unlock his collar. But something is nagging at me, that same feeling of nails scraping at the back of my mind. It's like I left a wild animal locked in a tiny closet, and they're trying to tear through the door.

I pause at the feeling.

"Now, Vivian," his voice comes harder than before, and it jars my mind a little further as if someone has cracked the door to the room with the wild animal in it.

Leon must notice I'm coming out of the fog because he quickly settles his mouth over mine for another claiming kiss. His fingers come down and start rubbing circles on my clit. The fog and heat from the bond begin to trickle back in, but whatever is in the small corner of my mind doesn't want to go back into the closet. It doesn't want to be trapped anymore.

I can hear it now. Whoever was locked up in my brain is really pissed off. I can start to make out the word now between outraged screams.

'NO,' the voice screams in my mind.

I try to split my attention between the searing kisses, Leon's fingers slowly driving me into bliss, and the outraged voice that is yelling inside of my head.

As the voice grows louder, it's like something is starting to shake me from the inside out. Still, the voice comes, yelling 'NO' over and over.

Frowning, I realize I recognize the voice.

It's mine. It's not actually coming out of my mouth, but a part of my mind is screaming.

Why am I screaming?

I try to remember.

Leon's hips press into me, and I can feel him pressing against my centre again.

Why am I here, on the table?

How did I get here?

The screaming becomes deafening, to the point that it blocks out the ringing in my ears from the bond.

I remember.

The plan to risk my home.

Leon's demand that I release him.

His demand that I obey.

His insistence that I'm a possession, that I belong to him.

Again, the voice screams, and at that moment, my mouth rips from Leon's as I scream with it. "NO!"

With my shout, a surge of energy bursts from me, and Leon's body flies across the room, slamming into the opposite wall.

CHAPTER 25

LEON'S BODY SLUMPS ONTO THE GROUND IN A crumpled heap. My eyes widen as I realize what just happened.

I scramble over to him. He isn't moving.

"Leon?" I ask, unsure if he's hurt.

Leon's eyes snap open at my voice. They're back to shining the same electric blue, and he's looking at me with a completely new emotion.

Suspicion.

"What the fuck was that, Vivian?"

I try to help him up, but Leon slaps my hand away. Recoiling at the quick snap of pain, I sputter, "Leon, I'm so sorry. I have no idea what just happened. I just got angry and…"

His eyes remain narrowed at me, utterly unmoved by my apology. A new kind of tension fills the air between us as Leon straightens himself completely. He takes a step towards me, and instinctively, I take a step back.

"There's something you aren't telling me, Vivian. I can fucking feel it. I've fucking seen it. The night the forsaken appeared. The storm. Your suddenly exceptional luck at escaping a garage full of those murderous beasts. What the fuck aren't you telling me?" He's yelling at the top of his lungs, and the building quakes.

I shake my head at his words, denial quick and ready to make an appearance.

With my wordless answer, Leon's face contorts into rage. He moves for me again, looking like he might throttle me. I keep backing up until, once again, I'm pressed against the table.

He gives me no avenue for escape, planting a hand on either side of my body.

Trapping me.

"It doesn't make any sense," he growls. "Keepers are not meant to hold any kind of power. Mortals!" He yells again. "Mortals are not supposed to hold power. You are a magic-less race – at our mercy. And yet you..."

He pauses to caress my cheek. I flinch, and he grabs my chin hard to hold me still. "My precious, innocent little human. An enigma of magic follows you around like a fucking stench of corruption. What. The. Fuck. Are. You?"

The vein in his temple is throbbing. I think my pulse is racing at the same speed. My instincts scream at me to run. He's scaring me, and I have nowhere to go, no one to turn to but myself.

I'm alone, not even in my own world. "Leon, I swear I don't know," I reply, my tears threatening to spill free.

Leon stares down at me like he's trying to tell whether he can believe a word I say. He nods slowly, but the air of danger around him remains. His arms still hold hostage against the table. "What other powers do you have? I know you caused the storm, and I know you just threw me using energy alone."

"I – I don't think I caused the storm, Leon. I think that was you." I start, hoping to avoid the question he's asking. I might not be able to think too hard about it, but every time I think of Need and the Council learning anything about me, my anxiety skyrockets. There's something going on, and I know they can't be trusted.

Leon's eye twitches. "I am perfectly *capable*," the twitch comes again as he emphasizes the word, "of knowing when I am using *my* power, Vivian. Now I am going to ask you again, and you will tell me the truth. All of it. What other powers do you have?"

My heart races and my mind frantically tries to figure out the best way to answer him. I can't tell him about everything. His words confirmed what I'd been suspecting for days.

Being a Keeper isn't the reason I have magic.

The same puzzles that have plagued me for the last four years still lay before me, unsolved. I still have no idea why I can see ghosts and why I can release the spirits of broken souls.

Need's conversation with Rydon plays again through my mind, and I'm certain they were talking about me. But why? The fog starts to creep in as my thoughts teeter in the direction of treason. I reign them in, instead focusing on the very angry Destroyer that holds me captive.

"I – I don't know." My voice is flat, and I keep my eyes downcast.

"LIAR!" Leon roars.

In a frenzy, he flips the table I'm pressed against, and it crashes to the ground, splintering it into dozens of broken pieces. At the sudden loss of the tabletop that was supporting my weight, I fall back with it. A piece of wood embeds itself into my arm, and I scream.

Leon grabs my arm and wrenches me back up, oblivious to the pain he's causing. I can feel my body starting to become paralyzed with fear. I have nowhere to run and no way to fight this large man who is clearly out of control.

"Leon, please," I plead in a small voice, tears streaming down my face.

A cruel grin spreads across his face, and he tightens his grip on me as he takes in my vulnerable state. "Did you know, Vivian?" His voice is low again, threatening. "That every fucking time you lie to me, I know it. I can feel it coming right through our bond. As clear as a fucking beacon, it lights up, and I fucking know."

I try not to show any outward reaction to his statement. My arm is burning where the wood still impales me. Despite Leon's calm tone, I don't believe he's in control, not for a second. I can't imagine what would happen if he lost control without his collar. The devastation he could rain down before gaining his senses again.

No matter which way this conversation turns or what he does to me, I will not uncollar this man. He can break my body and poison my thoughts, but I will not free him.

"If you would just use some fucking common sense, you would accept the bond, and this wouldn't be a problem anymore. I can't imagine why you are being this fucking obstinate. It's fucking destiny, Vivian! Your destiny! Not something you have a choice in. And yet, for some reason, you think you're strong enough to outrun it? Keepers and Destroyers don't break their bonds, save in death. From the moment that key was given to you, you became *mine*." His voice is feral, possessive.

His words hit me harder than any stone ever has. "But Need said…" I answer, not wanting to believe him.

Leon laughs harshly. "Need would have said anything to get you to do your part and come and wake me so that our bond could do the rest. You were promised to me before you were ever fucking born. From the moment you took your first breath – it was for me. And until you take your last, you belong to me. So, stop fucking fighting, and wake up. You never had a choice. Your freedom was always an illusion. All you are doing now is prolonging the inevitable and potentially at the cost of the lives of millions. Your selfish tantrum ends now. Unlock my fucking collar."

I can only look up at him in horror.

Death.

My only way out is death. My mind recoils at the thought of being bonded to him for the rest of my life, and the bond flares. The same sinister heat floods my body. I gasp for breath, stepping back from Leon as I try to stamp it down.

"No," I answer, between deep inhalations. The heat grows worse, but I know it's coming. I cross my arms against myself as if trying to physically hold my body in place.

Leon only shakes his head at me. "Still trying to fight impossible fights." His tone becomes bitter as he continues, "It's almost funny. You have a long history of making decisions that don't bode well for your survival. You make it exceedingly difficult to protect you. You always have. You don't make good choices, Vivian."

I frown, trying to figure out where Leon is headed with this. He steps towards me again, and his hand comes around to wrap at the back of my neck.

I still completely, fighting how the bond sends a surge of pleasure through me at his touch. "I'm going to keep you safe. No matter the cost."

As he finishes his declaration, a spot in the back of my neck begins to burn where Leon's fingers trace an obscure outline. I try to jerk away from the pain, but Leon's hold only tightens until he finishes what I'm pretty sure was searing a piece of my skin off.

"What the hell was that?" I cry.

"You obviously have some power within you that we don't understand. Until I know what it is, I'm sealing it off so that you don't accidentally hurt yourself," he answers, finally backing away.

My hand reaches out to touch the back of my neck, but I feel nothing, not even a scab. But the rest of me feels like someone just pulled the plug from the bathtub, and I'm draining. The feeling is rapidly replaced by a hollow emptiness inside of me. The bond is still there, but something is missing. Like, I'm wearing sneakers but no socks. It's not painful, but I don't like it.

I start to ask Leon how long I need to keep it, but he cuts me off, "I'm going to leave you here for a time, while I go speak with Need."

His arms are crossed against his chest, and he's still looking at me with the same bitter expression.

I pause at his words, letting their meaning sink in. "Wait, you're leaving me here? Alone? Won't that trigger the bond?"

Leon's words from the day before echo in my mind. That if he'd gotten more than thirty feet from me while I wasn't accepting the bond, I'd likely black out from pain. Considering my body is still fighting the waves of heat that pound against me, I'm sure the bond is in no way going to be okay with our being separated.

Leon shrugs. "It will undoubtedly be a less than positive experience for you. But all things considered, I think it's time you learn just how strong the pull between us really is. If this is what it takes for you to finally stop fighting us and give in to your destiny, then so be it."

"Leon, this isn't the right way to solve things between us," I answer between the gasps of air I'm still taking, trying to control the heat that burns through me.

Leon takes another step away from me. His gaze becomes detached as if preparing himself for what he's about to do. "The castle is warded. You'll be safe enough here. Sin and Morgana are likely still in the mortal realm."

"Leon," my voice is now edged with panic. "Leon, don't."

"Mine, Vivian. You are fucking mine. And you'd better come to grips with it while I'm gone."

And with those words, he disappears.

CHAPTER 26

PAIN.

Someone is holding a scalding brand and stroking it across my skin. There's only room for pain. I fall to the ground, still trying to take in air, but my lungs feel like they're being constricted by the bond, coiling my insides together.

My vision is hazy as dark spots dance in my peripherals. I try to focus, try to latch onto anything other than the sensation of my very blood boiling.

Air.

I need air.

The suffocating press of the bond is making me feel trapped inside my own skin. I can't breathe. I can hardly think.

Slowly, I raise a hand and start to try and crawl to the door.

Air.

There's air outside.

Each movement feels like hot pokers are being shoved through my body. My ears ring with a high pitch, making me even dizzier. Still, I press on, my legs scraping against broken shards of the table that litter the floor. If the splinters are embedding in my skin, I don't feel them.

I make it to the door but stumble as I try to lift onto my knees to reach the knob. My body collapses against it, trembling from the pain. There's more blood pouring down my arm where I fell against the wood shard still lodged in my skin. My eyes glaze over at the sight, replacing it with dark spots.

The ringing in my ears disorients me. I reach up with my good arm and slap at the door, trying to feel for the knob.

Air.

Get to air.

Finally, my hand finds the metal latch, and I let myself collapse against it. The night air rushes in, and I try to take more life-giving breaths. My lungs burn, not unlike the night I drowned in the ocean. I gasp, over and over, lying in the doorway. The air is cool, and I try to let it sooth the vice of fire within me.

It isn't nearly as effective as I'd hoped, but it's a start.

With a bit more oxygen, I use the door frame to pull myself up to sit, panting with exhaustion from the effort.

How long could this possibly last?

Would Leon stay out all night just to prove I'm not strong enough to fight the bond?

The thought has a definite Leon quality to it. The man is not going to back down until I give in and become his to command.

Tears run down my face at the thought, and the ringing in my ears reaches a new, head-splitting frequency. Even in this state, the bond punishes me for having less-than-obedient thoughts.

I let myself sob as I'm hit with wave after wave of blinding pain. It's quickly followed by a rising tide of nausea that rolls through me. I don't even bother to crawl; instead, I just let my body slump onto the grassy side of the doorframe. I throw up the small meal I had the day before and then continue dry, heaving in between sobs and gasps of pain.

The heat won't stop. The burning only gets worse with every passing moment that Leon is away. I rack my brain at how to fix this.

The burning. I need to stop the burning.

How the fuck do you stop a supernatural burning pain from a punishing magical bond?

A stupid TV commercial voice rings through my head, 'Only you can stop forest fires.'

Breathing hard, I decide to give in to my ridiculous subconscious mind and try the obvious. If my body feels like it's on fire, I need water.

Fucking brilliant, inner Vivian.

My vision still clouds with black spots and tears, and I manage to find the strength to look around. I try to remember where I saw an ocean yesterday when Leon was building wards around the castle. Disorientated and desperate, I grip the doorframe, forcing myself to stand.

"Breathe, Vivian," I whisper to myself. "Find the water."

The cool promise of water is enough for me to push through the searing pain that kisses every inch of me. If I can reach the water, I can climb into it and let myself rest until the pain stops.

I need water.

I keep repeating the logical thought. Even though nothing in my life makes sense anymore, a simple task like this does.

I stumble forward in the direction I think the water is in. It's still pitch-black outside, and there aren't any streetlights in this realm to guide me. There isn't even a moon to illuminate the darkness.

I continue forward, sobbing through the pain when I see it. Ahead, to my right, a slight glow in the darkness. My brow furrows at the sight. I know that glow. I've seen it before.

My head hurts so bad; the realization is slow to hit.

A forsaken spirit.

The slight glow looks to be rippling below it like it's casting waves in the ground.

No, not ground.

Water.

I don't care if this creature might want to eat my face. I spin and make my way towards it.

The forsaken doesn't move and watches me with its long claws dangling in the water. As soon as my toes feel the dampness leaking through my shoes, I let myself collapse into the shallow depths.

I don't even bother to look at the terrifying creature.

If it wants to hurt me, it can get in line.

The water is cold and feels like absolute heaven on my skin. Still, my insides feel like molten lava. Swallowing, I try to stamp down that fire to no avail. So, instead, I let myself just lay in the water, the small ripples coming from the forsaken lapping against my body. The water isn't doing much, but it's helping enough that I can take deep breaths now rather than gasping and retching.

Small wins.

I don't know how long I lay there, but when I finally feel like my body isn't about to spontaneously combust, I open my eyes to look at what is supposed to be a murderous creature. It's barely moved since I entered the water and only stands there, watching me.

Creeper.

I'm not afraid. Instead, we both stay still, considering each other. Through the pain, I feel sorry for the broken soul. I'm quickly becoming familiar with the feeling of being trapped. Looks like this creature and I have more in common than I thought. It seems like both of us have been dealt a shitty hand, to be trapped for all of eternity. I can't even help this one, considering Leon has cut off my powers.

"I'm so sorry," I croak at the creature. It's killing me that I can't free it.

As empathy floods my mind, the familiar silver light rises from me. It stutters like it's fighting against something, but still, it comes, extending out from me. I'm shocked to see it, considering Leon said he cut me off.

Still, the light reaches out towards the forsaken. The creature moves forward a step and extends one of its long, clawed fingers towards the light. As they touch, my power grows, and the light further extends to envelop the forsaken.

As soon as my light fades, a young woman stands before me. She holds the same glow and is dressed in light leather-looking armour. She has a bow with a quiver of arrows slung on her back. I continue to lay in the water, content to feel the cool press of it soothing my skin as I watch the spirit.

The spirit is less inclined to follow my relaxation regime. She waves at me, trying to get my attention.

I don't think I'll ever understand why ninety percent of ghosts want nothing to do with me and the other ten percent feel compelled to order me around.

Still, despite the blinding pain that pulses through my joints at the effort, I stand up. I've learned my lesson about not listening to spirits way before my life got boss-level paranormal.

The spirit beams at me and exhausted, I manage a thumbs-up, waiting for something to happen. The spirit just stands facing me now, giving me an expectant look.

I try to figure out what the spirit wants. She's waiting around and looking at me like she fully expects something to happen.

I frown. "What? What am I missing? Why aren't you leaving?"

The ghost spreads her arms wide as if to indicate something completely obvious.

I grow frustrated. "Look – I don't know what you want. Okay? I'm sorry. But spirits out here, they don't have a good afterlife. And at least one of us should be free. It looks like you've suffered longer. So, you should go. Go be wherever you need to be now."

As I speak the words, the spirit beams at me as if she's finally been given the magic words, and with them, she fades out from existence until I'm once again surrounded by darkness.

Alone with the burning pain of the bond again, my shoulders sag. The forsaken was a nice distraction from the searing heat in my body.

I'm happy for the spirit. At least I was able to help someone find their freedom today. It might not be my own, but it gives me hope that my time will also come.

Because it will come. I won't stop fighting until I'm free again.

Giving in to the call of the cool water, I walk deeper into the ocean.

I'll just let myself float the night away.

I'm in knee-high water when I hear someone walking into the water behind me. I start to turn, expecting to see Leon. However, before I turn even an inch, a large hand clamps down on my mouth. It's accompanied by a deep voice that doesn't belong to Leon. "Sorry, mortal – this won't feel very good."

And with that, the ground below my feet disappears as I'm wrenched from the realm.

THE END

Hate cliff hangers?

Me too! Keep reading for a sneak peek at Destruction's Desire, Book Two in the Broken Souls Trilogy.

Creation's Captive

TEASER – DESTRUCTION'S DESIRE

Sin's Point of View

THE MORTAL IS TINY.

She's weak, too.

She blacked out the second we hit the wards guarding the Shadow Realm.

I shouldn't be surprised. I've been watching her for years.

This mortal is nothing like the warrior we faced in Atlantis. She looks about as fierce as a kitten, passed out in my arms.

What does surprise me is the state I've found her in.

Fates above, I knew Leon was a piece of shit, but I didn't think he'd go so far as to hurt the mortal.

They're supposed to be destined for each other. The idiot has a piss-poor way of treating his fated.

Guilt and rage war with each other as I take in her sorry state.

She's bleeding from multiple cuts, and there's a piece of wood lodged in her arm. I can see bruises circling her neck and down her arms. She looks more pale than usual.

We led her to her own slaughter.

When we found the mortal four years ago, Morgana insisted we only keep an eye on her to ensure she survived long enough to find Leon. Once the two were reunited, we'd open up communication channels.

If the prophecy is to come to light, Leon and the mortal must be together. That's the only way this will work.

Our plans fell apart when Magnus, our spy in the black market, reported that the mortal might be in danger *from* Leon.

That changed everything.

The mortal stirs in my arms, but we aren't quite at Morgana's castle yet.

"Sleep," I command her.

My influence is fast-acting, and she once again stills in my arms.

I don't want her waking until I've had a chance to remove the wood shard from her arm. While I could just as easily use my destructive powers to remove the wood – I'd rather do it with medical supplies on hand.

Mortals are delicate creatures. Best not to take chances.

I try not to notice her scent. Or the silky feel of her hair brushing against my arm.

She might look like a siren, but she's just another Council puppet — an obedient little princess born to serve the whims of the corrupt.

She's only as useful as the influence her tight little cunt has over Leon.

Her existence disgusts me.

And yet – our sources say Leon is still wearing his collar.

She didn't release him.

And by the looks of her, I'm guessing she fought back.

I hold her a little more tightly as we enter Morgana's castle.

If the mortal fought Leon and didn't give in to the Council, then maybe, this kitten has claws.

ABOUT THE AUTHOR

Melody is an obsessive overachiever. When she isn't caring for her three young children, she's writing books, working on her PhD, or binge-reading books.

When the warmer weather sets in, she likes to plant fields of flowers and adopt more animals for her hobby farm.

Melody writes because she can't afford her book addiction.

ACKNOWLEDGMENTS

A huge thank you to my friends and family for putting up with my obsessive tendencies. Thank you to my alpha and beta readers. Seriously, your feedback is incredible, and I value you all so much!

Thank you to my amazing cover designers, Krafigs Design. You absolutely nailed the new cover!

Thank you to the amazing community on BookTok and Bookstagram – you guys are wonderful!

And finally, thank you to my readers! Becoming an author has always been a dream I kept close to my heart, but I never thought it could be a reality for me. I am so grateful to you all for taking a chance on Creation's Captive.

Please consider leaving a rating or review on Amazon. Rankings and reviews help authors continue to do what we love!

Creation's Captive

Made in the USA
Coppell, TX
11 June 2025

50593907R00192